No one could believe it. A robbery? With guns? At Le Croque, one of the most elegant restaurants in Bev Hills? It was beyond belief, it was amazing, it was definitely going to be on the front page of tomorrow's *Variety*.

"Jerry, is this a joke?" Marie whispered softly.

Jerry Zalman shook his head.

"It's not a joke," Happy Henke growled in fury. "It's a setup! I'm not going to take this," Henke said firmly, twisting his diamond ring so the stone was facing backward toward his palm.

Zalman stared down at the floor and tried to become one with his environment. He didn't want to get stuck in the middle of an argument between Happy Henke and a grumpy armed robber.

"Buzz off," Henke said to the robber in the Goofy mask.

Zalman shook his head. Definitely the wrong thing to say.

As Zalman covered Marie's body with his own, he heard the crack of gunfire . . .

PRAISE FOR THE JERRY ZALMAN MYSTERIES:

LET'S ROB ROY

"With its eccentric characters, zippy one-liners and nutty situations, *Let's Rob Roy* is reminiscent of a screwball comedy—but . . . this is first and foremost a mystery. . . . Enjoyable . . . a breezy read."

—*Rave Reviews*

SCREWDRIVER

"*Screwdriver* is a romp. . . . Ms. Kraft peoples her mystery with an amusing cast of the beautiful and eccentric. Cheers."

—*The Cincinnati Post*

Books by Gabrielle Kraft

Bullshot
Screwdriver
Let's Rob Roy
Bloody Mary

Published by POCKET BOOKS

Most Pocket Books are available at special quantity discounts for bulk purchases for sales promotions, premiums or fund raising. Special books or book excerpts can also be created to fit specific needs.

For details write the office of the Vice President of Special Markets, Pocket Books, 1230 Avenue of the Americas, New York, New York 10020.

Gabrielle Kraft

POCKET BOOKS

New York   London   Toronto   Sydney   Tokyo   Singapore

This book is a work of fiction. Names, characters, places and incidents are either the product of the author's imagination or are used fictitiously. Any resemblance to actual events or locales or persons, living or dead is entirely coincidental.

An *Original* Publication of POCKET BOOKS

POCKET BOOKS, a division of Simon & Schuster Inc.
1230 Avenue of the Americas, New York, NY 10020

Copyright © 1990 by Gabrielle Kraft
Cover art copyright © 1990 Stephen Peringer

All rights reserved, including the right to reproduce
this book or portions thereof in any form whatsoever.
For information address Pocket Books, 1230 Avenue
of the Americas, New York, NY 10020

ISBN: 0-671-66941-9

First Pocket Books printing July 1990

10 9 8 7 6 5 4 3 2 1

POCKET and colophon are registered trademarks of
Simon & Schuster Inc.

Printed in the U.S.A.

BLOODY MARY

"GET HIS LEGS!"

"I can't, he's too fast."

"Grab him! Grab his legs!"

"I can't! He's getting away from— Ow! He kicked me!"

"That's it, I've had it. I'm gonna kill him."

But it was too late. Rutherford, usually the world's most cowardly Doberman, leapt out of the bathtub. For a long wet second all four paws scrabbled madly for traction on the slick floor; then he beat it down the hall and into the living room, dripping a trail of soapy water on the carpet behind him.

Jerry Zalman slumped down on the bathroom floor and put his head on the nice cool tile. "I'm gonna slaughter that cretin," he said mildly. "I'm gonna rip out his stubby little tail and whack him over the head with it until he barks for mercy."

"He didn't mean it, honey," Marie Thrasher soothed as she tossed a wet sponge back into the bathtub. "It was an accident. He didn't mean it. He's just a dog."

Zalman looked up at her and shook his head emphatically. A soap flake drifted serenely to the floor. "No, Marie, that's where you're wrong. Rutherford isn't just a dog. He's a horrible hound from hell. I can hear him now," Zalman groaned. "I know the sound his tag makes on his collar. He's shaking water all over the living room, and I know he's ruining my beautiful new paint." Zalman cocked his head to one side, listening. "Now he's up on the couch, rubbing his disgusting wet snout on the new silk pillows. That's it, I'm gonna kill him."

"I told you we shouldn't leave him alone with the Brie," Marie sighed. "He's a dear little bunny dog, but he isn't trustworthy where food is concerned."

Zalman sat up and glared at her. "Marie, he's a Doberman, and a Doberman can't possibly be described as a dear little bunny dog. He's a fiend dog from hell, and he isn't trustworthy, period. It wasn't just the Brie, either," he said sadly. "He ate all the pears, too. And I like pears. I looked forward to my Harry and David Fruit-of-the-Month pack. It comes all the way from Oregon."

"I know that," Marie said, whapping him gently with a wet dog towel. "It's my auntie Wishniak who sends you the darn thing, after all. I'm sorry he ate your pears, Jerry."

"And the Brie . . ."

"And the Brie. But we had to wash him. All that gooey cheese on his snout! He was a mess."

In the living room, Rutherford began to howl, a wet dog with a satisfied stomach. "Now the living room is a mess, too," Zalman said as he got up off the floor and looked around for a dry towel to wipe his hands on. There wasn't one, so he had to use his pants. "I spent a fortune on the living room, doll," he groaned.

"Well, you had to, Jerry," Marie pointed out in a reasonable tone of voice. "Sergeant Pepper is adorable, but I must say that I never realized monkeys were so messy. I always thought monkeys were very well behaved."

"Well, you were wrong. And I still think it smells funky in there."

"Oh, it does not!" Marie said. "It's all in your imagination. But at least Lydia and your dad took him back to Florida with them after the wedding."

"I hate weddings. But thank God the monkey's gone. We could have been stuck with the little villain forever. I hate monkeys, too," Zalman said. "Filthy creatures. Marie, if Rutherford's ruined the paint, I'm going to kill—"

Luckily for Rutherford, the phone rang in the bedroom. "Damn, I thought we'd have a quiet Sunday evening for once," Zalman said. "First I kill Rutherford; then I'm gonna rip the phone right out of the wall," he mumbled as he went into the bedroom to answer it. "I've always wanted to do that. Marie honey, see what you can do with ferrethead, will you? If he's done anything really horrible, keep it from me. I'm a weak man."

"Ohhhh, poor Jerry-werry," Marie teased as she went down the hall to the living room.

Jerry Zalman searched around on the floor for the phone. It rang again. Last he'd seen, it was buried under all the ten tons of the Sunday edition of the *L.A. Times*.

Up till now, Zalman and Marie had been enjoying a pleasant Sunday together. They'd read the paper in bed, watched *King Kong vs. Godzilla* on TV, then nipped over to Century City to the Stage for a deli dinner. Everything was swell until they returned home to find Rutherford up to his eyeballs in Brie. And now the phone.

Zalman didn't like the phone ringing late on a Sunday evening; it inevitably spelled bad news in bright red capital letters. Jerry Zalman was a lawyer in Beverly Hills, and because he had an oddball practice consisting of weird people with even weirder problems, a phone call on a Sunday evening always meant some kind of trouble. He found the phone, under the funnies.

"El Rancho Zalman," he snapped as he picked it up.

"Hey, Uncle Jerry, that's cute. El Rancho Zalman. Very cute. It's me, your nephew, Jason Hanning."

"You coulda just said it was Jason," Zalman said as he sat down on the bed and started searching around on the night table for his cigar case. Last he'd seen, it was under a screenplay he was reading for one of his clients, a writer named Huston who was hitting the comeback trail with an epic called *The Southland Swelters*, a tall tale about a hot spell in Beverly Hills. "I know you're my nephew and I know your name's Hanning. What's the matter? Your mother all right?"

"Sure," Jason said. "She's fine." Silence.

"Your father all right?"

"Sure. Fine." More silence.

Zalman found a cigar, snapped his gold Dunhill lighter, and slowly puffed the Macanudo to life. "Okay, Jason, I'll bite," he said as he watched the smoke drift across the bedroom. "Why are you calling me? You're thirteen years old, you don't need a lawyer, I trust...."

"Funny you should mention it, Uncle Jerry," Jason Hanning said brightly. "I was wondering if I could drop by the office tomorrow morning, first thing. Like about eleven?"

"You think eleven is first thing?" Zalman snorted. "You grow up, you're in for a big shock, kiddo. Yeah, sure you can come in. What's the problem?" he asked gently.

Zalman didn't like Jason's phone call one bit. He knew that the only reason the kid would call and ask for an appointment was because he had big trouble.

Still, he didn't want to start yelling at the kid and scare him to death. Whatever Jason's problem was, Jerry Zalman would handle it, because with him, family always came first. But one thing was certain. After he'd cleared up Jason's problem, then he'd yell at him and scare him silly so whatever he'd done, he damn well wouldn't do it again.

"Nothing cosmic," Jason said, his voice a bit too offhand, a bit too breezy. "But I'd rather tell you in the office. I like to maintain a thoroughly professional attitude where business is concerned. Okay?"

"Sure it's okay, whaddaya think? See you at eleven." Zalman hung up, blew a double smoke ring, and frowned across the bedroom at his poster of Paul Muni in *Scarface*. Business? This was not a good sign. Not at all. What kind of business could a thirteen-year-old kid have with Jerry Zalman, Esq., first thing in the morning? Whatever Jason Hanning wanted, it wasn't going to be good, and Jerry Zalman, Esq., didn't like it one damn bit.

Zalman switched off the bell on the phone. At least he'd spare himself any more dumb phone calls, he thought as he went to the living room to ask Marie's advice.

Zalman loved a lot of things about the adorable Miss Marie Thrasher. He loved her curly auburn hair, he loved her brown eyes, he was crazy about her smart mouth, but one of the things he loved most was the level head she had planted firmly on her cute little shoulders. She had a great brain, and she never told Zalman anything but the whole truth, even when he didn't want to hear it.

Marie was sitting on the floor drying off Rutherford, and they were both watching *They Only Kill Their Masters* on TV.

"He shouldn't watch that," Zalman warned as he came in. "It'll give him bad doggy thoughts, twist his psyche into a pretzel. Marie, riddle me this. Why do you think a thirteen-year-old boy would want to see a lawyer? Anything you can think of, right off the top of your head?"

"Uh-oh," Marie said. "I smell trouble. Who was on the phone? Any particular thirteen-year-old boy?" she asked suspiciously, arching a delicate eyebrow. "Does he want to see any particular lawyer I happen to know personally?"

"Jason Hanning. Me."

Marie rolled Rutherford over on his back and began to rub his tummy with the towel. Rutherford stared up at Zalman and panted damply, his pink tongue hanging out of the side of his mouth. The dog looked as if he was smiling. "Hmm," Marie said, frowning. "I hate to tell you this, Jerry. I don't want it to come as a big shock, but maybe you've noticed that most of the time when a guy wants to see a lawyer it means he's got a problem."

"That's the first thing I learned when I stepped up to the bar, as the girl said to the sailor." Zalman grinned.

"Even a thirteen-year-old guy. And if he's coming to see you, it's probably a very big, very expensive problem."

"Hey!" Zalman said defensively, stubbing out his cigar in a silver ashtray on the bar. "I wasn't gonna charge him. He's my nephew, Marie! Besides, he's only thirteen. What's he gonna pay me with, a couple of used Nintendos? Maybe he's got some Gobots he's tired of and he wants me to take them in trade?"

Marie smiled up at Zalman and thoughtfully began to rub Rutherford behind the ears. "You know I love you, don't you, Jerry?" she asked.

"I take it that's rhetorical?" Zalman asked. "Of course it's rhetorical and of course you love me. I'm a great guy. What's not to love?"

Marie shook her head ruefully. "Did you ever wonder why I love you?"

"Not until now," Zalman said as he sat down next to her on the floor, bent over, and bit her on the ankle. "Because I'm taller than you are?" he said as he straightened up. "Because I'm brave, clean, and reverent? Because I let you buy me dinner?"

"All of the above," Marie agreed, leaning over to kiss him. "But mainly because of your sense of humor."

"I knew you had a good reason, but I was hoping it was something with a little more zip," Zalman sighed. "Like how I drive you into a mad paroxysm of passion, three shows nightly."

"Oh, well, of course there's always that," Marie said airily. "And I also love you because you're honest. You're a little selfish, a little greedy, a little self-centered, but at least you don't try to pretend. You have faults—"

"The hell you say."

"But you don't try to hide them," she continued. "And it makes you lovable. You know," she said thoughtfully, "honesty is a real turn-on in a man, because these days it's so unusual."

Zalman leaned down again and began to nibble on Marie's bare toes. "That wasn't what I was hoping for," he said between kisses. "But in life you take what you can get. Okay, enough idle chitchat. You think the kid's headed for summer camp in a Turkish prison? What's going on here? He says it's business, what kind of business can he possibly have? And why is he calling me? I'm just his uncle. If he's got a problem, why doesn't he go to his mother? My sister's in the rock-and-roll business; she knows all about the vagaries of modern life. Or why doesn't he go to Phil? Okay, Phil's not the brain of the century but he's the kid's father and—"

"You're tickling me, Jerry." Marie laughed as she wiggled her foot away. "C'mon, Jerry! Don't get feeble on me. Think back, honey, way way back into the dark days of puberty. Now, when you were thirteen, what was the one thing you didn't want to talk to your parents about, hmm?"

Zalman stopped kissing Marie's toes abruptly and looked up to see Rutherford drooling at him. "Ohhh," Zalman said slowly. "I get it."

"Exactly!" Marie laughed. "It must be love."

Zalman moaned and buried his head in his hands. "*Cherchez la* preteen *femme,* huh? Oh, no! This can't be happening already! He's only thirteen!"

"God, Jerry! Grow up! How old were you when you—"

"A gentleman never reveals that sort of information, Marie. You should know that. Besides, Louanne Springle and I had a deeply meaningful relationship, and I'll carry the memory of our shared love to my grave," he said as he looked up. "But that's not the point. The point is, how did this happen to me? Only yesterday I was a psychedelic rebel, the hero of the picket line, and now all of a sudden I'm a lawyer in Beverly Hills and I've got a smart-aleck nephew with woman trouble. Old age isn't creeping up; it's leaping up! I knew it was going to happen; I just didn't think it was going to happen so fast. Makes me feel old, that's all."

"Well, you're not old, and if you come over here, I'll let you prove it to me."

"I thought you'd never ask." Zalman laughed as he started kissing his way up Marie's leg. "Well, whatever Jason's got to say for himself, I'll hear all about it first thing in the morning. Like about eleven."

But when Jerry Zalman strolled into his office first thing in the morning, like about nine, he was amazed to see his secretary, Esther Wong, seated at her desk. Esther was both gorgeous and scrutable, and though she thrilled each and every client with her smooth ice-cube smile and her dark, lustrous hair, she rarely came to the office until ten, ten-thirty.

"Esther," Zalman said in surprise, tossing his briefcase on the chair next to her desk, "why are you here? You know you never come in until ten at the earliest. Are you all right? Is something wrong, dear?"

"Oh, Mr. Z.," Esther moaned as she searched in her purse for her hairbrush. "Pete Marchetti called me at seven o'clock this morning and woke me up! It was awful . . . the crack of dawnnnnn. . . . He'd been trying to get you for hours, but you weren't picking up your home phone, so he called me."

"Yeah, I switched off the bell. Even an attorney has the right to privacy once in a while," Zalman said.

"I thought it was something like that, but Pete's having a fit! He's at Le Croque, waiting for a very important delivery of calamari for the lunch menu, or he'd be here already."

"Calamari? Squid?" Zalman shook his head in disgust. "Call Spago and make me a lunch reservation, I ain't eating at Le Croque today, I can promise you that. I don't eat anything that's got tentacles and an ink sac. What's Marchetti want?"

"I don't know," Esther moaned. "But he's been calling me every half-hour since seven, so I thought I might as well come in to the office, since I was already awake. I've asked him what the problem is, but he won't tell me. He's really upset, too, Mr. Z. He's talking normally."

"You mean he isn't using that phony French accent of his? Or phony Hungarian. I can never figure out what country he's supposed to be from. Hmm,"

BLOODY MARY

Zalman said, puzzled. "This sounds serious. Well, I'm here, so next time he calls—"

The phone rang. Esther sighed and picked it up very carefully so she wouldn't chip her Slightly Scarlet, inch-long nails. "I bet that's . . . Hi, Pete," she said, rolling her eyes dramatically and pointing at the phone. "Yes, he just came . . . Yes, he . . . Just a minute, Pete, I'll put him . . ." Esther punched the hold button. "Talk to him, Mr. Z. He's in an awful state and he's driving me bananas."

Zalman picked up his briefcase, strolled into his office, and sat down in his big leather chair behind his huge Victorian partners desk.

Zalman looked around, enjoying, as he did every morning, his little corner of Beverly Hills. He loved his desk, he loved his office; matter of fact, he loved his entire world. Jerry Zalman had only one problem in life that a six-figure income couldn't cure: he was a short guy, five feet four and a half, although he invariably lied about it and claimed he was five-five. That's why he liked a big desk and an even bigger chair. It made him taller than his clients, even if the added height was only an illusion. What the hell. Zalman always figured that in L.A., illusion was the next best thing to reality.

He spun around so he could see Beverly Drive spread out below him. Beverly Drive always reminded him of a jumbo version of Uncle Milton's Ant Farm with a bad case of nerves, and this morning was no exception. Even though it was early, Beverly Drive was buzzing with trendy street life. He punched the speakerphone. "Pete!" he called, one eye on the early morning shoppers below him. "How ya do—"

"Zally! Zally!" Pete Marchetti moaned. "Thank God you're in! What happened to you? I tried you at home, but you didn't answer! I almost had a heart attack! Jerry, you gotta help me. I got a big problem.

Serious problem! Only you, Jerry Zalman, can help me out, save my life. When can I see you? Christ, I got a guy coming into the restaurant with some fresh calamari any minute, and I gotta see him; I already got it printed on the lunch menu, so what time, Jerry, huh? Ten-thirty? I gotta see you!"

"Pete, what the hell's the matter with you! Shut your yap a minute, will you? What are you telling me about squid for? Nobody wants to hear about squid at nine o'clock in the morning, and don't think you can fool me by calling it calamari. A squid's a squid in any language and they're always disgusting. C'mon, what's the matter, Petey-pie," Zalman cajoled. "Tell Poppa."

"Please, Jerry!" Pete cried. "You gotta help me! I gotta see you! I don't want to talk about it over the phone," he said, lowering his voice. "These guys that work for me, they claim they don't speak English, but I don't believe a word of it."

"Okay, okay. Come about eleven-thirty, quarter of twelve," Zalman said, remembering Jason's troubling visit. "Best I can do for you."

"Ayyy, the lunch hour! My busy time . . . but I'll be there, Jer! We gotta talk!"

Zalman clicked off the phone and went over to the bar for some coffee. "Thanks for putting on the coffee, Esther," he called into her office.

"Bring me a cup, please, Mr. Z.," she called. "It's so early, I feel dizzy. I drove in on the freeway. I couldn't believe all those people were already awake and driving!"

"They're not already awake; they're still awake," Zalman said as he poured a pair of coffees, went back into Esther's office, and put her cup down on her desk.

Esther was opening the mail. "Umm, thanks," she said as she took a dainty sip of her coffee. "So what did Pete say? What's the big problem?" she asked as she threw a Neiman-Marcus catalog on the coffee table.

"Nothing, he just whined for a few minutes about how tough it is to be a successful restaurateur in Beverly Hills, told me about his squid delivery, and begged for an appointment. I told him eleven-thirty, quarter of twelve," Zalman said. "I've got a high-paying customer coming in at eleven."

Esther looked up from the Horchow catalog. "Oh, goody, is he single?" she asked expectantly.

Zalman laughed. Esther was forever on the trail of true love, though so far all she'd managed was modern romance. "Yeah, he's single, but he's also thirteen years old, Esther, so forget it. Jason Hanning called me last night, wants to come in and see me."

Esther looked shocked. "Jason? Is it serious? Does Lucille know?"

"I don't know. He wouldn't talk over the phone. God, everybody's so paranoid about the phone these days." Zalman laughed as he sipped his coffee. "Like what could a thirteen-year-old have to say that the CIA would want to hear?"

"If he wants to come in and see you, it must be serious. After all, today's a school day," Esther said primly.

"School. Jeez, I never thought about school," Zalman said. "I forgot you have to go to school when you're thirteen. Kiddie jail. The slammer for tykes. I wonder how he got out of it? I bet he got Phil to write him a note. Phil, he'd write you a note. Now, my dad would never write me a note unless we were going to the track. Something serious. He always told me to use my free time in a constructive manner." Zalman grinned.

"But is it serious? Do you think Jason's in trouble?" Esther pressed. "What does Marie think?"

BLOODY MARY

"Marie thinks he's in love," Zalman said with a laugh.

"At his age?" Esther said in amazement.

"C'mon, Esther, grow up!" Zalman said sagely.

Esther stared at him wordlessly, then picked up the phone. "I think I'll run out at lunch and get an herbal body wrap," she mused as she poked the buttons with a silver pencil. "Jason? In love? All of a sudden I feel very wrinkly."

Zalman took his coffee and retreated into his office where he was safe from the distressing problems of love-struck kids and mollusk-ridden restaurateurs and dug into the pile of papers on his desk.

At five of eleven, Zalman was on the phone with Huston the writer, explaining to the old pro that even though *The Southland Swelters* was a damn good screenplay, it needed more violence if there was to be a shot at a development deal with a major studio, but Huston was skeptical.

As he coaxed his recalcitrant client, Zalman spun around in his chair and looked out the window at Beverly Drive and saw a beautifully restored pink '68 Cadillac Fleetwood with black glass windows and glinting chrome fenders glide to a stop right below his office.

A tough, louty kid dressed entirely in black leather and silver studs slouched out of the driver's seat, surveyed Beverly Drive with the cold eyes of a Secret Service agent, and spat carefully into the gutter. The kid slicked back his greasy black ducktail with one palm and nonchalantly pulled open the back door of the Caddy.

Jason Hanning nodded to the lout in black as he got out of the car, adjusted the lapels of his sharp gray silk suit, shot his cuffs, and reached into the car to give the little lady a big hand.

BLOODY MARY

A dainty foot in a navy blue ankle-strap heel peeked out of the car; then the rest of the blonde followed it. She was twelve, maybe pushing thirteen, and she was wearing a demure navy blue suit with a white silk blouse and a snappy blue chapeau. Even from his upstairs office, Zalman could see a string of pearls the size of Jujyfruits around her neck.

"What the hell? Huston, I gotta go," Zalman barked as he stared at the scene below his office window in amazement. "Talk to me later." He slammed down the phone and took a closer look at the three kids.

The lout parked a casual hip against the Caddy's hood and began to snap his fingers and whistle to himself as Jason patted Blondie on the cheek and she gave him a worried glance. Even from his second floor vantage point, Zalman could see the glazed look of puppy love burning fiercely in Jason Hanning's eyes. As always, Marie was right. Jason Hanning had woman trouble.

Zalman shook his head in disbelief as he watched Blondie take out a heavy gold compact and begin to powder her nose, staring critically at her reflection. Blondie was perfectly togged out for a 1940s Warner Brothers gangster flick, and though Jason Hanning's duds were contemporary, he matched her high-style look perfectly.

Zalman shook his head again and laughed out loud. He was a longtime film noir fan and loved the look. Besides, both Jason and Blondie had plenty of pizzazz and he admired them for it. Even in Hollywood, a good act was hard to find.

But who was Jason's lady love? Who was the lout in black? If Jason and Blondie were living in grainy black-and-white, the lout was emulating full-color, lip-twitching Elvis, maybe in *Spinout* or *Blue Hawaii*. And where did they get the car? What the hell was going on here?

BLOODY MARY

As Jason and Blondie disappeared into the entrance of Zalman's building, the lout leaned up against the car and pulled out a smoke, snapping his fingers and whistling to his own interior sound track.

Zalman went over to the bar and made himself a Bullshot, just in case. He wondered if he ought to call Lucille right away and let her know she had big, big trouble with her firstborn, but he didn't want to panic his sister so early in the morning. Maybe nothing was wrong. Maybe Jason was kidding about his business problems, and maybe it was just a social call. Or maybe it was just a tricky question on the algebra final. And maybe if Grandma had wheels she'd be a trolley.

Zalman frowned thoughtfully. How could this happen? Lucille and Phil Hanning spent plenty of quality time with their three kids. Lucille was an important manager in the rock-and-roll biz and worked a sixty-hour week, but Phil was a househusband and he'd always been there for the kids, picked them up after school, trucked them off to piano lessons, ballet, whatever. Phil and Lucille gave their kids a stable upbringing, good schools, summer camp, the whole nine yards, and look what happened.

Thank God I don't have kids, Zalman thought. Rutherford is bad enough. He heard the door to the outer office open and Esther's voice murmuring.

The intercom buzzed. "Yeah?" he said, trying to sound casual but businesslike. If something was wrong with Jason, it would break his sister's heart in a thousand pieces. Zalman knew that was a dead-certain fact. So whatever trouble Jason and Blondie had cooked up for themselves, Zalman knew he had to keep it from Lucille if it was humanly possible.

"Jason's here," Esther said. "And he has a friend with him. A young lady," she added pointedly.

"Oh?" Zalman replied. "How nice." He wasn't

going to tell Esther he'd seen them out the window, and he wasn't going to admit that he was already plenty worried. "Be right out."

Slowly Zalman got out of his chair, walked across the room, and opened his office door. Here comes trouble, he thought, a great big fake smile plastered on his face.

"Jason, gladda see you," he said as he shook hands with his nephew.

"Uncle Jerry, thanks for the meeting," Jason Hanning said as he came in. "I know what your time is worth."

Jason flashed a cocky grin at his uncle. He was a good-looking kid, with his father's regular features and his mother's smart eyes and dark, curly Zalman hair. The kid looked right at home in his snappy silk suit; Jason Hanning was only thirteen, but he'd already acquired a patina of ennui that came from an upper-crust upbringing in the wilds of Toluca Lake, an exclusive enclave in L.A.'s San Fernando Valley.

"This is Brenda," Jason said. "My close friend."

Brenda smiled, batted her eyes, and gravely extended her little hand to Zalman. "So kind of you to see us, Mr. Zalman," she said softly. "So kind."

"Please, sit down," Zalman said, offering her a chair. If she wanted to play a breathless ingenue in a 1940s gangster flick, it was okay with him; he'd play along. What the hell, he knew all the dialogue by heart.

Brenda took one of the deep leather armchairs across from Zalman's desk, and Jason perched protectively on the arm of her chair. Carefully he reached into his jacket pocket and took out a slim silver cigarette case, opened it, and offered her a licorice stick. Brenda shook her blonde head no.

"Yeah, I appreciate the meeting," Jason said as he selected a stick for himself, snapped the lid closed, and replaced the case in his jacket pocket. "Means a lot, a guy has family he can depend on."

Zalman sat down behind his desk, folded his hands carefully, and began to play "here is the church, here is the steeple, open the doors, see all the people." "Of course, Jason," he said smoothly. "You got a problem, you come to see me first. Okay? Never forget that," he told the kid expansively. "See me first. But look, you gotta be straight with me, okay? Never forget that either. So the first thing you gotta tell me is what the hell's going on? Who's the stooge downstairs, huh? Driving the Cad? The moose boy in black?"

"Tyrone?" Brenda said innocently, the faintest trace of a pout on her pretty face. "He drives for us. We're not old enough to drive. He's sixteen, so he drives us, picks us up."

Jason nodded. "I needed someone to help me out," he added.

Zalman closed the doors, squashed all the people, and regarded the kids closely. Help me out? What did that mean? "He works for you? You're saying he works for you?" he asked Jason.

"Well, yeah. In a manner of speaking, he does," Jason answered.

"Jason, Jason, Jason, I told you, you gotta be straight with me, right? So tell me this. I know your mother doesn't give you enough money for a chauffeur and a Caddy, even an old one. I know your father—a wonderful man and a helluva cook—so I'm not maligning him, okay?" Zalman said. "But not a financial genius."

Jason shook his head sadly. "Dad's a great guy," he said. "But I know you're right, Uncle Jerry. Not good with money. Lucky for me, I take after Mom. And of course, Ernie."

BLOODY MARY

"Don't call your grandfather Ernie, will you, Jason? Show a little respect."

"I told you before, he wants me to call him Ernie!" Jason protested. "But look, Uncle Jerry, here's what we wanted to see you—"

"First things first, kiddo. You didn't explain to me about the kid and the Caddy. How do you get the dough to employ this fine young man?" Zalman asked, jerking a thumb toward the window. "First, let's talk about that. Then we'll talk about your problem."

Jason grinned happily and shot his cuffs. "Okay, Uncle Jerry, have it your way."

"I usually do," Zalman said sharply. He couldn't believe it. The resemblance was horrifying. Jason Hanning was the image of his gambling grandfather, Ernest K. Zalman.

"The dough, huh? You want to know about the dough? Well, me and Brenda have a nice little business going."

"What are you telling me, Jason?" Zalman exploded, fearful visions of teenage illegality dancing in his head like stale sugarplums. "You're thirteen—"

"And a half!"

"And a half. What kind of business can you have? You got a paper route? You deliver *Fortune* door to door in Beverly Hills, what? Tell me, Jason, I want to know!"

Jason got up off the arm of Brenda's chair and leaned on the back of the chair next to her. He was twirling his licorice stick in his fingers like a tiny cane. "Uncle Jerry"—he smiled knowingly—"don't you trust me?"

"Sure, I trust you, Jason," Zalman lied. "Like you were my own son. And you trust me, right?"

Jason grinned. "You bet, Uncle Jerry."

"Okay. Since we trust each other so much, why

don't you just set my worried mind at ease, huh, kiddo? Tell Uncle Jerry. . . ."

"Simple," Jason said, still smiling. "It's Achenbachs."

"Well, that's great, Jason." Zalman smiled paternally. "Now that I know it's Achenbachs I feel one whole helluva lot better about it. Makes all the difference. Clears everything right up. So what the hell are Achenbachs, Jason? Explain it to me, will ya?"

Zalman was getting worried. The kid was clearly bonkers, a mental condition that ran through the entire Zalman clan, but which had miraculously skipped Zalman himself. He could never understand how it was that everyone in his family was nuts except him. An amazing piece of luck, he often thought, and a tribute to his own mental stability.

"It's a long story," Jason hedged.

"I got time," Zalman said as he sipped his coffee and smiled benignly. "And if I didn't have time, I'd make time for you."

Jason shrugged. "Well, about a year ago I got bored in school, and Mom decided I was having deep-seated emotional problems. Not true," the kid said, wagging his finger. "But she got this idea in her head, and you know Mom. She figured she oughta send me to a shrink so's I wouldn't get weirded out. You know how she's always saying she doesn't want us to grow up like Beverly Hills brats. Which I've never quite understood, since we live in Toluca Lake. I tried to tell her I was just bored with school—I gotta tell you, Uncle Jerry, you know me. I'm planning to be a Renaissance man and go into the diplomatic corps, and I need a topflight education if I'm gonna achieve my personal goals."

"Yeah, yeah, I heard you play 'Stormy Weather' last time I was at your house," Zalman said. "I know you're smart. Go on, tell me about the rabbits, Jason."

"Steinbeck, right?"

Zalman nodded. *"Of Mice and Men."*

"Ya see, that's the kind of thing they don't teach you in school. That's why it's so boring. Here I am, reading Steinbeck and the teachers are telling me it's too adult, I should try *Travels with Charley* 'cause it's got a dog in it. Gimme a break. School's a drag. So Mom sends me to this guy, got an office around the corner here on Canon Drive. Dr. Pudzowski. You hearda him?"

"No, but I bet I know what you call him for short."

Jason grinned. "Yeah. Ol' Dr. Pud. He gives you an Achenbach test. It's a behavior profile, and he gives 'em to all his patients. All shrinks do. It's gotta be scored on a computer so you know how nutty you are. So, I like Dr. Pud, it's kinda relaxing. We play chess in his office, and besides, that's where I met Brenda."

Brenda smiled and crossed her legs daintily. "It was my lucky day, Jason," she said as she reached out and patted his arm gently.

"So then what happened?" Zalman prodded.

"So I go to see Dr. Pud for a while and we get to be good friends. We talk. We share. He tells me all about how he wanted to be an architect, but his dad was a doctor so he had to be a doctor, too. Dr. Pud kinda fell into the kiddie shrink end of the racket, and now he's making so much dough his wife won't let him quit. He wanted to go back to school and give himself a chance to grow as a person, and he felt he was stuck in a dead-end job. Talking to crazy kids all day long can be a drag, I guess. He said I was the first person he'd been able to communicate with on a sincere level in a long, long time. So then he meets this girl. She's his research assistant, right?"

"Jason," Zalman warned, "I said I had time; I

didn't mean a lifetime. Tell me about the Achenbachs, okay?"

"I'm getting to it. One thing led to another. Dr. Pud had to break up with his girlfriend when his wife found out. But the girlfriend was scoring the Achenbachs for him, so he was stuck. I told him it was no problem; I'd handle it for him on my home computer. I started doing his Achenbachs, and he got me referrals from every kiddie shrink in town," Jason said, as he leaned forward conspiratorially. "See, I got no overhead so I can afford to undercut the competition. Me and Brenda knock 'em out on weekends. I got a couple other kids working for me; I'm making a fortune!" Jason said smugly.

"You take after your grandfather, that's for sure." Zalman laughed. "Okay, Jason, you've relieved me of some nagging tension. I know you're on the straight and narrow, and I have nothing to worry about, right?"

"Yeah, except for this little problem I got." Jason sighed, nibbling nervously on his licorice stick.

Brenda leaned forward in her chair and stared hopefully across the big partners desk at Zalman. "Actually, Mr. Zalman, it's my problem. Jason's only trying to protect me."

"Proves he'll be a gentleman when he grows up," Zalman told her kindly. "Tell me all about it, okay? Whatever it is, I'll do my best for both of you, okay? C'mon, tell Uncle Jerry what happened. . . ."

Brenda looked at Jason, who nodded his assent. "Go ahead, honey," Jason urged. "It's okay."

"Well," she began. "Last Saturday one of the girls from school had a birthday party."

"It was a lovely party," Jason added. "Pete does a great job."

A cold finger of fear tickled its way up and down Jerry Zalman's back. "Pete?" Zalman said slowly.

"Pete who? Who Pete?" He knew he didn't want to know. He just knew it.

"Oh, that's right, you know Pete, too," Jason said. "I forgot. Pete Marchetti, owns Le Croque? You know Le Croque, don't you, Uncle Jerry?"

"I ought to," Zalman snapped. "I eat there practically every day of my life. Except for today 'cause the special's calamari and I don't even like to look a squid in the eye," Zalman said slowly. "Go on."

"Well, Angela Marchetti—that's Pete's daughter by his second marriage? We all go to the same school in Encino together, and since her father's got the restaurant, she had her birthday party there. I had the veal piccata, sliced nice and thin the way I like it, and Brenda had the—"

"Jason," Zalman warned, wondering if he ought to take Maalox right away or wait until the heartburn he could feel festering in the pit of his stomach was in full, fiery flower. "Skip the menu. Give it to me straight, okay? Now?"

Brenda sighed and a small tear threaded its way down her cheek. "I'm so ashamed," she said brokenly. "So ashamed of myself . . ."

"It's a compulsion, honey," Jason soothed, patting her arm. "C'mon, you know Dr. Pud says you can't control a compulsion without years of treatment. Besides, it only happens when you feel deprived."

"Jason!" Zalman warned.

"Okay, I'm getting to it! So there were about thirty of us from school, but the regular Saturday lunch crowd was there, too. Now, since it was Angela's birthday, she was getting all the attention. The regular stuff—presents, cake, singing 'Happy Birthday.' All the waiters sang 'Happy Birthday.' But every time another girl gets a lot of attention, Brenda feels deprived, like she isn't getting the love she's entitled to. Dr. Pud thinks it's because her mother died when

BLOODY MARY

Brenda was little and a sense of abandonment triggers negative feelings in Brenda. I agree with him," Jason said sagely. "He's got a point. But when she feels this emotional deprivation, this hollow void inside her, there's only one thing she can do to fill that void, see. It's a compulsion, like I said."

"What does Brenda do?" Zalman said softly. He felt like throttling both kids and heaving them out the window, but he controlled the urge. After all, he was an adult.

"She takes things that don't belong to her," Jason said.

Brenda extracted a lacy white handkerchief from her purse and buried her face in it, sobbing softly.

"She steals," Zalman said with his usual practicality. "We call that stealing. When you take something that doesn't belong to you, that's called stealing. Okay, that's the good news, I take it. You want to hit me with the bad news? What did Brenda steal? I'm dying to know."

Jason reached into the pocket of his gray silk suit and silently handed his Uncle Jerry a small package wrapped neatly in three-ring notebook paper. "This," the kid said. "And I think it's gonna be a problem."

Zalman took the package and hefted it in his hand. It weighed only four or five ounces. Carefully he unwrapped the package and laid the contents gently on his desk. "Well, I'll be damned," he said as he stared at one of the most beautiful things he'd ever seen in his life.

A SOLID-GOLD MEDALLION WAS NESTLED IN THE WHITE square of notebook paper lying in the middle of Zalman's desk. The medallion bore the graceful image of a woman's profile, and a loosely sculpted dove hovered behind her three-eyed head. The dove's spread wings were etched with a delicate tracery of lacy engraving in strange, almost hieroglyphic patterns.

It was beautiful, it was brilliant, it was strong but graceful; innocent, yet the woman's lips curved with a secret, sensuous passion.

Although it was unsigned, the gold medallion was clearly the work of a great artist, and Zalman had a good idea who the creator was. Carefully he picked up the medallion and turned it over. There was a pin on the back and also a small gold jump ring so it could be worn as either a brooch or a pendant.

"It's absolutely beautiful," Zalman said in admiration. "I've never seen anything like it before."

"Few people have," Brenda agreed.

Zalman thought he heard a trace of pride in her voice, but he let it pass. He turned the medallion over again and gazed at the woman's profile. "Well," he said. "I'm no art critic, but if this ain't a Picasso, I'm Pee Wee Herman."

"It is and you're not," Jason told his uncle. "I went through some art books Mom had at home after Brenda, uh, Brenda got it. Critics think it's one of five, though nobody seems to be too sure. See, back in the forties, Picasso had this rich lady friend, and she wanted him to make her a nice piece of jewelry. She thought a piece of Picasso jewelry would have more cachet than Cartier."

"I always heard Picasso was a girl's best friend," Zalman said dryly.

"I think you're right," Brenda added. "Tell him the rest, Jason."

"So this lady friend of Pablo's gave him a bunch of her jewelry and some Mexican escudos she had lying around, and Picasso took the stuff over to his dentist, a guy named Chataignier, and told him what to do."

"This thing was made by a dentist?" Zalman asked incredulously, turning the medallion over and over in his hand like George Raft's lucky dollar. "Are you sure?"

Jason laughed happily. "Yeah, ain't that something? Dr. Chataignier melted the stuff down, put it all together just like Pablo ordered, and the lady got the pin she wanted. It's a pretty rare piece. There were some others made, but nobody's really sure how many or where they are, so this is worth a bundle. A similar one got hammered down at Christie's last year, and judging by the picture in the catalog, this one's better by a long shot."

Zalman rubbed his fingers over the medallion longingly. His taste in home decor ran to film noir movie posters, Oriental rugs, and shiny silver walls—until the unfortunate episode with Sergeant Pepper the incontinent monkey. But even so, Jerry Zalman harbored a deep passion, a secret desire for the truly beautiful, and he'd always hoped that someday he'd latch on to an original piece of hard-core art. In fact, one of the worst moments of his life was when he discovered that his ex-wife Tracee, may she rot, had sold a Toulouse-Lautrec etching of his to finance

BLOODY MARY

World O' Yip, her current husband's New Age health spa.

"A Picasso medallion." Zalman sighed greedily. "It's a gem. Okay, Brenda, time to fess up. Give me the whole story. How'd you get this?" he asked.

Brenda reached for Jason's hand as she leaned toward Zalman's desk. "At Angela's birthday party," she said quietly. "I . . . uh . . . I got so mad, and there were four ladies sitting next to us at another table. Like Jason said, it wasn't just us kids from school. There were regular people there, too. And when I saw the medallion on this woman's mink coat I had to have it, that's all!" Brenda said defiantly.

"Bad habit, Brenda," Zalman said sternly.

"It was so beautiful, I couldn't help myself. Surely a man like you can understand that, Mr. Zalman," Brenda said as her eyes swept over Zalman's office, taking in the Victorian furniture, the rugs, the polished look of wealth and stability that Zalman had created around him. "You're a man of taste, a man of feeling," she said. "I can tell. I just slipped it off her coat when she got up to go to the ladies' room. She didn't notice me. Grown-ups never notice us kids." Brenda pouted.

Zalman looked at his nephew. "You have anything to do with this, Jason?" he asked quietly, giving the kid the full blast of his harsh-lawyer stare.

"I didn't know a thing about it until after the fact," Jason said quickly. "This was Saturday. I didn't know anything until Brenda called me Sunday morning, and that's the truth, Uncle Jerry. I thought about it. Later on I decided we'd better ask you to help. If I go to Mom, she'll just freak out, and Dad, this kind of stuff's not in his area of expertise," Jason said diplomatically.

"Hmm," Zalman said, still stroking the Picasso

medallion with a loving forefinger. "I take it you want me to return this for you?"

"You bet," Jason said strongly. "Brenda's sorry and she's going to talk to Dr. Pud about the whole episode in tomorrow's session, but I want it returned right away, before the insurance companies get involved. Maybe we'll get lucky and the police aren't in on it yet."

Brenda snuffled loudly and hiccuped.

"Can you do it for us, Uncle Jerry? Look, I know Marchetti—"

"Mr. Marchetti to you, Jason," Zalman snapped. "Don't be so fresh!"

"Yeah, yeah, right. I know who he is, but if I go in there, try to work it out with him, he's gonna flip, call Mom. Brenda'll get in big trouble. Her stepmother already doesn't like her, and this could be the big excuse the old bat's looking for. She wants to send Brenda to some dumb East Coast boarding school."

"She hates me! She wants me out of the house and I don't want to go to Foxcroft! I love L.A.!" Brenda cried. "Please, Mr. Zalman. I'm sorry about the medallion. Won't you please take it back for me? I need your help so badly, Mr. Zalman. . . ." She dabbed at her blue eyes helplessly as tears ran down her cheeks like tiny diamonds. "I have nowhere else to turn."

Zalman shook his head. Brenda was going to be a killer-diller when she grew up, no doubt about it. The blue eyes, the tears, the Mary Astor dialogue . . .

"Okay, okay, turn off the waterworks," he said gruffly. "I obviously don't have a choice. Brenda, I'll help you, but you have to promise me you'll talk to your shrink tomorrow. I'll return the medallion for you, don't worry about it. But I want your word that you'll get some help. I know Pete Marchetti. He's a friend of mine, and he'll get the medallion back to the lady. This time it'll be handled. But you keep stealing and one day you'll steal from the wrong person, Brenda. Foxcroft's gonna look damn good to you, you hear me? You know what I'm talking about here?" Zalman said, wagging a warning finger. "You can't steal and get away with it forever, Brenda. Take it from me. That's my professional advice to you as an attorney. People pay me lots of money for my advice, and you're getting it for nothing, so attend to my words," Zalman said as he got up out of his chair. "Now, you two get out of here. Go back to school or do whatever kids your age are supposed to do. Trust me."

Jason and Brenda stood up, and Jason leaned across the desk and extended his hand. "I knew that coming to see you was the right thing, Uncle Jerry," he said as they shook hands. "Thanks. When I grow up, I won't forget this."

"I hope not," Zalman said as he walked the kids to the office door. "Good-bye, Brenda. Remember what I told you."

Brenda pressed both her tiny hands into Zalman's and looked up at him trustingly, her blue eyes wet with tears. "I'll never forget this either, Mr. Zalman, I promise you."

Brenda and Jason left, and Zalman went back into his office and stared down at them through the big window as Tyrone opened the back door of the Caddy and the kids got in. Tyrone the lout hopped into the driver's seat, and the car screeched off down Beverly Drive, burned a patch of rubber at the corner, and squealed onto Wilshire Boulevard.

"Kids," Zalman said to the ceiling. "What the hell's the matter with them?" He turned and saw the Picasso medallion shimmering on his desk like a dream in the night. Damn shame he couldn't keep it, Zalman thought longingly as he walked over to his desk and picked up the medallion.

BLOODY MARY

A guy like him really appreciated a thing of beauty. A guy like him could give it the care it deserved. Imagine some silly woman wearing a Picasso on her mink coat as if it was a two-bit rhinestone trinket. Imagine wearing a Picasso medallion out to lunch. It was a crime, Zalman thought, shaking his head. Some crazy world.

Twenty minutes later, Zalman was still admiring the Picasso medallion and wondering if there was any way he could possibly avoid giving it back to Pete Marchetti. Of course, the minute Jason told him the kids were at Le Croque, Zalman had put two and two together. Pete's hysterical phone call and impending office visit plus Brenda's attack of light fingers equaled the Picasso medallion.

Too damn bad, though, Zalman thought as he admired the warm glow of the gold in his hand. Too damn bad I'm so honest.

"Mr. Z.," Esther called. "Pete's here."

"Oh, goody," Zalman said to himself, slipping the medallion into his pocket.

Pete Marchetti burst into Zalman's office and stood in the doorway, his thin, ratlike face twitching. He was a nervous little guy with patent leather hair he kept slicked back because a casting director from Fox had once told him he was a dead ringer for Pat Riley, and Pete never forgot a compliment.

Pete Marchetti and Jerry Zalman went back a long way, ever since Pete Marchetti left Cleveland in a big hurry after a nasty dust-up with the IRS and moved to California to seek a second fortune.

After a few abortive attempts at various business schemes, Pete had found his true niche in life when he opened Le Croque, an ultra-chic French eatery on the outskirts of Beverly Hills. Very quickly he turned the joint into the trendiest restaurant in town. Of course, he had an unlisted phone number, and in an amazing show of reverse snobbery, he also refused to take reservations, which meant that those citizens who wanted to chow down at Le Croque had to stand in line. But instead of being insulted, L.A.'s glitziest thought Pete's chutzpah was cute, and Le Croque was standing room only seven days a week.

But Jerry Zalman never stood in line, not, as he often said, to see Moses wrestle a bear. In return for a constantly reserved table and free food in perpetuity, Zalman had done all the legal work on Pete's tax-fraud case, and Pete had gone legit, although he insisted on calling himself Pierre. He also began to affect a constantly shifting foreign accent, presumably French, though Zalman thought it had a mere hint of Mittel European flavor.

Now Pete Marchetti stood in Zalman's office door, his thin face a twisted mask of anguish. "Jerry!" he cried in terror. "Christamighty, I got a big problem here!" Pete moaned as he threw himself into the leather armchair recently vacated by Jason Hanning and buried his pointy face in his hands.

Zalman smiled benignly at his old friend and client. "What's the matter, Petey-pie, your squid didn't show up?" he said.

"Zally, Zally, don't noodle me about the squid, will ya? Other people like squid. I got a restaurant to run. Just because you don't like squid . . . Nyah!" Pete cried in pain. "What are we talking about squid for? My God, in twenty seconds I could be a dead man, and you're noodling me about the squid!"

"Calm down, Pete. You want a drink? Coffee? Calm down and tell me what happened." Zalman sighed. This Monday was turning out to be grimmer than a fried Santa Claus.

Pete shook his head. "You gotta help me, Jer!" he wailed. "Besides, you don't help me, I could be outta business. No more Le Croque for me, and that means no more free lunch for you. Not only could I be outta business, I could also be dead! This is serious," he said, twitching in the leather chair like a smelt in a hot frying pan.

"Tell me your tale of woe, will ya, Pete? I don't have forever." Zalman knew he had to lean on Pete. Otherwise the restaurateur would be whining all day.

Pete settled down a little, yanking at his clothes like a toddler who had to go to the bathroom. "Okay, okay, here's what happened. Last Saturday, a good day, I got the usual big crowd, and I also got a lotta kids in the joint. My daughter Angela had all her friends in for a big birthday party, so I'm very busy. But everything's hunky-dory, people are eating like crazy, everything's great." Pete stared at Zalman. "Then what happens?" he asked.

"What am I, the Amazing Kreskin?" Zalman said irritably. "C'mon, c'mon. . . ."

Pete sighed and continued his story. "So about five o'clock I get a phone call. At first I'm not sure who it is, what it's about. It's noisy, now we got the late afternoon drinkers in the bar, very raucous. Everybody's oiling up so they can face the family over the dinner table. You know how it is."

"I can imagine," Zalman said, the medallion heavy in his pocket.

"So I get this phone call, and finally I figure out it's from Happy Henke. You know who Happy Henke is, Jer?"

"Happy Henke from Henke's Hideaway, the guy who sells the fake jewelry on TV? Guy who says, 'A Henke ring, it's a beautiful thing'?" Zalman asked.

"Yeah, that's the guy. Y'know, Jer," Pete said conspiratorially, "Henke was originally a chemist, but he's also got the major piece of Henke's Hideaway. Strictly credit, but Henke does good. He's in it with a partner. Henke invented the Diamette and the

Emerelle, and those rocks are the biggest thing alive in the faux gem racket, so he's got big buckskis. He tells me all this over the phone, like I don't already know. He tells me what an important guy he is, how he's got all kinds of friends." Pete laid a finger on his nose and pushed it to one side. "You know, Jer, flat-nose types. He's also mucho mucho richo. 'A Henke ring, it's a beautiful thing,' " Pete repeated. "That's the guy. He's been in a few times. I seen him around, and I knew his girlfriend was in at lunch with some other babes. Henke tells me he's very unhappy. Why is that? I ask him. And why tell me about it? He says his girlfriend had a great lunch today, enjoyed the pork 'n' punkin stew, but when she got back to her place she realized this fancy pin thing Henke gave her was missing. Except now Henke's turning stingy, says he didn't really give it to her, it was only a loaner. Can you believe it?"

" 'Neither a cheapskate nor a piker be,' as my dear old dad so often told me," Zalman said brightly.

"Henke doesn't care if the gizmo's lost, strayed, or stolen. He says since it disappeared in my joint, it's my responsibility. Whaddamy gonna do, Zally?" Pete said in desperation. "He says get it back. Or else."

"Or else, hm? Sounds bad, Pete," Zalman said. He loved watching Pete squirm, but he wouldn't let it go on too long. He'd give him the medallion back. Any minute now. "Why doesn't he call the cops? Why's he playing tough guy?"

Pete conked his head with his open hand. "Ayy, police in Le Croque? Forget about it, Jer. Bite your tongue. The rich and famous don't want to frequent joints where there's thievery."

"Nice choice of words, Pete. I don't think I've heard 'thievery' used in a sentence recently."

"I heard it on 'Sixty Minutes,' " Pete admitted. "He won't go to the cops. Henke's a married man, and he doesn't want the wife to find out about the girlfriend. The usual story. C'mon, Jer, you're a man of the world, you know how it goes. You gotta get it back for me, Jer. Okay? Huh? Jer?" Pete said expectantly.

"No problem." Zalman smiled, the weight of the gold medallion still heavy in his jacket pocket. "No problem at all."

Pete stared at him blankly. "Really?" he whispered. "You can do it just like that? Wow, that's amazing!"

"True, true." Zalman smiled happily. As Pete had spun his tale of terror, Zalman realized he had the opportunity of a lifetime. If he strolled into Le Croque that evening with the medallion, his reputation would be phenomenal. It would get around town that he could cure a rainy day, and his position as the premiere fixer of the vexatious problems of Hollywood's glitterati would be assured for the rest of his life.

Of course, the kids knew, but they'd never squeal. Nobody else knew Brenda had copped the Picasso, and so Zalman could keep her out of trouble and increase his legal stature among the cognoscenti of Babylon by the Freeway at the same time. It was a great shot, and Zalman jumped for it.

"Yeah. I got connections, Pete," he said, affecting an air of menace—early Bogart, late Lawrence Tierney. "It's no problem. Tell you what. Set up a dinner meeting tonight with me and Happy Henke, and I'll give him the gizmo. I promise."

Pete's eyes were glowing as if the Tooth Fairy had left him a little bit of heaven underneath his pillow. "Zally," he said as he jumped to his feet, "you don't know what this means to me. You've saved my entire life, my entire career! Jerry, how can I thank you?"

"Siddown, Pete," Zalman said, still wrapped in his

gangster persona, "and I'll tell you how. You're gonna open that new joint in Century City, right?"

"White Asparagus," Pete said happily. "Smooth as silk on satin."

"Twenty percent," Zalman said, figuring he'd aim high and settle for ten so Pete would feel that he'd won something.

Pete buried his thin face in his hands. "Jerry, how can you do this to me!" he cried in obvious pain.

"It's easy."

"I thought we were friends!"

"We are friends, Petey-pie. But I'm your attorney, and I know your financial position is in the negative cash flow situation. I'm a businessman, too," Zalman said defensively. "I've got overhead! Now, you want the pin back, you pay me in cash or I'll take it out in trade. Hey, if I don't get it, you don't have to pay me anything. Look at it that way."

"Don't say that, Jer," Pete wailed. "Please. Henke could have me wearing cement booties! Okay, okay, but no more than five percent," he bargained craftily.

"Ten."

"Ten?"

"Ten."

"You're killing me, Jerry, but what can I do?" Pete said as they shook hands.

Zalman knew Pete felt better, figuring he'd screwed Zalman a little bit. Zalman always liked a guy to go out feeling he'd won something; he wouldn't blow the man's entire macho cover.

"Eight-thirty," Pete breathed. "I'll set it up with Henke. You're gonna deliver, right, Jer? No kidding here? This is my life we're playing handball with, so don't fail me."

Zalman took Pete by the arm and led him out

through Esther's office into the hall. "Don't worry about a thing, Petey-pie," he told the restaurateur. "I'm a man of my word."

"Honestly, Jerry," Marie Thrasher said with exasperation as she leaned forward over the bathroom sink and stared into the mirror. "You're impossible!" Very carefully, Marie began to outline her lips.

Zalman stood in the open doorway of the bathroom in Marie's Studio City house and smiled, rocking back and forth on his heels and admiring the Rockwell Kent lithos that lined the hallway. Rutherford lay at his feet, peacefully gnawing a Nyla-Bone.

"Why do you say that, doll?" Zalman laughed as he watched Marie put on her makeup. "A guy's gotta make a buck in this world. Look, the kids come to me, they want help. They want me to take the medallion back to Marchetti. I tell them I'll do it, right? They think I'm a great guy."

"They're only kids, Jerry. I'm talking about Pete! Do you like this lipstick?" she asked, swiveling a tube of hot pink in his direction.

Zalman blew her a kiss. "I know I will," he said. "It looks yummy. But Marchetti, he comes to me, I don't work for free. Not for him. He's a client, Marie! I thought I gave him a good deal! He already can't pay me what he owes. This way, he settles his debts like a man and I get a piece of White Asparagus. Another place we can eat free for life."

"You don't need the money, Jerry. Don't give me that!"

"It's not the money, it's the principle," Zalman said righteously.

Marie shook her head and laughed as she brushed out her curly auburn hair. "It's the money!" she said. "And you know it. You had the medallion in your pocket. You could've just given it back to Pete right there in your office, been a nice person."

Zalman was shocked. "I'm a lawyer, Marie. I don't want to be a nice person; it would ruin my reputation. Besides, there's something you don't understand. Pete'll think less of me if I do work for free. He'll get suspicious; he'll wonder. He'll start to think maybe Jerry's on the way out; maybe his bulb's getting dim in his old age. If I charge him a bundle, he'll know he's getting value for his bucks."

"What do you think of this dress? Tracee helped me pick it out," Marie said, smoothing the pink and black silk over her hips. "Ruthipoo, take that bone into the kitchen, please? It's all wet and nasty!"

Rutherford promptly picked up his bone and trotted off into the kitchen with it.

"Tracee, may she rot!" Zalman said, shivering at the mere thought of his ex-wife. "Is your dress supposed to be that low in front?" he asked anxiously, eyeing Marie's substantial cleavage. "Are you sure you don't have it on backwards? Marchetti and Henke, they'll forget all about the Picasso when they get a geeze at your chest, doll. That's what I call a real work of art. How is Tracee, may she rot?"

Marie laughed as she slipped her diamond studs into her ears. Marie and Tracee had become fast friends as well as business partners in World O' Yip, and Marie was making a fortune on her investment in the fabulous spa. "Tracee is fine, and did you see the Smokey the Bear salt and pepper set she gave me? It's just adorable."

"Oh, sure I did," Zalman fibbed. He had few quibbles with Marie, but her taste in Star Trek decor and her passion for oddball collectibles remained a mystery to him. He just didn't understand the humor of Howdy Doody on Mars. "Let me just kiss you on the—"

"Don't try to change the subject, Jerry." She laughed. "You always start admiring my bosom when you feel threatened. I can tell you didn't even notice my new Smokey."

"Have you been reading self-help books again?" Zalman asked skeptically. "You're not going to start wanting to share or get up close and personal, are you? Do we have to have a relationship? Can't we just be in love?"

"You bet." Marie laughed again. "But don't think I'm going to let up on you about the medallion, Jerry Zalman. You know you should've given it to Pete. You know I'm right," she said, shaking a school marmish finger at him.

"Weeellll . . ."

"Say it, Jerry. . . ."

"Okay, okay," he said. "You're right. Kinda right. Not all the way right. Just a little bit right."

"That'll do for now, Jerry," Marie said. "It's a start anyway. Okay, admire my cleavage one more time and then let's go. I'm starved."

"I admire your cleavage any more, we're not going anywhere," Zalman told her. "Good night, Rutherford," he called into the kitchen. "See you later, gatemouth."

Zalman pulled his silver-gray Mercedes 280 SE into the parking lot next to Le Croque and jumped out.

"What a car!" the parking attendant breathed, running a hand over the Mercedes's silver skin. "What year is it?"

"It's a 'sixty-eight, and it's in perfect shape," Zalman snapped. "You scratch this baby and your life is over permanently. Open the door for the lady, huh?"

The kid obediently trotted around to the passenger side, opened Marie's door, and helped her out. "That's really something," he said, staring down her dress.

"You better be talking about the car, kid," Zalman warned.

"Oh, you bet!" the kid replied quickly as he slipped into the driver's seat and zoomed off.

"I can see that dress is going to give me nothing but trouble tonight," Zalman sighed.

"You'll fight for my honor, won't you, darling?" Marie murmured as they strolled up the brick pathway to the front door of the restaurant.

"How about I negotiate for it?" Zalman countered as they went inside.

Even though it was a Monday night, Le Croque was jumping. Pete Marchetti, who was standing at the far end of the crowded bar, saw Zalman and Marie come in and scurried through the packed room to greet them.

"Ah, zee beautiful Mamzelle Thrashair! Quelle frock! Très risqué! And M'sieur Zalmann, eet ees zee plasair to zee—"

"Cut the comedy, Pete," Zalman said. "Talk American, will you? I can't take that phoney accent all night long."

"C'mon, Jerry," Pete whispered. "People come to a French restaurant, they expect a French accent! We're in Hollywood, man! This town thrives on illusion! Besides, everybody says I sound just like Maurice Chevalier in *Gigi*!"

"Okay, okay," Zalman said. "But I still think you sound like Werner Klemperer on 'Hogan's Heroes.' "

"You got the medallion, Jerry? Huh? You got it?" Pete was damp with anxiety.

Zalman patted his jacket pocket and smiled. "It's in the bag, son," he said. "Happy Henke here yet?"

Pete nodded happily. "Right these way, m'sieur et mamzelle," Pete said loudly, Frenching it up for the benefit of the paying customers.

Zalman and Marie threaded their way through the

noisy dining room. Le Croque was tingling with the excitement of cash on the hoof, flush with the dull roar of deal-making, and behind it all, the music of silver on china tinkled like wind chimes as the elite scarfed up their dinners. Potted palms studded with tiny lights glowed throughout the room, and overhead hanging ferns waved like a lacy cloud of greenbacks.

In addition to being one of the best restaurants in town, Le Croque was a very trendy spot for upscale singles. The long glass and walnut bar faced a wall of antique mirrors, allowing those who frequented the place to hunt for their prey discreetly. Here they were safe. Pete never allowed anybody in who didn't have the right look, the right car, or the right address, and he knew most of his patrons personally. Le Croque was a big club for the best and busiest Hollywood hotshots and Beverly Hills babies.

Happy Henke was sitting at a large round table at the back of the room, and there was a willowy redhead seated next to him nibbling pensively on a bread stick. Henke looked up as Pete Marchetti brought Zalman and Marie to the table.

"Happy," Pete said nervously, "this is Jerry Zalman, the lawyer I told you about. You got a problem, Jerry Zalman's the man to see. Whatever you got wrong, he can fix it for you without going to court. And he says it's in the bag. Right, Jer?" Pete asked hopefully.

"So you're Zalman," Henke said, his cold blue eyes sweeping across Marie's low-cut dress, over to Zalman, and back again. "I hearda you. My partner, Maxie Phalen, knows your brother-in-law, Phil Hanning. They took some real estate investment seminars together." Henke half stood up and shook hands with Zalman across the table.

"Yeah? Great," Zalman stalled as he and Marie sat down. He rubbed his hand surreptitiously under the table. Happy Henke had a grip like a pit bull's fangs. "Hanning's a great guy," he lied.

Jason's father, Phil Hanning, was a perpetual albatross around Zalman's neck and caused him nothing but grief. But the worst part was that Phil Hanning had once saved Zalman's life and that put Zalman in the uncomfortable position of being a debtor as well as a brother-in-law, and he didn't like it. Zalman knew there was no way he would ever be able to pay off. Once a man saved your life, he owned a piece of you forever.

And to make matters worse, Hanning was endlessly involved in a variety of nutty investment schemes in a futile effort to promote himself out of his role as househusband and into the ranks of movers and shakers. Hanning's schemes invariably went belly up, and Zalman invariably had to clean up after the elephants.

"I think I've met Maxie Phalen," Zalman said. "Isn't he . . ." Zalman saw Happy Henke's eyebrows shoot up and stopped himself in the nick of time. Maxie Phalen was known all over town as Failin' Phalen because, like Phil Hanning, he was always involved in a losing proposition. But unlike Phil, Failin' Phalen didn't have Jerry Zalman to look after his interests, hence the nickname. "He's the guy with the Dinky Rinks, isn't he?" Zalman continued smoothly.

"Yeah, that's right," Henke said. "Too bad about that. Before its time, Dinky Rinks."

"Dinky Rinks?" Marie asked, smothering a laugh.

"Yeah," Henke said. "Dinky Rinks, don't you remember 'em? Portable roller-skating arenas small enough to be set up in a mall, a parking lot, or even a garage. Great concept!"

"They had a brief vogue among ten-year-olds," Zalman added. "Then they died out."

"Well," Pete Marchetti said nervously. "It's great you guys are getting along. You don't need me, so

I'm gonna go meet and greet, okay? Jerry here'll take care of everything, right, Jer?" Pete said as he slipped back into the happy throng like a sleek seal in a tank of sardines.

Zalman ignored Marchetti. "This is Marie Thrasher," he said, smoothly maneuvering the conversation away from both Phil Hanning and Failin' Phalen.

Henke nodded hello. "Mary Rose Peek," he said, jerking a thumb at the redhead. He was wearing a diamond pinky ring the size of a bowling ball.

Mary Rose Peek was incredibly pretty, with large china blue eyes, flawless white skin, and a cascade of deep red hair pouffed up over her forehead like a Gibson girl and trailing down around her bare shoulders in soft waves. "How do you do," she said, smiling. She reached across the table to shake hands, but her bread stick brushed up against a bud vase of pink roses. The vase toppled and fell, dumping water and roses all over the table. "Oh, gosh darn it!" she said, a becoming blush spreading across her cheeks. "Oh, darn! Ah'm always . . . Happy, give me your napkin, hon," she said as she pushed her chair back and dabbed at the water seeping across the table. "Ah'm awfully sorry, what a mess!" She had a faint southern accent, just enough to conjure up wistful visions of Scarlett O'Hara scampering around a prewar Tara.

"God, you're clumsy," Henke said mildly, tossing his napkin across the table to her. There was no animosity in his voice, just bored recognition of established fact. "Waiter!" he barked. "Clean this up, will ya?" He gestured at the soggy table.

A young man ran over, whipped the tablecloth off, and quickly reset the table. Henke didn't bother to get up. "Yeah, Zalman," he said, ignoring the waiter. "I hearda you. You got my medallion? Like I told Marchetti, I got more friends in this town than you got hairs on your head." He smiled coldly. "So for Pete's sake, I hope you got what I want."

Zalman cocked a sarcastic eyebrow. "For Pete's sake, I'm here. Aren't I?" Already Jerry Zalman knew he wasn't warming up to Happy Henke. Already he didn't see them as being buddies for life.

"Phalen's on his way over; he'll be here any minute. I wanted him to see this," Henke said. "I told him if you deliver the goods, maybe I'll throw a little business your way."

"How nice." Zalman smiled thinly. One of the advantages of his position as a legal lone wolf was that he didn't have to take clients he didn't like, and Happy Henke certainly fit into that category. Zalman studied Henke across the table. The jeweler was thin and fit, with short gray hair and calculating blue eyes. He was wearing a black suit, a maroon silk tie, and a maroon silk shirt, and he looked like a costume designer's idea of a rich gangster.

Zalman had seen Henke on TV, of course, doing his jolly promotional spiel, constantly reminding the bleary-eyed late night audience that a Henke ring was a beautiful thing. Every night Henke was busy pitching thick gold quad herringbones, heavy gold ropes, and nugget-style rings to L.A.'s jewelry-starved masses during the breaks in ancient black-and-white movies. But the real Happy Henke wasn't jolly at all. He was cold and tough, real tough, not just Hollywood tough, and he didn't fit Zalman's fantasy of the distracted inventor turned jewelry entrepreneur.

"So you're the guy who invented the Diamette," Zalman said. "Very famous item, the Diamette."

"And the Emerelle," Henke added proudly. "Don't forget about the Emerelle." A sunny smile spread across Henke's taut face, and for a moment he looked honestly happy. In that smile Zalman caught a glimpse of the smooth TV huckster hiding underneath Henke's stony exterior. "Faux gems are more important than ever. They're gonna be the coming thing. Don't let anybody tell you different," Henke said, stabbing the air with an angry finger.

"You should know," Zalman said noncommittally.

"But I thought quality was the big seller these days," Marie said delicately. "Do upscale people really want to wear fake jewelry?"

Henke gave her a penetrating stare, then shrugged. "A Henke gem is tops in quality, dear. Let me explain it to you," he said. "Take a good look around this room and tell me what you see."

"The local yokels out for a good time, same as in Shamokin, P.A.," Zalman replied, motioning for the waiter. "Beverly Hills is a small town, too, only here we play bingo for real money. Bullshot for me, vermouth cassis for the lady," he told the waiter. "Miss Peek, something else for you?"

"Oh, gee, no. Uh-uh," she said, reaching out nervously for another bread stick. She knocked over the basket, and bread sticks fanned out across the table like a winning hand. "Oh, darn, ah did it again!"

"It's nothing," Marie assured her, righting the basket and collecting the bread sticks.

Henke ignored Mary Rose. "Yeah, but you see more than that," he continued. "Now, most of the ladies in here are wearing lots of jewelry, right? I bet you a hundred there isn't a woman in here who isn't wearing at least one diamond ring, one piece of gold. Little girls in Beverly Hills, their moms got 'em on trainer jewelry." He snorted. "Stones, plenty of gold, what have you, right?"

"Of course," Zalman said. "Goes with the territory. Ladies get up in the morning, they put on jewelry first thing. They go out at night, they put on more. Some magpie instinct, I guess."

BLOODY MARY

Marie kicked him under the table. "Magpie! Magpie! I don't think I like that one bit, Jerry!" she said.

Henke grinned and wiggled his big diamond pinky ring. Little chips of fire sparkled as the huge stone caught the light and scattered it over the table. "Magpies are smart, Marie. They collect bright shiny things that hold their value in a town like this. Life gets tough, the jewelry's always with you, waiting to be turned into cold cash. But you're right, too, Zalman," Henke continued. "You're an observant guy. I like that in a lawyer. Okay, think about it. I bet there's a half mil worth of rocks in this room, probably more. A guy gets rich in TV, the record biz, first thing he does is buy some snazzy jewelry to hang on his wife, so's all the guys in the screening room will know he's hit the big time and think he's worth talking to, am I right?"

Zalman nodded. "I wouldn't fight you on it," he told Happy Henke.

"And I'm being conservative in my estimate," Henke continued. "Now, probably every person in this room has a home alarm, a car alarm, a boat alarm, an office alarm, right?"

"Of course." Zalman shrugged. "Like I said before, it goes with the territory."

"And in a few years, we'll all need personal alarms, right?" Henke said, sipping his wine. "To protect us from the negative elements on the street, as it were."

"A friend of mine has a personal alarm." Zalman smiled benignly. "He calls it a three fifty-seven Magnum."

Henke choked on his wine. "That's good!" He laughed. "That's really good! But that's my point. In a few years, life's gonna get real tense for the rich. People will be afraid to wear real gems outside their own homes. It'll be too dangerous. But it's no fun being rich if you don't look rich, so they'll still want quality, like you said, Marie. And that brings me to the Henke line of gemstones. The Diamette and the Emerelle are just the first in my line of quality faux gems." He chuckled. "Very soon, I'll be introducing the Rubyola, the capstone of my career."

"The Rubyola?" Marie asked. "I've never heard of the Rubyola."

"Happy isn't even finished inventing it yet," Mary Rose said proudly. "It's a secret. No one knows how to make it but Happy, 'cause he's a genius. Isn't that right, hon? And he's promised me the first one, haven't you, hon?" she asked.

"You bet, baby," Henke said. "I'm modeling the color of the Rubyola after the color of your hair. And you got just the right skin tone to wear it, too. Show it off beautiful when I take my full-color spread in *Vogue*. Just you and the Rubyola on a bed of mink, nothing else. Your body, my Rubyola."

Mary Rose laughed, a little uncomfortably, Zalman thought.

"So the Rubyola is going to be a new false gem?" Marie asked curiously. "False gems have been around for a long time, haven't they, Mr. Henke?"

"Call me Happy," he told her. "Why do you think man invented glass?" He laughed. "Well, Marie, first thing you gotta learn is there's two kinds of what I like to call faux gems. Never say 'false,' Marie," he frowned. "Wrong word. False is fake and fake is phony. There's your synthetic and there's your imitation. Now, your synthetic is your gem made by man. In the case of the Diamette, the Emerelle, and very, very soon the Rubyola, that man is me," Henke explained proudly. "Your imitation, well, glass was one of the first imitations in the gem line, and hey, I like glass. It makes a great window! But a Henke gem?" Happy Henke shook his head and laughed harshly. "No comparison. That's what I always say.

BLOODY MARY

A Henke ring, it's a beautiful thing, a gem any woman can wear anywhere, anytime. There's nothing false, fake, or phony about a Henke. It's a man-made creation, the real thing. And when I introduce the Rubyola, there's gonna be a gem revolution. The Rubyola is gonna be better than a ruby. More lustrous, more beautiful, it'll have the depth of a molten ocean, the clarity of an exploding sun," Henke rhapsodized. "And the color? It'll have the color of this little lady's hair," he said, patting Mary Rose paternally. "And the dough?" He grinned. "Beyond your basic dreams of avarice."

"No business like faux business, huh?" Zalman said. He couldn't resist.

"Did you have to?" Marie groaned.

"Maxie! Babe!" Henke said, waving across the room at a stocky man scanning the crowded restaurant.

"Hi, y'all!" Mary Rose called. "We're over here!"

Failin' Phalen saw Henke and made his way to the table followed by a tall, good-looking kid in expensively torn jeans and a Moscow Summit T-shirt.

"Happy!" Phalen wheezed. "Mary Rose, you look gorgeous, as always," he said as he bent down and kissed her on the cheek.

Mary Rose giggled and dropped her napkin.

"Don't tell me, I already know," Phalen said expansively as he turned to Zalman. "Jerry Zalman, one of the best lawyers in town! Mr. Fixit, huh, Jer? This is my assistant, Tony."

"Marie Thrasher," Zalman said as everyone shook hands.

"Hey, guess who I just left?" Failin' Phalen said as he slipped into a chair next to Zalman and started to pitch without missing a beat. Tony sat down next to Mary Rose. "Phil Hanning! What a great guy! Too bad that Jack-the-Zipper deal blew up in his face, huh? But tomorrow's another deal, that's what I say.

Now look, this is ears only," Failin' Phalen said, lowering his voice and looking cautiously behind him for eavesdroppers. "I wouldn't say this to just anyone, but me and Phil, we're thinking seriously of setting up this fast-food franchise thing we got going, Snaxamillion? We got room for investors and it's a great opportunity. You could do the legal bit for your end, Jerry. Whaddaya say? Has Phil talked to you yet? I'm telling you, it's not too late to get in on the action."

"Snaxamillion, huh?" Zalman said, envisioning hours of unpaid labor on Hanning's behalf when the thing went down the tubes. "Phil hasn't mentioned it."

"Let's buzz him," Phalen said, looking around for a waiter. "I just left him, so he's still in his car."

"Not now, Maxie," Happy Henke said sharply. "Talk garbage food on your own time. Mr. Zalman's here on business for me, but I wanted to wait till you got here so you could see the show. Ecch, this bread stinks," he said as he tossed a soggy, half-eaten bread stick on the table.

"Hey, Tony!" Phalen said sharply. "Run over to Musso and Frank, will ya? Get a long, long loaf of that sourdough bread they got and bring it back here, pronto."

"Awww, Maxie," Tony whined. "I gotta?"

"Tony, Tony, you want to learn executive skills? Go for bread when I tell you," Phalen said. "And don't gimme a hard time about it."

"And on your way out," Happy Henke added, "get the waiter to send over some champagne and caviar. Plenty of both," he ordered. "Then maybe we'll see if Mr. Zalman can deliver the goods."

Zalman stared across the table at Happy Henke, barely controlling the urge to punch Henke in the beezer and keep the medallion for himself. After all, he was man of style and taste. He'd appreciate it, admire its perfect beauty every day for the rest of his life, and Happy Henke was obviously one step removed from pencil-necked geekdom. Besides, Henke only saw the monetary side of Pablo's golden oeuvre; he'd never experience the true joy of owning an artistic masterpiece. Sadly, Zalman stifled his larcenous urge, but not without a good reason.

First of all, he knew he couldn't get away with it—not for long, anyway. And second, he'd promised Jason and Brenda that he would return the medallion to its rightful owner and there wouldn't be any trouble about it. If he copped the medallion, there'd be trouble and nothing but trouble. So even though he wanted to ram his fist down Happy Henke's miserable gullet and rip his lungs out, Zalman grudgingly tossed the little package, still wrapped in three-ring notebook paper, on the table in front of him. "There ya go," Zalman said in a passable John Wayne.

Happy Henke's hand shot out for the package as fast as a ravenous diamondback for a dear little mousie, his huge pinky ring scattering chips of reflected light over the table. Quickly, he tore open the package and grinned with hungry glee when he saw the Picasso medallion glowing softly in his palm. The woman's profile smiled on, untouched and unmoved by her recent adventures.

"Ha!" Happy Henke laughed. "Okay, Mr. Jerry Zalman! Okay! Great, huh, Maxie? Look here, it's back! You owe me a hundred."

Failin' Phalen reached into his pocket, pulled out a gold money clip, and handed a crisp hundred dollar bill to Happy Henke. "You were right, Hap," he agreed, his eyes on the huge black mound of beluga caviar the waiter was putting in the center of the table.

"Great, huh?" Henke said again, spinning the medallion on the table like a top.

"Yeah, Hap. Great," Phalen said, still gazing hungrily at the caviar.

"Oh, Happy!" Mary Rose squeaked. "Ah'm so relieved. Yes, ah am! Ah thought it was lost and gone forever! And if that had happened, why, ah would've been so upset!" she cried, jostling the waiter's arm as he poured her a glass of champagne. "Oopsie! Sorry!"

"You gonna tell me how you got this so fast, Zalman?" Happy Henke asked as he rewrapped the medallion and slipped it into his jacket pocket.

Zalman shook his head. "Not a chance," he replied smoothly as he leaned back in his chair. "I recently met a lady magician, and she says that the first secret of magic is that a magician never reveals the source of her illusions. Neither does a smart lawyer, if you take my point. After all, Happy, you wouldn't tell your competition how to cook up a Rubyola, would you?"

"Not a chance." Happy Henke laughed knowingly.

"How ya doing on the Rubyola, Hap?" Failin' Phalen asked, still anxious, still sweating. Like Phil Hanning, Phalen was always damp and anxious. Maybe that was why the two losers got along.

"Any day now," Henke said serenely. "I'm almost there. I gotta say it's been tougher than I thought," he revealed, bemused by his own inability to spin the fabled Rubyola out of straw in an instant.

Mary Rose poked a bread stick into the mound of caviar, bit down delicately, and grimaced as a fine spray of bread crumbs shot out over the table.

Happy Henke stared at the redhead and shook his head. He was about to say something rude when Marie caught his disgusted glance and stepped in smoothly to protect the hapless Mary Rose.

"That's a lovely dress, Mary Rose. I've always

wished I could wear lacy things, but I think I'm too short for it. Makes me look like the Pop 'n Fresh Doughgirl." Marie smiled.

A faint frown creased the redhead's perfect brow. "Ah didn't know there was a doughgirl." Mary Rose looked puzzled, settling a stray lock of hair behind one ear. "Just the little man who goes hee-hee-hee when you poke him in the tummy. Did you know there was a doughgirl, hon?" she said to Happy.

"Get me out of here," Marie whispered to Zalman. "I'm about to lose control, and I think I hate it."

"But anyway, ah'm glad you like this dress," Mary Rose continued obliviously. "Ah'm thinking of wearing a dress just like it when Hap and ah get married. But white, a course." She beamed. "We're engaged," she confided to Marie. "And we'll be married real soon. Just as soon as Hap's divorce comes through. Isn't that right, hon?"

Happy Henke kept his mouth shut.

"Oh, how nice," Marie said. "How long have you been engaged?"

"Two years." Mary Rose smiled. "Almost from the day we met. Ah was just crazy about Hap right from the start."

Henke nodded but said nothing. "Where the hell's Tony?" he mumbled as he grabbed a slice of hard-boiled egg and stuffed it into his mouth. "Musso and Frank's not so far. He oughta be back with the sourdough. I like that sourdough with the fish eggs."

"Barking," Failin' Phalen said, his mouth full of caviar. "Brobably had trouble barking."

Zalman considered slaughtering the entire company, but in his heart he knew the crime wasn't worth the time. On the other hand, he couldn't take much more of Happy Henke. "Well, Happy, it's been great meeting you," he said genially. "Sorry we can't stay for dinner. I'm afraid Marie and I have—"

BLOODY MARY

But the horrified look on Happy Henke's face stopped Zalman cold, and he followed Henke's eyes across the room. Standing at the back of Le Croque he saw two men wearing black clothes, heavy black windbreakers, and masks.

One was tall and one was short, but even though they looked like two of the Three Stooges, they were both carrying dull black machine pistols, and the ugly weaponry erased any trace of comedy from their act.

Shorty was wearing a black ski mask that covered his entire head, and he had his pistol jammed into Pete Marchetti's ear. Pete looked terrified, his thin face shivering visibly. The rest of the kitchen staff was cowering nearby, obviously afraid to move.

The tall man, who was wearing a rubber Goofy mask, stepped calmly up to a table where a nervous young guy was busily impressing his date with his knowledge of wines. Goofy grabbed the young guy's wine bottle out of its silver cooler and casually whacked it against the wall. Red wine and bits of broken glass spouted across the table and over the carpet.

"Hey, bud!" the young guy howled in protest as he jumped up and out of his seat, his clothes dripping with wine the color of dark blood.

But before he could finish, Goofy whacked him, too, right across the side of the head with the pistol. The nervous young guy flopped down on the floor, and his girlfriend began to squeal like a pink piglet who had just realized where bacon came from.

The cheery noise in the big room sank to a frightened silence, as if somebody'd flipped off the fun switch. Shorty gave Pete Marchetti a sharp poke in the ear with the pistol.

"Ow!" Pete whimpered as he climbed up on a chair. "Okay, okay, just gimme a minute, will ya?"

Pete waved vaguely, motioning to the crowd to settle down. His thin face was pale, and his eyes were twitching wildly back and forth in his head like the eyes of a crazed Chatty Cathy. He swayed on top of the chair and lamely clapped his hands for attention.

"Uh, folks," Pete said, his voice quavering with fright. "I hate to break it to you, but this is a robbery! Now, if everybody stays calm, no one's gonna get hurt, right?" he asked Shorty. "Everything's under control."

The crowd of diners yakked softly to themselves like frightened geese, and faint shrieks and astonished mumbling filled the room. No one could believe it. A robbery? With guns? At Le Croque, one of the most elegant restaurants in Bev Hills? It was beyond belief, it was amazing, it was definitely going to be on the front page of tomorrow's *Variety*.

"Jerry, is this a joke?" Marie whispered softly.

Zalman shook his head.

"It's not a joke," Happy Henke growled in fury. "It's a setup!"

"Maybe so," Zalman said quietly. "And maybe not. Just keep your yap shut, Henke. We can all get out of here in one piece if we stay calm."

"I'm not gonna take this," Henke said firmly, twisting his diamond ring so the stone was facing his palm.

What a cheap trick, Zalman thought. I hate this guy.

Pete Marchetti motioned for the crowd to calm down again, and this time he clapped his hands sharply when they ignored him. "Now, this guy here," Pete continued, pointing at Shorty, "is gonna come around and collect cash and jewelry. No wallets, no credit cards, and nobody moves until he tells you to, okay? He'll tell you what he wants, so everybody keep their hands on the table and their mouths shut! He told me to tell you that," Pete said apologetically. "He said it, I didn't."

"Son of a bitch!" Henke snarled. "I'm not gonna—"

BLOODY MARY

"Hon, please!" Mary Rose sniffled. "Please don't start anything!"

"Yeah, Hap," Failin' Phalen pleaded, wiping his damp hands on his pants. "These guys have guns!"

"Oh, I forgot to tell you," Pete said. "If anybody tries anything, this guy says he's gonna blow my head off, and I believe him. So I'd appreciate it if you'd all just follow his instructions," Pete added as Shorty pulled him down from the chair and pushed him over to a table.

Shorty began to move efficiently from table to table, his masked face unknowable, as Goofy covered the crowd. Shorty didn't speak, just pointed swiftly at each victim with the barrel of the machine pistol. He bagged cash and watches and jewelry, but he limited his take to authentic Piagets and Rolexes, no cheesy knockoffs. Zalman thought the guy was very picky, and he had very good taste, especially for a thief. He only took the best, stripping thick gold chains from the ladies and the choicest rocks from their fingers and wrists.

Shorty continued smoothly around the room, stopping briefly at each table, quickly stuffing handful after handful of jewelry and cash into the leather pouch he carried. As Happy Henke had noticed only moments ago, there was a lot of expensive jewelry in Le Croque, and every lady in the room was forced to donate a trinket or two to the robbers' bag.

Zalman didn't like it. He hated it when guys waved machine pistols around and threatened to fire them. Violence always made him queasy, and he wished he had a roll of Tums in his pocket. He looked over at Marie. "When he gets here, give him the earrings and anything else he wants. Don't give the guy a hard time about it, promise me?" he said under his breath. "I swear we'll go over to Tiffany's first thing in the morning and I'll get you a pair of earrings twice as big, okay, doll? I don't want a problem here."

"I hear you, Jerry," she whispered softly. "I'm not crazy. I don't think a pair of diamond earrings is worth anybody's life, especially mine."

Zalman was relieved. Marie was such a feisty little package, it would be just like her to give the guy some lip, and Zalman loved her just the way she was—unperforated by bullet holes.

Mary Rose was crying softly, great big tears rolling down her perfect skin. "Ah'm scared, Hap!" she snuffled.

Henke growled way back in his throat like a nutty dog. "Somebody set me up!" he said. "And I don't like it! I'm not taking this crap offa these yo-yos. Hey, buddy!" he yelled as he stood up and stared across the room at Shorty, who was stripping a lady's wrist of a sparkling tennis bracelet. "Hey, c'mere!"

Shorty stood stock still, the tennis bracelet dangling on the end of his gloved finger like bait from a hook, and stared across the room at Happy Henke. "God, this is tacky," Shorty said in a harsh voice as he stashed the tennis bracelet in his bag. "You kidding?" he asked Happy Henke. His grating voice was muffled, and he sounded as if he had a thick slug of bubble gum in his mouth. "This is a robbery!" Shorty mumbled, waving his pistol in Happy Henke's direction. "Shut up!"

"Yeah, zip it, buster," Goofy growled from the front of the room. "You won't get hurt. This'll all be over in a minute."

But Happy Henke wasn't the kind of guy to take yes for an answer. "C'mere, I said!" he yelled again.

"Idiot," Goofy said. "Cover 'em," he barked angrily at Shorty. "I gotta get this guy in line."

"Great," Zalman muttered. "Henke, if I get out of this whole, you're dog food."

BLOODY MARY

Goofy zigzagged through the cowering diners to Henke's side and poked him sharply in the ribs with the machine pistol. He pushed his masked face close to Happy Henke and looked him slowly up and down. "You're an idiot, buddy, you know that?" he snapped. "I told you nobody gets hurt if they listen up, so I guess you forgot how to listen up, huh? Is that the problem? Your mom didn't teach you how to listen up?" He sighed.

"I'm not standing still for this," Henke warned.

Goofy shrugged. "Look," he said reasonably. "Let me put it to you this way." Very calmly, Goofy stepped over to Failin' Phalen and clobbered him over the head with the pistol. Phalen sank wordlessly to the floor, down for the count.

"See? That's called an example," Goofy explained. "Next time the example could be you, get it? Now, shut up!"

Zalman stared down at the floor and tried to become one with his environment. He didn't want to get stuck in the middle of an argument between Happy Henke and a grumpy armed robber. It was a losing proposition from the start.

"Buzz off," Henke said.

Zalman shook his head. Definitely the wrong thing to say.

Goofy sighed and stuck his pistol in Henke's stomach, hard. "Buzz off?" he mumbled, enraged. "Buzz this off, Henke," he said, pushing Henke hard.

"Uhhhnnnkkk," groaned Henke as he fell over his chair and slammed into the floor.

"You didn't listen up before, so listen up now!" Goofy snapped. "Shut up, you won't get hurt!" He reached down, stripped off Henke's watch, and quickly patted down his pockets. "Hey, what's this?" he said as he felt the lump in Henke's jacket pocket, then pulled out the Picasso medallion wrapped in white notebook paper. The medallion tumbled out onto the floor, the woman's profile unruffled. "Lookee here," Goofy crowed. "What we got here?"

"Get away, scum ball," Henke said, making a grab for the medallion.

Goofy planted his foot on Happy's hand and bore down with all his weight.

"Ow!" Happy Henke yelled. "Get offa my hand!"

"No kidding around. Gimme that thing and gimme that ring you're wearing or I'm gonna kill you right here and now!" Goofy snapped.

"I'm shaking," Henke sneered.

"Shit," Goofy said sadly. "Just gimme the stuff, will you? I don't wanna make a bad example of you, too." He bent down and, with his foot still firmly planted on Henke's hand, picked up the medallion and then yanked at Happy's flashy pinky ring. "Gimme that!"

"Get offa me," Henke yelped. He grabbed Goofy's ankle with his free hand and began pulling.

Goofy started to lose his balance and teetered as Henke yanked his leg.

"Let go of him!" Shorty boomed from the front of the room. His voice was loud but mushy, and he sounded as if he was wearing Styrofoam teeth. "Let go or I'll kill Marchetti!"

"Me? What'd I do?" Pete howled.

"Gimme that ring," Goofy growled again as Henke scrambled to his feet.

"The hell I will. This is a real diamond! Plenty carats and it's not faux. It's worth a fortune!" Henke cried angrily.

Zalman smelled blood in the air, and it wasn't going to be his. He saw Henke make a fast grab for Goofy's gun, and in Jerry Zalman's opinion that was a really dumb move.

Across the room, Shorty raised his machine pistol

BLOODY MARY

and squeezed down gently on the trigger. Zalman knew what was coming and without thinking he made a sideways grab for Marie, threw her onto the floor, and rolled as far away from Happy Henke as he could get.

As he covered Marie's body with his own, Zalman heard the crack of gunfire and looked up, even though he knew he'd be sorry. He was right.

There was a soft plop as Shorty drilled Happy Henke neatly between the eyes. A big hole exploded in the middle of Henke's forehead, his head flipped back, his mouth fell open, and his blue eyes stared in empty pain, as wide and round as a pair of dirty softballs. He was already dead, but he still looked surprised and angry, like he couldn't believe he'd actually been murdered, that a guy with national TV exposure could die in a restaurant robbery. He stood there wavering for a moment, then fell backward into his seat.

The crowd screamed as Shorty ran quickly across the room, bent down, and roughly wrenched Henke's pinky ring from his dead finger.

Zalman ducked, concentrating his complete attention on Shorty's feet. They were small and thin, and he was wearing black boots that gleamed with the sparkling polish of an army spit shine. The boots had high heels like flamenco dancer's, Zalman noticed. Elevator shoes, he thought, what a jerk. I'm the same height as he is and I'd never wear elevator shoes. It's degrading.

He kept Marie's head buried under his arms, though she was wiggling like a worm and he knew he was holding her too hard. He didn't want her to see this, even though she wasn't as squeamish as he was and she'd seen dead bodies more than once. Still, Zalman liked to be a gentleman when he had the chance. He took a fast look at the mess on the table and looked away, gulping for air. Henke's brains and blood were soaking into the caviar, and the once beautifully sculpted half-pound of black beluga looked as if it had been sprinkled with Red Hots. It wasn't pretty, and Zalman knew he was going to have bad dreams about it for weeks to come.

People screamed as they realized that Henke was dead, and most of Pete Marchetti's patrons followed Zalman's example and hit the deck. Sadly, most of the gents weren't gallant and abandoned their wives and best friends as they scrabbled for cover. Every guy for himself was the motto of the day.

"HAPPY, OH, NO! *Noooo!*" MARY ROSE SHRIEKED AS she knelt down and cradled Happy Henke's body in her arms. "What's wrong, Hap?" she cried.

But it was no use. Happy's third eye stared grimly at the crowded room and he looked like a Miracle Picture of Elvis with eyes that followed you.

"*Shaddup*, lady!" Goofy yelled at Mary Rose.

"What happened?" Failin' Phalen moaned from the floor as he struggled to get up. "My head, I'm bleeding! What the hell happened?" He looked up, and his stunned eyes slowly began to focus on the mess on the table. "What's tha . . . oh, Hap, my God," Failin' Phalen said as he fell back down on the floor, gagging.

BLOODY MARY

"Jerry, let me up!" Marie said angrily, wriggling like a hooked trout in Zalman's protective embrace. "I want to see what happened!"

"No, you don't," Zalman said firmly. "Trust me on this." His hand was still over her eyes, and he was trying to shield her, just in case there was any more shooting. He felt the warmth of her body pressing up against him, and he realized all over again how much he loved her, how much he wanted to spare her the grim ugliness of the mess on the table in front of them.

"I do, too!" Marie said, still wriggling.

"This isn't a special effect, this is for real," he warned. "Believe me, you can live without this scene imprinted on the back of your eyeballs for the rest of your life."

But Marie struggled out of his grasp anyway, raised her head, and took a fast peek at the late Happy Henke sprawled in his chair with his brains splashed all over the table as if he'd been run over with a Garden Weasel.

"Yecch," Marie moaned. "You were right. Why did you let me see this?" she said as she burrowed back into Zalman's arms. "It's gross."

"Yeah, and it's a helluva waste of a half-pound of beluga," Zalman muttered, trying to keep it light.

Mary Rose was standing over Happy Hanke's body, shrieking as high as Yma Sumac.

Goofy fired a pair of shots into the ceiling.

"*Shaddup*, lady!" he yelled at Mary Rose. "Everybody stay on the floor!" he snapped.

"Yeah, settle down," Shorty rasped over the noise of the squealing crowd. "We're outta here!"

Shorty and Goofy sprinted for the kitchen door at the rear of Le Croque. Shorty had a firm hand on the leather bag of jewelry; Zalman could hear it clanking as it knocked against his legs.

BLOODY MARY

As the two robbers disappeared, there was a brief silence in Le Croque, and in that moment Zalman heard another sound, the sound of Shorty's feet clicking on the hard kitchen floor. The swinging doors pivoted slowly back and forth and finally stopped, trembling.

The big room was still quiet. It was the same intense silence one sometimes heard on a Sunday afternoon when a huge wave gathered up the full force of twenty tons of foaming seawater and was about to slam it down on the waiting beach like the Jolly Green Giant backhanding a pesky sand flea.

Then Le Croque exploded in angry yelling. Zalman jumped up and took a fast look around the chaotic room.

Mary Rose, the long, lacy sleeves of her dress trailing in Happy Henke's blood, was standing over the body of her late lover. "Hap!" she cried. "Oh, Hap, honey, get up!"

"Coast is clear, babe," Zalman said to Marie. "Just watch where you look, okay?"

"Uhh," Failin' Phalen groaned.

Marie opened her eyes again and squinted around the room, very carefully not looking at Happy Henke.

"Hap!" Mary Rose cried again. "Hap, hon, what's the matter?"

"Marie, take Mary Rose out of here, pronto. I can't take any more screaming, and besides, I think she's in shock," Zalman said as he tossed his handkerchief to Failin' Phalen. "She hasn't figured out that he's dead yet."

"You're right, Jerry," Marie said, sneaking a squinty-eyed peek at the body. "Yecch," she said again. "I don't think the view is going to get any better, either. C'mon, Mary Rose," Marie said as she went over to the redhead's side. "Let's go to the ladies' room, huh? C'mon, dear, that's a girl." She put her arm around the weeping Mary Rose and led her away.

"Thanks, babe," Zalman said.

"Jerry," Marie called over her shoulder, "you're in charge. But you want my advice, call my dad right away. Let him hear it from you, honey. Don't let him find out down at headquarters or over his radio. As soon as they find out it's you, the guys'll laugh, and you know it drives Dad nutsoid when they make fun of him."

"Oh, God," Zalman moaned as he looked at Happy Henke's bloody body and shook his head in disbelief. "You're right. We're stuck with another stiff! Not again! Why me? How can this be happening to me? Tell me it's all a nightmare!"

"Stop complaining, Jerry," Marie advised. "Just call my father, will you?"

Zalman knew she was right. He had to call Captain Arnold Thrasher right away, but the one thing Jerry Zalman didn't want to do was face Detective Captain Arnold Thrasher over yet another cooling corpse.

LAPD Detective Captain Arnold Thrasher was Marie's father, and he and Jerry Zalman went back a long way together. Way back to the misty past Zalman didn't like to think about, that dim, unlamented time before he became a hotshot Bev Hills lawyer. That horrible time when he was just another pathetic pisher on the picket line and Captain Arnold Thrasher was known as the Radical's Curse.

Arnie Thrasher was a behemoth who looked nothing like his beautiful daughter Marie, and he had hated Zalman and Zalman's best buddy, Doyle Dean McCoy, the first time he chased them off a picket line. Soon afterward, in a lone moment of brilliance, Thrasher advanced his cop career by ten giant steps when he sent McCoy for an unpleasant vacation to San Quentin on a trumped-up charge of kidnapping. At least

McCoy always claimed it was trumped up; Thrasher sanctimoniously claimed that he'd merely oiled the wheels of justice after McCoy stashed the dean of men in a broom closet during a demonstration.

Some years later, when Zalman met Marie Thrasher and they discovered the body of a local low-life named Sticky Al Hix stuck in a Frigidaire, Thrasher quickly learned to loathe Zalman all over again, and the hideous thought of his former enemy as a prospective son-in-law turned Arnie Thrasher bilious.

How had this happened? Zalman wondered as the crowd around him writhed and shrieked in high-class agony. Not Thrasher again! It was a fate to hate.

Pete Marchetti, his thin face taut and drawn, was up at the front of the room. He was busily trying to calm the anxious crowd, most of whom were frantically craning their necks so they could get a look at Happy Henke's body and have something to talk about in case they were interviewed for the eleven o'clock news.

"Pipe down!" Pete yelled over the racket as he came trotting over to Zalman's side. "Don't nobody leave!" By this time, Pete had totally abandoned his floating French accent and reverted to Clevelandese, which suited him a lot better than his cornball attempts at an ooh-la-la Maurice Chevalier.

"Pete," Zalman began, but before he could finish his sentence, Pete cut him off.

"Jerry, Jerry, you gotta help me!" Pete said. "What now, Jerry? C'mon, you're my lawyer, think fast! Thank God you were here. What a lucky break for me!"

"Yeah, some break," Zalman said reaching into his jacket for his cigar case. Last time he'd taken a nose dive under a table, he'd crushed his cigars, but he'd picked up a new hard-body Dunhill cigar case only a few weeks ago and that particular misfortune hadn't struck again. Zalman slowly pulled out a Macanudo, lit it, and looked around the room at the tumult raging in Le Croque.

Failin' Phalen was slumped in a chair, Zalman's handkerchief pressed to the gash leaking blood down his forehead, moaning and whimpering to himself like a lost puppy.

Most of the other diners, now stripped of their jewelry, watches, and cash, had flopped down at their tables, leaving a *cordon sanitaire* around the late Happy Henke.

The cooks, the waiters, and the rest of the staff were clustered around the long bar, belting back Pete's best brandy.

Zalman knew Marie was right: he had to call Captain Arnie Thrasher. But he was waiting until he could get his breath—not stalling, just waiting.

"You'll take care of this, Jer, right? It's like, uh, part of the deal, right?" Pete Marchetti begged.

Zalman turned slowly toward Pete and stared at the nervous restaurateur. "What deal are we talking about, Pete? What the hell's the matter with you? First thing this morning you're torturing me about squid, last thing at night I'm looking at brains in a bowl! And now you're yapping about some deal you think we have. What deal are we talking about, Petey-pie?" Zalman snapped irritably.

"The medallion . . ." Pete began.

"I returned the medallion. It's not my fault it's been snatched again!"

"Aw, don't be that way, Jer! You know what I mean! What we was . . . were . . . talking about this morning. The medallion, White Asparagus. You're gonna get a good piece of the action as your fee, Jer. And besides," Pete said righteously, "you promised you'd help me with Happy Henke, Jer. You gotta be a man of your word. I mean, it's all part of the same deal."

Zalman sighed. He hated to do it, but he had to agree with Pete. It was all part of the same deal. Besides, there was something else, something much more important.

Zalman knew that if he stiffed Pete in the face of Happy Henke's unexpected demise, his carefully cultivated rep as the guy who could fix anything would certainly suffer. People wouldn't understand. They'd think he was trying to weasel out of a deal, and Pete would trash him all over town. He had to help Pete; he had no choice.

"Yeah, Pete. Same deal," Zalman said, slowly blowing a stream of cigar smoke across the table. "Look, we got no time now, Pete. I have to call the cops. But tomorrow we gotta talk. Did anybody know Henke was gonna be here tonight?" Zalman said.

Pete looked unusually thoughtful. "Everybody. Nobody. I don't go around saying 'Guess who's coming to dinner,' but most of the staff knew he was coming. See," Pete said slyly, "even though I don't take reservations, I hadda keep a table for him tonight. 'Cause of the medallion. I told the guys to keep this table back," Pete said.

"Happy Henke drops in to pick up a stolen Picasso medallion and he happens to get killed in a heist? I wonder . . ." Zalman said.

"He asked for it," Pete added. "If he'd shut up, none of this would have happened. It was his own fault."

"Maybe so," Zalman said thoughtfully. "Look, I gotta go call the cops. Let's not discuss the medallion unless we gotta, okay?" he said. If there was any chance of keeping Jason and Brenda out of this mess . . . "I'm not telling you to lie. If they ask you, tell the truth. Just don't go volunteering anything. Pretend you're in the army and don't volunteer. That's my advice to you as an attorney."

"I gotcha, Jer," Pete said wisely.

"Now I'm gonna go call the cops," Zalman said.

"Hey, great. You got a personal in with them or something, Jer?" Pete said, relieved that the burden was off his skinny shoulders.

"Oh, yeah. Right," Zalman said grimly. "Kissing cousins."

It wasn't long, maybe ten minutes after he called LAPD, before Zalman heard the squad car in the distance, wailing toward Le Croque. A minute later Pete Marchetti led Captain Arnold Thrasher through the front door of the restaurant. The captain was followed by a pair of uniformed cops who remained at the door, steely eyes darting around the room like minnows.

As soon as Thrasher saw Zalman, he lowered his head and came charging through the crowded dining room to Zalman's table, snuffing and snorting like an unpleasant goat.

"Hiya, Arnie," Zalman said, puffing on his cigar. He was trying to sound chipper, but he didn't offer to shake hands. He knew any physical contact with him would drive Thrasher crazy.

The big cop glowered down at Zalman and shook his head. Thrasher was about six-three and looked like a raw recruit's worst nightmare of a marine drill sergeant. He weighed in at two-fifty, and his prickly iron gray hair was shaved as close to his head as any barber could get with a pair of number one clippers. He was wearing a wrinkled, dark blue fifty dollar suit and, as always, a horrible polyester tie. Thrasher had a whimsical fondness for crustaceans, and this particular tie was flecked with a cunning design of interlocked lobsters wearing pink crowns.

"Where's my little girl?" the captain snapped.

"Relax, Arnie, she's okay," Zalman said.

"She better be okay, you shrimp son of a bitch."

"Don't start with me. I ain't in the mood," Zalman told him. Arnie was the kind of guy you had to stand up to right off the bat. Show him who was boss. Otherwise he'd kill you and toss your broken bones down some handy ravine out in Palm Desert. "Of course she's okay. You think I'd let anything happen to Marie? She's gone to the ladies'. The other girl at the table got hysterical, seeing as it's her boyfriend over there with the hole in his head," Zalman said, pointing at the motionless body of the late Happy Henke.

Thrasher frowned as he stared at the three-eyed jeweler. "Dead, huh?" he said.

"Brilliant deduction, Arnie," Zalman said airily. "I guess so, since he got his brains splattered all over the damn table. Guess that means he's dead, wouldn't you say?"

"Don't get smart with me, shrimp bait," Thrasher growled as he walked around Henke carefully and stared at the body from all angles.

"Hey, Chief!" a deep voice rumbled from the front of the room. "Sorry I'm late!"

Zalman turned and looked across Le Croque in the direction of the booming baritone. The guy approaching them was incredibly handsome, with the chiseled jaw and piercing blue eyes of a full-color cartoon hero. Maybe Steve Canyon. Indiana Jones. He was six-two, easy, with big wide shoulders and carefully combed blond hair, and he looked just like a male model in *Esquire* but much more manly. Women sighed and smiled up at him as he came striding through the room, and he smiled back, so they wouldn't feel left out.

BLOODY MARY

The cartoon guy came up to Thrasher and saluted smartly, though he was wearing well-cut civvies.

"Hey, saluting, that's cute. You train him to do that?" Zalman asked Thrasher. "Now you toss him a sardine or what?"

"This is my assistant, Lieutenant Yarrow," Thrasher said shortly. "And he's smart. A lot smarter than you are, so put a damn lid on it, Zalman."

"Nice you got some help, Arnie. You're gonna need it," Zalman said.

Lieutenant Yarrow turned the full blast of his perfect smile on Zalman. "And who are you?" he asked snidely. "Are you someone I should know?" His voice was deep, and he sounded like a positively motivated life insurance salesman trying to close a big policy.

"Jerry Zalman. I'm an attorney."

"My daughter goes out with him," Thrasher said, his voice gloomy. "God knows why. How'd it happen, Zalman? Or I might ask how'd it happen *this time?* Since you're so used to murders and dead bodies, you can probably wrap it up with a big red ribbon for a pair of dumb mug cops like us, huh?"

Zalman sighed. "No need to have an attitude, Arnie. You want to know what happened? No problem. Here goes. Marie and I were having dinner with Happy Henke, the big jeweler. Guy who has the commercials on TV. Him," he said, pointing at Happy Henke.

"You mean, 'A Henke ring, it's a beautiful thing'?" Thrasher asked. "His stores are all over town."

"That's the guy," Zalman nodded. "But now he's all over the table. And Henke's partner, Mr. Phalen," Zalman said, pointing to Failin' Phalen who was sitting quietly in his chair, his head in his hands. "And Henke's lady friend, the one who flipped out. So we're having a lovely evening when all of a sudden two guys wearing masks burst in. One's wearing a black ski mask and one's wearing a rubber Goofy mask. Halloween mask," Zalman explained. "They've got guns and there's a robbery. Henke tries to mouth off when the guys tell him to fork over the big diamond pinky ring he wears. The short guy, the guy wearing the black ski mask, gives Henke a bullet in the skull for his trouble. If he'd kept his mouth shut and given 'em the ring, he probably wouldn't be dead now. Big-mouth guy made the wrong move. End of story."

"Pretty messy," Lieutenant Yarrow observed. "Shot in the noggin, huh?"

Zalman stared at him open-mouthed. "Yeah, that's right. See the little hole in his forehead? That's where the bullet went in. See that gunk on the table? Bullet goes in, brains come out. Get it?"

"Don't push me, Zalman," Thrasher warned. "Just don't."

"Hi, Daddy!" It was Marie, with Mary Rose standing helplessly at her side. The redhead's eyes were vacant, the long sleeves of her gown were stained with blood, and she looked like a pale southern-fried version of Lady Macbeth.

Marie ran over to her father, and he bent down to give her a kiss, rumpling her hair affectionately.

"How's my baby?" the captain said fondly, instantly reverting to his mushy role as the doting dad. "What are you doing here with him?" Thrasher said, pointing a bratwurst finger at Zalman. "You shouldn't see this, honey, a nice girl like you," he clucked. "Go sit over there. Take her with you. I'll want to talk to you in a few minutes, miss," he told Mary Rose.

Marie looked back and forth between Zalman and her father and sighed. "Yes, Daddy," she said obediently, winking at Zalman. "But don't think you can keep me out of this," she warned him. "After you guys haul the stiff outta here, I want to hear all the gruesome details!" she said, leading Mary Rose away.

"Who taught her that kinda language?" Thrasher demanded. "Not me, Mr. Beverly Hills, not me! And she shouldn't be wearing such a low-cut dress, either," he said, lowering his voice. "Say something to her, will you?"

"Arnie!" Zalman said with exasperation. "She's twenty-eight years old!"

"Twenty-nine," Thrasher said with certainty.

"Wait a minute, I thought she was twenty-eight." Zalman was puzzled.

"I'm telling you, twenty-nine," Thrasher said. "I oughta know, I was there! Besides, what difference does it make?"

"Excuse me? What's going on here?" Tony, Happy Henke's assistant, was standing in front of Happy Henke's body, a long loaf of crusty sourdough bread tucked under one arm, his face twisted up like a damp washcloth. "What happened, Mr. Phalen?" he asked as he started to put the bread down on the table, thought better of it, and stuck it back under his arm.

"Who the hell is this guy?" Thrasher demanded.

"My assistant, Tony," Failin' Phalen moaned, his voice tired and weak. "I sent him out to pick up some sourdough bread for Happy right before all this started. Hap liked sourdough with his caviar."

"Yeah, I hadda go over to Musso and Frank for it," the kid said. "The traffic on Hollywood Boulevard was terrible, but Hap liked his sourdough."

"Buncha goddamn nuts," Thrasher mumbled under his breath. "Yarrow, interview this guy with the bread and then this guy," he said pointing at Failin' Phalen. "I'm gonna talk to the lady."

"Wise choice," Zalman said brightly. "Mind if I tag along?"

"Yes. Does it make any difference?"

BLOODY MARY

"No."

"I knew that. Why did I know that?" the big cop sighed. "Okay, then, Zalman. You wanna play detective?" Thrasher said, glancing speculatively from Marie to Lieutenant Yarrow and back again. "You come hang around with me, maybe you'll learn something."

"Sounds like more fun than I can imagine," Zalman said. "But I got a client to protect."

"Who is it this time?" Thrasher snorted.

"Pete Marchetti," Zalman said. With any luck, he thought again, he could keep Jason and Brenda out of the investigation. After all, the medallion had nothing to do with Happy Henke's death. "Let's go, Arnie." He smiled brightly. "I know I'm gonna love this."

Thrasher lumbered over to the table where Marie and Mary Rose were sitting side by side. Marie had her arm around Mary Rose and was trying to comfort the pretty redhead, but it wasn't doing any good. Mary Rose had the glazed eyes of a two-year-old lost in a crowded shopping mall on a Saturday afternoon, and it was clear she had no idea what was playing at the triplex.

Pete Marchetti had wisely sent champagne to all of his unhappy guests, and Le Croque had the air of a hysterical morning-after party. The crowded room hummed with nervous laughter as the victims chattered their stress away.

But Mary Rose Peek was oblivious to the activity around her. She sat quietly in her chair, absently twirling her glass around and around in her hand, staring vacantly at the fizzing bubbles in her champagne.

Thrasher glowered down at Mary Rose, but before he could start barking, his daughter seized the initiative. Marie reached out and shook Mary Rose gently.

"Mary Rose?" she said. "This is my father, Captain Thrasher."

Mary Rose lifted her head and looked weakly at Captain Arnie Thrasher. "Him?" she asked. "I don't believe it."

Zalman covered a grin.

"It's true," Marie said firmly. "He's my father and he's a cop. He needs to ask you some questions about Happy. Do you think you can talk to him?"

Mary Rose looked at Captain Thrasher, her blue eyes clouded with pain. "What happened?" she asked, her voice dull and listless. "Where's Happy? I don't understand. . . . Where's Happy?" She buried her face in her hands; her champagne glass wobbled precariously, but Marie quickly reached out and grabbed it before it spilled.

"Great save," Zalman said admiringly. "Arnie, Miss Peek is in no condition to answer questions tonight. That ought to be obvious, even to you. So, since you've gotta wait, why don't you be a good guy and let her go home?" Zalman said, peering into Mary Rose's eyes. "I think she's in shock," he added.

"You representing her, too, Mr. Zalman?" Thrasher said sarcastically. "How is it you automatically represent everybody in the room every time there's a murder on my turf? Shouldn't you leave a few chunks of cheese for the rest of the rats to chew?"

"Arnie, you got some helluva negative attitude about me, and I don't understand it! I'm a lawyer, I represent people," Zalman snapped, dodging Thrasher's question. He didn't represent Mary Rose, but he wasn't about to let technical details get in his way where Arnie Thrasher was concerned. "That's how I make a living, and it's a damn good one. Do I come around bothering you every time you make an arrest?" Zalman asked the big cop. "No, I don't. That's how you make your living, and I respect that as a concept. So don't gimme a hard time about my chosen profession. I guarantee you Miss Peek didn't see any more than the rest of us, and she's a solid citizen and won't leave town, okay? So lighten up and let the lady go home."

Thrasher's eyes narrowed, and he glanced across the room at Yarrow, who was bending over Failin' Phalen and talking a mile a minute into the entrepreneur's ear. Phalen wasn't paying any attention to him. He was massaging his bruised head, and his face was the pale green color of a new cabbage leaf in spring.

"Hmmm," Thrasher said slowly, his eyes glowing with piggy glee. "Good idea, Zalman. I'll do that little thing. Yarrow!" he called. "Yarrow, c'mere."

Yarrow looked up, smiling like a happy Sun God about to toast the planet on a hot August afternoon. "You bet, Chief," he said as he trotted over to Thrasher's side. "You want something?"

"Yeah," Thrasher said. "First, I want you to take this lady home," he said, pointing to Mary Rose. "Then I want you to take my daughter home. This is my daughter, Marie," he said fondly as he reached out and patted Marie on the shoulder with his hamlike hand. "And check out her house and make sure there's no criminals hiding under the bed. Look in the backyard. Be thorough. Make sure she's secure, you get me?"

"You bet, Chief!" Yarrow said, saluting. "You'll be safe with me, Miss Thrasher. I'd never let my chief down."

"I'm sure you wouldn't," Marie said, smiling up at the handsome officer.

"Saaaay," Zalman said suspiciously. "I smell a big fat rat in cop's clothing. I'll take Marie home, Arnie. That's my department. I don't want Yarrow taking her home."

"You represent Marchetti, right?" Thrasher said, grinning. "Well, I'm letting the ladies go home, just like you wanted. But I ain't through questioning Marchetti by a long shot, so you'd better stick around, Mr. Attorney. Yarrow, take the ladies home. And take your time." Thrasher emphasized the last words heavily.

"You bet, Chief," Yarrow said happily. "Let's go, ladies. I've got a nice clean patrol car right outside."

Marie stood up and kissed Zalman on the cheek. "Don't worry about Yarrow, Jerry. He's just a big baby," she whispered. "I'd better go with Mary Rose. The poor thing's orbiting Pluto, and I don't think she can make it home by herself. Call me in the morning, okay?"

"Grrrr!" Zalman snarled. "I hate this, but I'm trapped."

Yarrow helped Mary Rose to her feet and led her across the restaurant with surprising gentleness. "You want to know how I joined the force?" he asked Marie. "It's a very interesting story. You see, about five years ago I was working as a security guard over at Twentieth Century–Fox. I still have the badge they gave me. All brass, with the logo. I had it framed for a souvenir."

"Oh, are you a collector?" Marie said. "I collect salt and pepper sets."

"So did my grandmother," Yarrow said in surprise. "Mostly fruits and vegetables . . ." His baritone trailed off as the threesome left the restaurant.

"I know what you're up to, Arnie," Zalman said, glaring at Thrasher. "And believe me, it won't work. You think you're a matchmaker? You saw *Hello, Dolly!* on TV and now you think you're a matchmaker? What, Arnie? Tell me, I wanna know!" Zalman said incredulously. "It ain't gonna work! Marie isn't gonna go for that big hunk of cream cheese, not when she's got a great guy like me to come home to! Besides, she's much too smart for him."

"Oh, yeah?" Thrasher said gleefully. "Yarrow's a great guy! Women go for him like crazy!"

"How do you know?" Zalman asked in surprise. "You double-date?"

"He tells me all the time! He says women go for him like crazy! Leave messages on his phone machine saying come on over and lick my toes."

"Yecch, how unsanitary."

Thrasher continued undaunted. "He's smart, he's a nice-looking guy, and he's got a great future in the department, Zalman. Got a steady job. And besides," Thrasher said maliciously, "he's a lot taller than you are!"

"That's a cheap goddamn shot, Thrasher!" Zalman snapped. "And I won't forget it, either."

Jerry Zalman didn't mind being a short guy. He'd realized long ago that short guys were usually more successful than tall guys because they had to fight harder when they were kids and work harder when they were men just to stay even, so being a short guy didn't bother him. But it really jerked his chain when a tall guy, especially Arnie Thrasher, made a wisecrack about his height.

"You want to question my client? Pete!" Zalman hollered across the room. "Get over here, will ya?"

Pete Marchetti looked apprehensively at Thrasher. "Who, me?" he asked. "I didn't do nothing! I was robbed!"

"Thrasher here wants to ask you some questions, Pete, but don't let his bad manners throw you. He had a lousy upbringing," Zalman said. "Go ahead and question him, Thrasher. But don't think you're gonna get any help from me on this, you sneaky bastard. Trying to break me and Marie up. God, I thought even you had some standards!"

BLOODY MARY

Thrasher shook his head happily and showed his teeth. Maybe he thought he was smiling. "Not where you're concerned, Zalman."

It was three-thirty in the morning by the time Thrasher finished pestering Pete Marchetti and the rest of the eyewitnesses to the Le Croque robbery and the murder of Happy Henke. The big cop hadn't learned anything earthshaking, and it had been an aggravating evening. Lots of pain, no gain.

Zalman returned to his empty lair, disgruntled, discouraged, and displeased. No Marie to cuddle up to. No Rutherford to hog the bed.

Zalman was beat, but he was still mad at Thrasher and he was too antsy to sleep, so he made himself a Bullshot and climbed wearily into the Jacuzzi, hoping he could bubble his troubles away.

But he couldn't. Imagine the nerve of that guy! Trying to fix up Marie with Yarrow, that yutz! Okay, so Thrasher hated him. Big deal. Zalman didn't mind that. But the old ferret was trying to set Marie up with a yutz! That rankled.

Zalman thought about calling Marie, just to say hi, how are you, everything all right, but he knew he'd wake her up. He thought about asking her to marry him, but he'd already asked her a few times and she didn't want to, so he'd dropped it. He'd been married twice already, once to Tracee, may she rot, and once to another lady he still remembered semifondly, so marriage wasn't a big deal for Jerry Zalman. Except for the logistical problems of driving back and forth between the Hollywood Hills and Studio City and keeping a few clean shirts in the trunk of the Mercedes, it wasn't a big deal. Still, if Marie had said okay, that would've been great with him.

But Marie didn't want to get married again. She'd

had a bad experience on her first go-round and even though Zalman tried to tell her that when you get married young it doesn't count, the first one's free, and other patent untruths, Marie didn't buy it. Why try something again, she reasoned, when you didn't like it the first time?

She'd been hooked up with a guy around town, a fancy chef who was now running a trendy Irish stew and soda bread emporium on Melrose Avenue called Muggins. It was done up with a thatched roof, horse prints on the walls, all brass, and comfort food. It was very chic and lots of Hollywood types went there at lunchtime to break bread on the company's money. Marie's ex had cheated on her more than once, and it hadn't been an easy breakup. Marie still had a low-level hate on for the guy and said she'd had such a bad experience with Chef Boyardee she wasn't marching up to the altar again unless it was at the point of a .45 automatic.

Wisely, Zalman had dropped the idea even though on lonely nights the concept floated up and into the forefront of his brain. He finished his drink, got out of the tub, and put on a new pair of jade green silk p.j.'s he'd picked up on sale at Neiman-Marcus for a hundred and twenty bucks a few weeks ago, and climbed into bed. He knew tomorrow was going to be a tough day from first to last and Jerry Zalman was going to be ready for it. Guaranteed.

And he was right. He went into the office a little late, about ten-fifteen, and Esther was already sitting at her desk, the phone stuck in her ear and a harried look in her eyes.

All of Zalman's lines were blinking furiously, and Esther raised her penciled eyebrows as Zalman came in and scribbled him a note. "Pete Marchetti on two, Mr. Phalen on three, and Mary Rose Peek on four," the note read. "I'm talking to Jason on one," she mouthed.

Zalman groaned, went into his office, tossed his briefcase on the couch, and pushed the speakerphone button. "Jason," he snapped. "One hour. Be here." He pushed line two. "Pete. Twelve o'clock. My office. Be here." He pushed line three. "Phalen. My office, one o'clock. Be here." He pushed line four. "Mary Rose. How're you feeling, dear, any better? Hmm, look. I'll be over to see you this afternoon, about three. What's your address? Got it," he said as he scribbled the number down.

That done, Zalman punched McCoy's number. He needed help, fast, and his old buddy McCoy was the guy to call.

Doyle Dean McCoy picked up the phone on the second ring, the sound of barking dogs in the background. McCoy lived way the hell out in Newhall in a strange compound of mobile homes, barns, and kennels jammed every which way on a dusty acre of land left to him by his father, and he eked out a modest living renting his surly, smelly, bad-tempered Dobermans as guard dogs for construction sites, movie sets, and used-car lots.

But since his longtime association with Zalman had led to various odd jobs of a paralegal nature, McCoy had begun to fancy himself a bit of a detective, and he'd recently had cards printed up featuring a lurid unblinking eye with the legend "The Real McCoy" and a pair of crossed revolvers underneath in an effort to drum up business.

"McCoy," he said, his deep voice rumbling over the barking dogs.

"It's Jerry. You want work? I got work."

"You got money, I want work. What is it this time, Zally? Do I need to break out the semiauto or is it gonna be another boring day job?" McCoy asked.

BLOODY MARY

Zalman sighed. Now that he thought he was Mike Hammer, McCoy was building up a hard-bitten character for himself, complete with a line of tough-guy patter. He claimed it helped him get girls. "Dean, come into my office at two. No guns, please. No knives, no grenades, no plastique, no nothing. Just your own wonderful self. We gotta do some fast and fancy footwork here."

"What is it this time, Jer?" McCoy asked.

"Oh, God," Zalman groaned. "I take Marie out to Le Croque last night, I had a little business with Happy Henke. The jeweler?"

"You mean the dead jeweler, don't you?" McCoy snorted. "I caught the footage on the eleven o'clock news. Pete gives a good interview. Comes across very sincere, which is surprising for a guy who's a total sweaty weasel. But I didn't figure you were dumb enough to get yourself caught up in a robbery-murder, Jer. You always told me you had brains and here I believed you." He laughed.

"Don't push me, McCoy. Anyway, there's a robbery, Henke gets himself shot, now I got big problems. Not the least of which is I got Arnie Thrasher on my tail again."

"Let me give you some advice, Jer."

"Shut up, Dean."

"Marry Marie, move to Taos, open an art gallery. Take up breeding them yappy little shitso dogs, get into a passive line of work. You got a death wish or what? Can't you stay away from Thrasher?"

"Like I said, Dean, shut up. I got an idea. Since there was a robbery and a lot of fancy jewelry was stolen, maybe you and me'll run out to Wacky Winger's place, see if he knows anything about it. Maybe some of it turned up in his pawnshop."

"Okay, good idea. But if we're gonna go see Wacky,

lemme do the talking, Jer. I don't know why, but the guy gets steamed if people treat him like a fence."

"Why? He is a fence."

"Yeah, but he doesn't like to be treated like one. Bugs him. He likes to think he's just a guy who has a big string of pawnshops and makes a phenomenal living."

"Everybody's got an attitude these days," Zalman said with a sigh. "Okay, you talk to Wacky. I'll pretend I'm looking for a sterling Cartier flatware service for twelve and I only wanna pay a hundred bucks for it. How's that sound?"

"You got the picture. See you later."

Zalman tried Marie, but there was no answer. He made sloppy kissing noises into her machine and hung up. Twenty minutes later, Esther buzzed him. "Jason's here," she said. "With Brenda."

Zalman peered down through the window at Beverly Drive. Yep, the pink Caddy was there, complete with the lout in black leather, one foot on the fender. What was his name? Tyrone, Zalman remembered as he jumped up and yanked open his office door. The kids stared at him, startled. They looked like a pair of fawns caught in the high beams along the side of a country road.

Zalman smiled. He thought he'd try being paternal and see if that worked. He could always start screaming later. "Ah, good," he said. "You're both here. How nice." He ushered them into his office and sat down behind his desk. He smiled again, waiting.

Jason Hanning fidgeted in his seat and Brenda crossed and recrossed her legs, staring intently off into space. Brenda was wearing a dark blue silk dress, the same big pearls, and a hat with a short veil. She lifted the veil and sighed deeply, and Zalman could see she'd been crying.

"You have to help me, Mr. Zalman," she said. "I have no one to turn to. I'm all alone now. Completely. There's no one I trust, no one but you. And Jason, of course," she said as she reached out and squeezed his hand.

"You see, Uncle Jerry," Jason said uncomfortably, "there's something we forgot to tell you yesterday."

"Forgot?" Zalman asked sharply.

"Okay, okay," Jason said, holding up his hand. "Not forgot. Something we didn't tell you."

"That's better. Okay, now that we have that out of the way, go ahead and tell me what it is. We both know it's important or you wouldn't be here, right?"

"Well, it's about Brenda," Jason began.

"Don't be angry at Jason, Mr. Zalman. It's all my fault," she said. "But I need your help so badly. Won't you give me that help, Mr. Zalman?"

Zalman thought he recognized the dialogue from *The Maltese Falcon,* but he wasn't positive. He made a mental note to check the tape sometime soon. "Brenda," he said sternly, "tell me the truth. Then I can try to help you. A man was killed, Brenda, and that's serious business. A lot more serious than your Miss Junior League klepto act at Le Croque. Better tell me the whole story, kiddo. At least I'm on your side."

Brenda looked at Jason; Jason looked at Brenda. "Go ahead," Jason told her.

"I'm Brenda Henke," she said softly, tears coursing down her preteen cheeks. "Happy Henke was my dad. . . ."

ZALMAN SWUNG HIS CHAIR AROUND, LOOKED OUT THE window, and asked himself the eternal question, the inevitable question every human being spinning wildly on the face of the crazy planet Earth asked when confronted with an impossible situation.

Why me?

Why was he the only guy in Beverly Hills with bodies popping up on his doorstep? Why was he the only guy in Beverly Hills whose father-in-common-law was a cop? The only guy whose thirteen-year-old nephew had a film noir girlfriend with a taste for larceny? What did I do to deserve this? Zalman wondered as he swung around again and looked at the kids.

"I want both of you to listen to me," he said, frowning. "You two lied to me yesterday, but you're in luck. I'm a lawyer, so I'm used to lies."

The kids nodded contritely.

"Now," Zalman continued, "I'm gonna tell you this once and once only, so embed my words in your brain. I don't care how old you guys are, if you ever lie to me again or shade the truth or fool around with me in any way, I'll throw you both to the wolves. Tell me the exact, complete truth and I'll do my best for both of you. It's the same thing I tell all my clients, and just because you're a pair of squirts I don't see why you shouldn't get equal treatment. You two receiving me?" he asked, giving them a penetrating stare.

The kids nodded again, eyes downcast.

Zalman smiled. It was a good rap; he used it all the time to throw the fear of God into new clients, and it invariably got great results. All of his clients trembled before the wrath of Zalman.

"Yes, Uncle Jerry," Jason said. "I promise."

"I'm really sorry, Mr. Zalman," Brenda began. "It's just that . . ."

Zalman shook his head and held up his hand to stop her. "Not necessary to explain, Brenda. As I said, people lie to me all the time. Just don't do it again and don't make the mistake of thinking I don't mean what I say. Don't mess with the truth where I'm concerned. Okay? End of lecture," he said. "Next case.

"Now, Brenda," Zalman continued. "I want you to give me the whole story, without leaving anything out. Let's have the bad news all at once. Believe me, I'm tough, I can take it."

"Okay, Mr. Zalman," Brenda said. "Well, first of all, my daddy's dead and I need help. I'm in a terrible situation and I don't know where to turn!"

"What do you mean, exactly?" Zalman asked her.

"I'm afraid, Mr. Zalman," she said simply. "My daddy's dead and I don't know what's going to happen to me. Like I said yesterday, my stepmother, Doris, doesn't like me. She always thought Daddy and I were too close," Brenda said, narrowing her eyes defiantly. "I just know she's going to try and send me to boarding school and cheat me out of my money, I know it! It's my money, all of it. I don't want Doris sinking her claws into my inheritance."

"Well, Brenda," Zalman said reasonably. "Maybe you don't like her, maybe she doesn't like you, but she was your father's wife, so she's going to get a piece of the estate."

"Not if I can help it," Brenda said, shaking her head again, her blond curls whipping from side to side, the righteous fervor of burning cash lighting up her blue eyes. "It's my money! It came from my real mom. All of the money Dad used to finance his experiments with the Diamette and the Emerelle and now the Rubyola came from my mom's money. She was a fat heiress."

"She was fat? What does that—"

"No, no, no," Brenda said impatiently. "She wasn't fat. Our money comes from fat. Grease. Lard. My granddad pioneered the grease industry in this country. When he was a kid he used to collect it from restaurants, then render it and sell it to cosmetics companies. He used to say he was the first man in America who made fat into a fortune. Most of the stuff that ladies pay fifty bucks a jar for at Saks to slap on their wrinkles comes out of the back door of a restaurant. Fat. He made a fortune in fat."

"Fat, huh?" Zalman wondered.

"So, Mr. Zalman," Brenda continued, "I need to know where I stand. Now that my daddy's dead, who's gonna take care of me? I don't trust Doris; she's just my fake mom. I know I'm only twelve, but I'm afraid that if I don't have somebody to look out for my financial interests, Doris is gonna send me off to Foxcroft and spend all my money, and I think it's a gyp!" she said defiantly. "Just because I'm a twelve-year-old orphan, why should I get stuck?"

"You're a true child of Beverly Hills, Brenda," Zalman said thoughtfully. "And you have a point. Now, tell me about the medallion. Did you really steal it?"

Brenda looked ashamed. "Yes," she said. "I do have this problem with stealing, just like I told you yesterday, but ever since I've been going to see Dr. Pud, I pretty much have it under control. But the medallion belonged to my mom, and when I saw Mary Rose wearing it, I kinda lost that control."

"Personal growth is a process, honey," Jason told her. "You have to expect setbacks."

"You knew about your dad and Mary Rose?" Zalman asked curiously.

"Sure."

"How'd you find out?"

"Oh, you grown-ups think just because we're kids we don't have any eyes! Dad and Doris have been married for five years and Doris is a royal pain in the poop. What a whiner! Last year I figured out Daddy was carrying on with somebody, so one day after school we followed him over to Mary Rose's apartment. Ever since I met Jason and we have Tyrone to drive us around, it's just as good as being a grown-up," Brenda said. "See, I never had a car before, and if you don't have a car in L.A. you're a prisoner, no matter how old you are."

"Very true," Zalman admitted. "So you stole the medallion . . ."

"Well, I took it," Brenda admitted grudgingly, her chin jutting out with determination. "After all, it's mine!" she added when she saw Zalman's questioning glance. "I wasn't about to let Dad give it away to some bimbo. Just like I'm not about to let Doris slime me out of my money."

"Tell Uncle Jerry what happened this morning," Jason said.

"God, Doris comes into my room first thing and tells me that Dad was shot and what a tragedy it is for me and how much we both loved him. What a crock! Then she starts being so super-sugar to me, really greasing it up. She thinks I'm a mental midget? I'm not going to fall for her act. Yesterday she's trying to pry me out of the house; today I'm the little princess. Y'know," Brenda said thoughtfully, "now that Dad's gone, I think she's afraid of what's in the will. Maybe she isn't in control anymore. Maybe everything's in trust for me. But don't you see, Mr. Zalman, no matter what happens, I need a lawyer. Somebody who's on my side. And I need protection from Doris."

"Okay, Brenda. I'm on your side and don't forget it. Now, you two reach into your pockets and give Esther five bucks on your way out. That means I'm officially your lawyer and I can officially tell people to go to hell on your behalf, something I'd usually do for free, but in this situation I think we'd better try to keep it legal. So go home and act normal," Zalman advised as a troublesome thought hit him. "Jason, before you go, what did you tell your mom about this?"

"Lucky for me, she's out of town. Bland's on tour, promoting his new album, *Dead Rat in the Swimming Pool*. Have you heard it?" Jason asked. "Great album. Mom says it's got lots of social consciousness, and it shipped double platinum. She won't be back for a week."

"Where's your dad?" Zalman asked.

"At home. He's no problem," Jason said confidently.

"I hope not, for your sake. I'll keep quiet about this as long as I can, okay? That's all I can promise, but if your folks ask me, I won't lie. Now beat it," Zalman said, looking at his watch. "Marchetti's due any minute, and I don't want him to see you, Brenda. He might remember you from the party. Talk to me later, kids," Zalman called as Jason and Brenda left his office.

Pete Marchetti showed up a few minutes later, barely missing Jason and Brenda. "Ayy, Jerry!" he moaned as he collapsed in one of the leather armchairs across from Zalman's desk. "My life is over! I'm finished! A murder at Le Croque! A robbery is bad enough, but a murder, ayy! Should I close for a few days, Jer? I got the place open but the pre-lunch booze crowd was slow. Everybody's rubbernecking at the blood on the dining room floor! Nobody's buying! What, Jer? Tell me what to do! My life is in your hands."

Zalman went over to the bar and made a pair of Bullshots. "First off, drink this and quit your bitching," he said as he shoved the glass in Pete's hand. "You got nothing to worry about and remember that you heard it here first. Business is going to pick up. It's gonna be phenomenal in the next few days, I'll swear to it. I saw the same thing happen after that murder at Mitzi's Magic Cavern."

"Oh, yeah," Pete remembered, narrowing his eyes. "You were involved in that one, too."

"I wasn't involved!" Zalman said defensively. "Not at all. But I'm telling you, Mitzi's business doubled! Happy was a great guy. . . ."

"He was a sleaze ball," Pete said. "Now he's a dead sleaze ball."

"Whatever. But I'm telling you, homicide can be a real boost to your balance sheet. C'mon, Pete, you were the lead story on the eleven o'clock news! You were interviewed! You can't buy that kind of publicity, so don't worry, okay?"

Pete shook his head, running his hands nervously up and down the sharp lapels of his brown silk suit. "I dunno, Jer. Maybe yes, maybe no. But I'm operating on a thin margin here. A few days with no customers, it's down the dumpo for old Pete. And you know what that means, Jer."

"It means you may have to work for a living, Pete."

"Yeah, and you may have to pay for your own lunch!"

Zalman grinned and sipped his Bullshot. "I'd hate

that, Pete," he said. "It would go against everything I hold dear."

"I'm serious, Jer! This could be the end of my impossible dream. No White Asparagus! I've come so far," Pete said, sniffling. "So far from Cleveland, from the banks of the mighty Cuyahoga. It would kill me if I had to start over, Jer, no kidding. You gotta help me!"

"Don't worry about it," Zalman soothed. "It's in the bag."

"That's what you said about the medallion and now it's stolen again, and what's worse, Happy Henke gets croakified in a pile of my best beluga," Pete whined. "What am I gonna do, Jer?"

"Finish your drink, get out of my office, go back to Le Croque, and hire some extra help for the next few days. You're gonna have so many folks bellying up to the trough you're gonna need five new waiters. Tell you what," Zalman said thoughtfully. "You're a gambling man, so how's about we make a little deal? I'm in for ten percent of White Asparagus, right? If business at Le Croque doesn't double in the next week, I'll cut my end down to five. If it doubles, I get fifteen."

Pete brightened. "And you'll throw in all the legal work? That guy Thrasher is a real monster. That was some going-over he gave me last night, and for what? I'm the victim, I was robbed! He's treating me like I'm the criminal here!" Pete said indignantly, shaking his head like a wet dog. "I don't believe he's Marie's father. There sure ain't a family resemblance."

"How do you think I feel?" Zalman said. "Is it a deal?"

"Sure," Pete agreed. "Why not? How could it get any worse?"

"You'd be surprised, Petey-pie." Zalman smiled.

*　　*　　*

BLOODY MARY

At one o'clock sharp, Failin' Phalen wandered into Zalman's office, sporting a large white bandage on his head that gave him the devil-may-care look of an Easter Bunny with a toothache. "I won't lie to you, Jerry," he said as he sat down. "I did a little checkup on you this morning. I called Phil Hanning, and he told me you're probably the one guy in town who can straighten me out. I've got major, major problems. Big problems."

Zalman stared at Phalen over his desk and smiled with a sincerity he did not feel. First of all, whenever a guy started off by saying he wasn't going to lie, Zalman knew exactly what to expect. Lies and plenty of 'em. And second of all, since when was Phil Hanning giving him recommendations? He wouldn't trust Hanning to recommend dessert, so where did he get off boosting him to Failin' Phalen, a guy with a big-time loser rep? But this wasn't the time to make a scene, so Zalman shifted gears from angry brother-in-law to professionally neutral lawyer. "Tell me about it, Phalen," he said sagely.

Phalen shifted uncomfortably in his chair and reflexively rubbed his bandaged head. "First of all," he ticked off, "Happy's dead. This is a killer, no pun intended. Hap and I were partners, yeah. But I gotta admit it up front, I was just the money man. Happy was the talent, and he was more than a TV pitchman; he was a chemist, an inventor, a genuis in the faux gem line! He and he alone came up with the Diamette and the Emerelle, and he was on the verge of a major breakthrough with the Rubyola! I'm telling you, Jerry, the Rubyola is going to be bigger than cold fusion! B-i-g." He spelled it out. "But now Hap's dead and I'm nowhere. Okay, I'm resourceful. I'm gonna work fast. If I can find his notes, I'll hire the best scientists bucks can buy, see if they can create the Rubyola. After all, the Rubyola was the completion of Happy's lifework. It'd be a tribute to his integrity, don'tcha think, Jerry?"

"Ummm." Zalman nodded noncommittally. "A tribute. Yeah. Sure."

"But here's the thing. Something's rotten in the state of Delaware," Phalen said with a frown. "I dunno why, but I got suspicious. I go down to the office this morning, whip through the books. I used to be an accountant before I hooked up with Happy, and even a quick run-through tells me I got a cash flow problem."

"Yeah? What kind of cash flow problem?"

"I ain't got a cash flow."

"That's a problem."

Phalen shook his head in agreement. "You're telling me. Looks like somebody's had a finger in the till. More like five fingers. More like both fists, if you take my point. I haven't been paying good attention, and now the dough's gonna dry up unless I do something fast. You're the man to help me, Jerry."

"You think it was Happy?" Zalman asked.

"I dunno." Failin' Phalen shrugged. "I hate to think it. But he had expensive tastes—big house, expensive wife, expensive best friend. The usual Hollywood story. But if it was Happy, I gotta recoup from the estate. Somewhere. Somehow. I can't take a bath on this, and after what Phil Hanning said, I decided you're the guy to straighten me out. Be like the bear that went over the mountain, Jerry. See what you can see. Phil says you handle all kinds of weird things, and it looks like you know that Captain Thrasher pretty well. I want you to keep an eye on the cops, too, just in case they find out anything about Happy's murder that they can't bring to trial. You know what I'm saying, Jerry," Failin' Phalen said. "They find out who did it, but they ain't got the evidence to make it stick."

"You don't think it was an accident?" Zalman asked. "You think he was set up at Le Croque?"

"I dunno," Phalen said, shrugging. "I dunno what I think. I know he's dead, I know somebody's been cooking the books, I know there was a big robbery and somebody made off with a lot of rocks. But I want to know what the cops know."

"Let me warn you right off, Phalen," Zalman said. "If you think I'm doing something illegal for you or anybody else, think again."

"No, no, no!" Phalen cried. "This is all straight up! I need to know what's going on."

"Okay," Zalman said. He figured that by keeping an eye on Failin' Phalen, he'd be helping Jason and Brenda. Pete, Phalen, and everybody else came second. Family loyalty was Jerry Zalman's number-one priority.

"And another thing," Phalen said. "I went over to the house this morning to pay my respects to Happy's widow, Doris. She was pretty upset, as you can imagine, but she needs some legal help right away. I hope you don't mind, but I asked her to drop by. First of all, she has something she doesn't want her regular lawyer to handle. She wouldn't tell me what it is. She wants it done discreetly, and after what Phil said, well, I think you're the guy to do it. But the main thing is—and I hate to think this way so soon after Happy's death—but if he did have his hand in the cash drawer and I run into a problem with the stores, I'll need you to smooth Doris over. Get it? Help me out with this, Jerry. There's enough here for everybody," Phalen said. "You'll make out okay," he said as he got up out of his chair and went to the door.

"I always do," Zalman said. "Talk to me later."

After Phalen left, Zalman leaned back in his chair and pretended to think. This case looked more like an Exxon oil slick every minute. Nice and glassy smooth

BLOODY MARY

on top, lots of black sludge and rotting goo underneath. Jason and Brenda. Mary Rose. Pete Marchetti. Now Failin' Phalen and the widow Henke. Absently, Zalman wondered what Brenda's fake Mom was really like.

HE DIDN'T HAVE LONG TO WAIT. TEN MINUTES LATER, Esther Wong poked her head through the door and made a hideous sucking-on-a-sour-pickle face. "A Mrs. Doris Henke to see you?" she said sweetly, as she crossed her eyes and stuck out her tongue. "And a Miss Forrester?" Here Esther smiled angelically.

Miss Forrester? Who the hell is Miss Forrester? Zalman wondered. "Show them in, Esther darling," he growled in his best Bogart.

Esther crossed her eyes again. "Get a load of this!" she whispered.

Zalman laughed despite himself. He was trying to maintain his legal composure, but Esther's antics made it tough going.

Doris Henke sailed into his office like a brave little tugboat in mourning. She was a short woman of about fifty, and it was clear that she considered herself extremely attractive even though she was carrying an extra twenty pounds in a thick roll of love handles around her waist.

But despite the added avoirdupois, Doris Henke wasn't ready to give in to blue hair and Sears prints quite yet. She was artfully made up, and her frosted blond hair was carefully coiffed. It was plain that she was determined to tough out the illusion of young middle age as long as she could.

She was wearing a chic black silk suit, but her short skirt and spindly ankle strap heels added a faintly suggestive air to her widow's weeds. Widow or not, Doris Henke had great legs, and it was obvious she wasn't willing to let a dead husband stop her from showing them off.

Even though she had good legs, her jewelry was an absolute showstopper. She was wearing a necklace of diamonds and emeralds, and each glittering stone glowed with a lush, concealed fire hidden in its secret depths. The square-cut emeralds were surrounded by a bank of pavé diamonds in a smooth gold setting, and Zalman was willing to bet the farm that the stones were real gems, not Diamettes and Emerelles.

As he admired her necklace, with its perfectly matched bracelet and earrings, Zalman thought that the coiled rocks around Doris Henke's pudgy neck were bigger, flashier, and shinier than anything Imelda Marcos ever dreamed of as she lay alone in the palace a few days before the coup. The only thing missing was a tiara, Zalman mused as he ushered the widow Henke into a chair.

"Mr. Zalman," she said, her deep voice purring like a well-tuned Rolls. "I'm Doris Henke . . . Annabelle!" she called sharply. "I want you with me."

"Coming, Mother," a woman's voice replied.

Zalman looked up just as she came in, and even though he was a guy who'd been around, he almost gasped out loud when he saw her standing in the doorway.

Annabelle Forrester was one of the loveliest women he'd ever seen in his life, and for a guy who'd been on the treadmill of love in Hollywood, California, for a number of years, that was saying something real.

She was twenty-two or -three and she was tiny, probably five-one without heels. She had long blond hair that reminded him of some soft, chewy taffy his dad had once brought him from Atlantic City, back when taffy meant a lot to a kid. Eyes? Blue. Blue like deep, dark sapphires, and skin as smooth as something rich and creamy he remembered spooning up at Le Croque late one night, some gushy delight meant to throw the entire body into an orgasmic paroxysm of sugar shock. Zalman realized that he was looking at a walking dessert, and he hoped he wasn't drooling.

"Won't you sit down, ladies?" he said smoothly.

"My daughter, Annabelle Forrester," Doris Henke said as she sat down across from Zalman's desk.

Annabelle took the other chair. She licked her Cherries Jubilee lips and looked Zalman up and down. It didn't take long.

Zalman had the eerie feeling that she had X-ray eyes and she'd just memorized the entire contents of his wallet, including the expiration dates on all of his credit cards.

"So kind of you to see me on such short notice," Doris Henke said.

"It's the least I can do, under the circumstances. I only met Mr. Henke for the first time last night, but even so . . ."

Doris Henke cut off Zalman's polite attempt at condolences with a short, harsh laugh that sounded like a cat choking on a hair ball. "Don't bother, Mr. Zalman. My late husband was a shit. Very few people liked him, very few people will miss him. I'm not one of them. Now, since I'm not here to pretend I'm sorry he's dead, why don't I tell you why I am here?"

"Please do," Zalman said.

Annabelle crossed her legs and tried to tug the skirt of her white suit down over her knees. Then she uncrossed her legs and began to rotate her little feet in front of her. Then she sighed and looked at her manicure.

"Don't fidget, Annabelle," Doris Henke told her daughter. "Actually," she drawled, cocking her head to one side like a parakeet, "the only thing I'm sorry about is that it didn't happen sooner. An early bereavement would have saved me a lot of aggravation. I'm here because I need you, Mr. Zalman. Maxie Phalen tells me you're the man to handle a few problems that have emerged," she said. "I think he's right."

Zalman watched as Doris Henke cast a businesslike eye over his office. In one smooth sweep, her heavily mascaraed eyes took in the expensive Persian rugs, the Victorian furniture, the framed prints, and the general impression of tasteful old money that Zalman liked to give.

He figured she was totting up the value of his goods in her head like a human calculator, and somehow he knew she had it all appraised to the nickel. If Sotheby's ever needed help, Doris Henke was the lady to see.

Zalman smiled professionally across his big partners desk at the widow Henke. "Well, at least you don't mess around," he said. "Drink?"

"Scotch, please. Straight. It's been a tough day and I've barely started it," she said dryly.

"Saratoga," Annabelle Forrester said, her voice soft and breathy.

"You have a family attorney, I presume?" Zalman said as he went to the bar and poured a glass of Johnnie Walker for Doris Henke and the fancy water for Annabelle.

"Umm," Doris hedged, sipping her drink. "Happy had someone to take care of his business interests, but I'm in the market for someone to take care of *my* business interests."

"He had a will?"

"Of course."

Zalman knew she was hedging again. It was probable Happy Henke had a will, but it was also probable Doris Henke wasn't positive about its contents and that was one big reason she was in his office. "You know what was in it?" he asked.

"I'm not sure," Doris said bluntly, her eyes harsh. "Look, Maxie Phalen spoke highly of you, Mr. Zalman, and I don't have time to go comparison-shopping for legal help. You seem like a smart lawyer to me. At least you have good taste," she said, waving her ringed hand at Zalman's furniture.

Zalman smiled and said nothing.

"Happy's dead. He left a child by his first marriage, and I'm sure Brenda will be well provided for," Doris said. "But I have myself to think about and, of course, Annabelle. She's my daughter by my first marriage," she went on, her eyes shifting back and forth over the room and lighting on Zalman as if he were a butterfly and she had the net.

Annabelle rattled the ice in her glass.

"I make up my mind fast and I think a personal relationship is what counts today, don't you, Mr. Zalman?" Doris Henke asked.

"Umm," Zalman said, shuddering imperceptibly. Was she being coy? He hoped not. The thought of a personal relationship with Doris Henke made him feel a tad nauseated. Better to stick your head in a python's mouth than to get up close and personal with a dame like Doris. "But first, let's talk about what you want me to do for you. How can I help you, Mrs. Henke?"

Doris Henke smiled. "Well, since you know what went on at Le Croque last night, the first thing I need is a liaison with the police. I don't know anything about the robbery, I don't know anything about the murder or how the police work, Mr. Zalman, so I want to keep in touch with the investigation. Some valuable property was stolen from my husband last night, and I want that property back."

"Everything was insured, I presume?" Zalman asked smoothly. Did she know about the medallion? he wondered.

"Oh, of course." She shrugged, draining her glass. "And you should see the premiums! But that Picasso medallion has a value far greater than mere cash," she said.

Too bad, Zalman thought sadly. Doris didn't deserve the damn thing either.

"And no matter what I get from the insurance company, it won't half cover the loss," Doris Henke said sharply. "This is a rarity, a piece of Picasso jewelry. Whatever it's worth this year, it's going to be worth twice as much next year and so on. It's a work of art, to be sure. But it has a potential value that no amount of insurance can cover. A future value, do you know what I mean?"

"Of course I do," Zalman said. "And what else do you want me to do for you?"

"There's Happy's ring, too. I'd like it back, but that's only money. A diamond ring is the kind of thing insurance can cover. That's only money," she repeated. "I'm hoping you'll be able to enter into negotiations with the men who have the jewelry, once the police find them. The police can't negotiate for me; maybe you can."

"Funny that your husband invented the Diamette, that he was a big promoter of faux gems, and yet he wore a real diamond ring. He died rather than give it up," Zalman said.

"Happy didn't like to give anything up," Doris said shortly. "It was one of his quirks."

"And is your necklace real?" Zalman asked, just out of curiosity.

"Of course it's real!" Doris Henke said, surprised by the question. "Happy was a shit, but he was no fool," she laughed as she rattled her bracelet in the air. "That was a very large diamond in his ring, and it's worth a fortune! The Diamette is beautiful, but a ten-karat diamond is so . . ."

"So solid."

"And so, so valuable. Then there's one other thing I want you to do," she said slowly.

"What's that?" Zalman asked. He wondered if she was going to cut to the human side of things at last.

"I want you to throw that little bitch Mary Rose Peek out of the apartment Happy kept her in," the widow Henke shrilled, her voice squealing like brakes on a wet highway. "Get her out of there today and tell her the free ride's over!"

Strike the human side of things. "I didn't know if you knew Miss Peek was at Le Croque last night," Zalman said. "Under the circumstances, I didn't want to bring it up."

"I know plenty!" The widow's voice shrilled again, crackling like broken glass on concrete. "She's out! Finished! Today! Happy owns the place; I know that because I happened to find the papers in his desk this morning."

"You work fast, Mrs. Henke."

"I have to," she said sharply. "Who's going to look out for me, for Annabelle, if I don't? Throw her out. Hire somebody, I don't care how you do it. Just get rid of her."

Zalman nodded. He had absolutely no intention of taking Doris Henke as a client, and despite the beautiful Annabelle Forrester, life was too short to ask for grief, terror, pain, and horror. Under normal circumstances, he would've tossed Doris Henke out in the street on her keester. But now he controlled his desire to give Madame Henke la boot.

Behind Zalman's own interests and his presence at the robbery and murder at Le Croque there lurked the troublesome question of Jason Hanning and Brenda Henke. Brenda said that she needed help, and now that he'd gotten a good geeze at Brenda's wicked stepmother and beautiful stepsister, Zalman knew he had no choice.

Brenda's twelve-year-old suspicions were valid. She needed protection from her fake mom, and she needed it fast. Doris Henke was tougher than old German army boots, and Zalman knew that if he didn't jump in and help Brenda Henke, the next few years of her life would be hell on ice. Her fake mom would stash her in a boarding school while she squeezed the grin off every dime she inherited from the late Happy Henke and put it right on Annabelle's pretty back.

Zalman steepled his hands and stared pensively at Doris Henke. "I can't promise anything. I'll check around, and we'll see what develops in the next day or so. I'm already committed to Maxie Phalen."

"At this point, my interests don't conflict with Maxie Phalen's," Doris growled. "We've had our differences in the past. He and Happy didn't always see eye to eye about the jewelry stores, I know that much. But most of the time, Maxie and I haven't had any problems. I'm not asking for a lifetime commitment from you, Mr. Zalman," she said as she stood up.

"I'll see what I can do," Zalman said gravely as he walked her to the door. "Let's be in touch."

Doris Henke and Annabelle Forrester said their good-byes and left the office. But before Zalman had a chance to sit down, the door to his office opened again.

Annabelle Forrester walked quickly over to Zalman, put her arms around him, and kissed him on the mouth.

He could feel those soft ice cream lips pressing his . . . lips that should have been sweet. But . . .

Annabelle stepped away from Zalman and ran her hand over his cheek. "I have my own interests to protect," she said. "I just thought I'd let you know what they were." She smiled over her shoulder as she walked out again.

Zalman sat down in his desk chair, spun around, and surveyed Beverly Drive. He'd kissed a lot of girls in his time, he thought as he tentatively put his hand to his mouth. But in his entire career as a single man, he'd never kissed a woman with lips of stone.

He tried Marie at her office over at Typeit, the script service she owned, in the San Fernando Valley, but her assistant, Linda, said she wasn't in yet. Zalman wondered where she was and wondered how she'd liked her evening with the delightful Lieutenant Yarrow. What a yutz that guy was!

Twenty minutes later, he heard the outer office door open and Esther shriek. Chester, Rutherford's brother Doberman, bounded into his office, jumped up on the couch, and began to lick the cushions like an unruly client.

"Get that mutt off my furniture," Zalman yelled at McCoy. "It's bad enough I got Rutherford to deal with at home, now I have to put up with this noise in my office? Get him off, Dean!"

Doyle Dean McCoy smiled, pulled a Lucky out of his crumpled pack, and snapped his fingers at Chester, motioning him down. Chester didn't move.

"And just as well trained as Rutherford, I see,"

Zalman said. "It's no wonder these dogs of yours are a hot ticket, Dean. Boy, I'd stake my life on Chester, no doubt about it."

McCoy shrugged, went over to the bar fridge, took out a pair of beers, opened them both, and drained one straight off. He offered the second beer to Chester, who took a dainty slurp and rolled over, scratching his back on the couch.

Zalman sighed as he looked at McCoy.

Jerry Zalman and Doyle Dean McCoy had been friends since the year zero, and Zalman often thought that if they met today they wouldn't like each other at all, because they had absolutely nothing in common. Besides, there was no way Zalman and McCoy would meet today unless they ran into each other jumping a stoplight.

Zalman, with his penchant for the upper crust, and McCoy, with his dirty pickup and his aura of dogs, guns, beer, and burgers, functioned in two different worlds. Maybe on two different planets.

But a good friend was hard to find, and even though they looked like Mutt and Jeff, Doyle Dean McCoy was one of the few guys Jerry Zalman trusted one hundred percent.

"Still alive, Zally?" McCoy grinned, shaking his shaggy head. "Thrasher ain't hung you out to dry yet?"

"Dean," Zalman warned. "I'm not paying you to abuse me. I'm paying you to help, as the girl said to the sailor, so shut up about Thrasher. Let's go over to Wacky Winger's and see what that gink has to say for himself. Maybe he's got a line on this hot jewelry and—"

"I'm telling you, Jer, be careful with Wacky! You start saying words like 'hot' around him, he'll get up on his hind legs! Besides, maybe later you'll come home and find your place has been cleaned out. Professionally cleaned out, get it? Like to the bare walls. Let me talk to Wacky, will ya?"

"Yeah, yeah, I get it, Dean," Zalman snapped. "You talk, I'll drive. But Chester rips my leather with his claws, he's gonna wake up dead. I just had the front seats redone, and it cost me seven hundred bucks per. Per each."

McCoy drained his beer and gave Chester the backwash. "Sure, you be the designated driver, Jer. Me and Chester like to go for drives. I'll even hang my head out the window if you want me to."

Zalman took Wilshire and cut up to Santa Monica on Fairfax. The smog was light, but traffic was brutal, so it took them thirty minutes to make what should have been the ten minute drive to Wacky Winger's main shop on Santa Monica Boulevard in West Hollywood.

You couldn't miss Wacky's place of biz because it had a big neon arrow firmly planted on the roof overhead, and hot pink Day-Glo letters that said Wacky Winger's Wanch on it in a lovely scroll. The Wanch part was Wacky's little joke. The pawnshop itself was a spacious affair with broad plate-glass windows that displayed a tasteful array of hocked goods—guitars, amplifiers, computers, VCRs, and a few trays of belt buckles and expensive gold jewelry, in case a customer had a few bucks left for treats on payday.

Zalman and McCoy parked the Mercedes on Santa Monica and left Chester in the driver's seat to guard the car. "Don't worry about it, Jer," McCoy said as they went into Wacky's. "You know what a villain Chester is. Leave a hundred on the dashboard, anybody goes for it, Chester'll bite his hand off. Nobody messes with Chester."

Wacky Winger himself scuttled up to greet them the moment they stepped inside his shop. "Mr.

Zalman," he said expansively. "Long time, Mr. Zalman! What a pleasure, Mr. Zalman! And Dean, nice to see you as well, my friend."

Wacky Winger was a little taller than Zalman, but not much. He was half bald, and what was left of his hair was carefully combed into an elaborate filigree of fur smack in the center of his skull. He was wearing an expensive blue pinstripe suit and several diamond rings on his delicate hands.

"Wacky," Zalman said as they shook hands. "Nice to see you, too."

Wacky Winger was a man with two reputations. Many people saw him as an honest businessman, a friend to those in need of ready cash, a guy who'd lend you a twenty out of his own pocket if you were on the skids and had nothing left of value to place with him for eventual sale. He was known as a regular guy and was an easy touch for hard goods like folding chairs for the senior center or bunk beds for a nearby halfway house for teen runaways. Wacky always said a good deed was like money in the bank.

But there was also the dark side of Wacky Winger. Wacky was a guy who'd started out scuffling, and he liked to keep his hand in when an opportunity came his way just so he wouldn't lose his touch. Thus, few people knew that once in a while—not all the time, just when it was a deal too good to resist—Wacky Winger didn't mind taking in a little warm jewelry through the back door of the Wanch, if he was two hundred percent positive he could get away with it.

Zalman started to open his mouth, but McCoy gave him the elbow. "Got a problem, Wacky," he said gravely. "Need your advice."

Wacky spread his hands and smiled. "Dean," he said, "for you, for Mr. Zalman here, anything I can do. You know that. Anything. I'm at your service."

BLOODY MARY

He looked around the shop. "But perhaps it's better to discuss private business privately. In my office?" He turned and led them behind the counter and up a small flight of stairs to a glassed-in loft that overlooked the shop. "I saw the news last night, Mr. Zalman," he said over his shoulder. "Pete Marchetti had a nice spot, did a very professional interview. Didn't know Pete had it in him. Word gets around you were there, at the Le Croque robbery?"

"Umm," Zalman muttered as McCoy gave him another elbow.

The three men sat down in Wacky's office, and Zalman offered cigars all around. Both Wacky and McCoy took one, and as they lit up, a thin haze of smoke began to waft toward the white acoustic tile ceiling.

Wacky peered at Zalman over a small pile of beepers lying on his desk. "So?" he asked. "How can Wacky Winger be of service to you two fine gentlemen?"

"You know Jerry is keeping company with the daughter of Arnie Thrasher?" McCoy said delicately.

Wacky raised his eyes skyward. "I heard this. I'm sure she's a lovely lady, Mr. Zalman, so no offense. But Arnie Thrasher, he is well known as a very difficult person. Hard to handle, shall I say? No offense," he said again, "but I'm wondering, can she be worth it?"

Zalman exhaled smoke and started to speak up in Marie's defense when McCoy jumped in smoothly.

"We were hoping you might be able to help us track down some of the proceeds from the robbery last night before Arnie Thrasher decides to have Jerry burned at the stake. Arnie Thrasher hates Jerry. He hates me, too, by the way, and he don't care who did the crime if he thinks he can nail Jerry with the time."

"Is this so? I'm amazed," Wacky said thoughtfully, staring down into his shop through the glass. Suddenly his attention was diverted as he caught sight of a young man in a blue Dodgers cap lugging in a huge Sony. Swiftly his hand shot out and pushed the intercom. "Eighty bucks tops on the Sony," he said to the clerk below. "Try for sixty. Otherwise, nix it." The clerk gave Wacky the high sign, and Wacky turned his attention back to Zalman and McCoy, then studied the wrapper on his cigar carefully before he spoke. "So little sense of responsibility in our public officials these days." Wacky sighed. "Imagine that a man like Arnie Thrasher would let a petty personal vendetta impede the flow of justice. But how can I help you? I only deal in goods with a perfect pedigree. The proceeds from the Le Croque robbery, I cannot imagine that the sales end of such a large transaction was not worked out during the planning of the crime. So much jewelry was taken and it's so very hot! How would I . . ."

Zalman coughed. With three men smoking cigars, the atmosphere in the little room was thicker than the air in Pasadena in the middle of August. Sadly, he stubbed out his cigar. A waste, but you gotta breathe, he thought.

McCoy frowned and leaned forward, the cigar clenched between his teeth. Zalman could tell his old pal was moving in for the kill. "Wacky, we've been friends a long time and I hope you take this in the right spirit. Jerry and I need your help, but after what I heard this morning, I think you need our help, too."

"What did you hear?" Wacky said cautiously. "About me? What did you hear? Where did you hear it?"

McCoy shook his big head. "Not in the best of places, I'm afraid. I dunno, Jer, maybe it's better if Wacky doesn't know."

"You gotta tell him," Zalman said, playing along. "It's his right to know."

"Know what?" Wacky Winger said, worried. "Know what about what?"

McCoy sighed sadly and took a meditative puff on his cigar. "Okay, Wacky. Jerry's right. You gotta know. On my way over to see Jerry this morning, I had a little business with Eddie Ramirez first, so I dropped in at the Dead Head to see him."

"That toilet!" Wacky said derisively.

"I never said Eddie was Mr. Klass," McCoy said mournfully. "Anyway, we're chatting, and he knows about the robbery from TV, and he knows me and Jerry are buddies with you, and he tells me two guys came into the Head last night and a girl told Eddie she overheard one of the guys mention your name—in connection with the sale of the proceeds of the robbery," McCoy added meaningfully.

"It's a lie!" Wacky yowled. "Pure as the driven snow, that's Wacky Winger! I wouldn't—"

"I know that, Wacky!" McCoy said, allowing the faintest tinge of exasperation to creep into his voice. "I know you're straight up on the narrow! But when a guy tells me a girl overheard two total strangers discussing someone who is a longtime friend of mine, I think he should know what's going around. So like I said, me and Jerry need your help, but I think maybe you need us, too." McCoy was sounding slightly aggrieved, the put-upon pal, the guy who'd tromp ten miles barefoot through toxic waste to help a buddy. It was an impressive performance.

Wacky's cigar trembled in his little hand. "I'm deeply troubled," he admitted. "This is a very unpleasant incident, and I'm deeply, deeply hurt by it. But what should I do?" he said as he turned to Zalman. "What would be your expert opinion as a lawyer, Mr. Zalman? And I'm not asking for freebies, either. Can I sue?"

Zalman shook his head. "This is all amorphous rumor, Wacky. There's never much you can do about rumors. I think Dean's point is that if rumors are floating around, the best thing for you to do is to help us track down the stolen jewelry. Then we go to the cops, Arnie Thrasher is forced to admit that I'm a great guy, and he's also forced to make a statement about how you helped the police break the case, by providing vital information."

Wacky nodded. "I see your point."

"Look," Zalman asked. "Is it possible some of the stuff was unloaded in one of your other stores? I can see that you're on top of things here, but what about the place out by the airport? Maybe one of your clerks is hustling action on the side?"

Zalman thought this was very clever. He was giving Wacky Winger an out. Wacky could pretend to make some calls, then miraculously come up with the vital information and blame his earlier oversight on some nameless stooge. Zalman thought it was a brilliant tactical move on his part.

Wacky leapt on it like lobster at a buffet. "I'll make some calls," he said excitedly. "I'll see what I can find out! You're right, Mr. Zalman. Maybe one of my boys is getting greedy, and if he is, he'll be no match for Wacky Winger! Let me make a few calls. I'll get back to you later this afternoon. Wacky Winger, a fence!" he said. "I'm insulted!"

"WHAT'RE THESE NOW, CONDOS?" MCCOY ASKED AS he peered up at Mary Rose Peek's apartment building on Selma, above Sunset Boulevard. "Used to be apartments. I think I knew a lady once on the third floor. Yeah, Maureen. She had a nice joint, fireplace, hardwood floors. She paid maybe three-fifty a month." He patted Chester's snout affectionately.

"Probably costs three-fifty to buy in now." Zalman snorted as he looked across the street at the graceful California Spanish building. "Three-fifty *K*, that is. Two *K* maintenance, maybe more. Who the hell knows? Everything's so crazy now. People love to throw money around, then complain about how they got screwed. Nice building, though. Very Raymond Chandler."

"Yeah." McCoy laughed. "Probably this is where Carmen Sternwood moved after they let her out of the bin."

Zalman grinned as he jumped out of the Mercedes. "I always figured she moved to Carmel, opened up a yarn shop," he told McCoy as they trotted up the broad red stairs into a small hallway faced in cheery yellow and blue tiles.

"Or maybe she went into drug counseling and tried to forget," McCoy said.

Zalman punched the intercom button on the shiny brass mailbox next to Mary Rose's name, and a moment later a wispy, dispirited voice said, "Yes?"

"Jerry Zalman."

"Second floor," Mary Rose said.

The buzzer sounded, Zalman pushed open the beveled-glass door and went inside and up the stairs, McCoy right behind him.

Mary Rose was standing in a doorway at the end of the hall, framed by a brilliantly bejeweled stained-glass window of Saint George pricking a cranky dragon with his sword. The little flecks of twinkling light cast a heavenly aura around Mary Rose, who was wearing a red silk kimono that set off her burnished hair to perfection. Her hair was loose, trailing down her back in soft waves, and she was holding an apricot-colored toy poodle in her arms.

The little dog stared up at her with hazy eyes, and in the soft glow of the multicolored stained glass she reminded Zalman of a dog's vision of a madonna. Our Lady of the Milk-Bones.

"That's the other woman in the case?" McCoy whispered, breathing heavily. "I think I just won the lottery of love."

"Oh, Mr. Zalman," Mary Rose said softly as she led them into her apartment, bumping her arm on the door frame. "Ouch, darn it." The poodle closed its eyes sleepily, then nestled in the crook of her arm. "Thank you so much for coming."

"I thought we ought to talk right away," Zalman said. "This is my associate, Doyle Dean McCoy."

McCoy shook hands with Mary Rose, then reached out and patted the dog on its walnut-sized head. "Nice doggie," he said.

Mary Rose brightened and kissed the dog. "This here's my little baby Triscuit," she said. "Ah don't know what ah'd do without him. He's such a comfort. Mr. Zalman, what's gonna happen to me?" she wailed, depositing Triscuit on the floor. "Come into the living room. I'm sorry everything's such a mess."

BLOODY MARY

The apartment was spacious, with beamed ceilings and white plaster walls. At the end of the living room there was a balcony with twisted wrought-iron rails overlooking a courtyard below. Outside the window, a palm tree rustled its dry fronds together like chapped hands in the California breeze.

Inside, the furniture was big, overstuffed, and comfortable, yet the apartment was faceless, devoid of character or a personal stamp. It didn't look like a home; it looked like a high-class hotel room where Mary Rose was camping out until, like every other hungry Hollywood citizen, she got her big break.

Zalman was surprised as he glanced around at the place. He'd figured Mary Rose for a closet homebody, one of those ladies who baked bread on Sundays while she rinsed out her undies in the bathroom sink. But even the pictures on the walls were anonymous seascapes, ten minute oils done in a back room in Hong Kong, then picked for size and color at a Sunday art sale at the mall.

Mary Rose flopped down on the nubbly wheatcolored couch and buried her head in her hands. "Ah just don't know what to do!" she cried, the long red sleeves of her kimono trailing on the floor. "Poor Happy!"

"I met with Doris Henke this morning," Zalman began.

"So she did know about me," Mary Rose said, lifting her head. "Ah wasn't quite sure. Happy said she didn't, but ah always wondered. He told me he was going to divorce her," she said. "And ah believed him. She never loved him!"

"Mary Rose," Zalman said gently, "I know that last night was an awful experience, but you have to face reality. No matter what went on between you and Happy Henke in your private lives, it's all going to go public now. It'll probably hit *Showbiz Today*, the *Hollywood Minute*. An armed robbery at Le Croque, lots of fancy folks, it's bound to be a hot media ticket. The police are going to investigate, and with any luck they'll catch the killer. That means an arrest and a trial. This isn't going away, dear. You'll have to steel yourself for the worst. And I'm afraid Doris Henke is only the beginning of the bad news."

McCoy picked up Triscuit, put the dog over his shoulder and jiggled him as if he was burping a baby. Triscuit let out a short sigh, closed his eyes, and began to lick McCoy's neck ecstatically.

"What does Doris want?" Mary Rose asked, her voice shaky.

Zalman didn't like it, but he figured it'd be better all around if he gave Mary Rose the bad news straight, no chaser. "She wants you out of this apartment. Today."

Mary Rose stared angrily at Zalman, and a hot flame he hadn't noticed before flared up in her blue eyes like a pilot light. "It's a damn shame Doris didn't get the bullet in the brain instead of poor Happy. That woman is a bitch from bitchtown," she said. "But ah don't give a damn about this place," she said, looking around. "There's nothing here that means anything to me. Just my clothes and a few things in the bedroom. Ah'll pack now, get the rest of the stuff later. The car was Happy's, too," she added. "So maybe if you wouldn't mind dropping me off at the Beverly Wilshire, Mr. Zalman?"

"Can you afford the Beverly Wilshire?" Zalman asked.

Mary Rose shrugged helplessly. "Ah'm not sure," she said. "Now that ah think of it, maybe not. Better go someplace cheaper."

"So you don't have a car, either?" McCoy asked as he put Triscuit down on the floor.

Mary Rose frowned thoughtfully. "Ah'll have to

figure something out in the next few days. When ah moved in here ah put most of my stuff in storage," she said. " 'Course, ah just have this silly ol' southern stuff, family samplers, buncha cracked Blue Willow dishes that belonged to my grandma. Happy picked out all this furniture," she said, waving her hand around the room. "My ol' stuff wasn't classy enough to suit him, so ah just tucked it away in one of those storage locker places. It'll take me a few days to get organized, find a place to rent. Till then ah'll stay at a motel, ah guess. Don't know what else to do. Can you all wait while ah get dressed? Won't take me long, ah promise," she said, already disappearing into the bedroom. "There's coffee on the stove. . . ." Her voice trailed off, and Triscuit trotted after her, his nails clicking like a toy typewriter on the hardwood floor of the hallway.

"Damn shame," McCoy said as he watched her leave.

"It's the woman who pays, as the girl said to the sailor," Zalman commented as he went over to the phone and dialed Wacky Winger's Wanch. "Wacky? Jerry Zalman. Anything new?"

"Mr. Zalman, Mr. Zalman, it's only been an hour or so, but Wacky Winger's on the case," the pawnbroker said proudly. "I already have a piece of information that may be of use to you. Now, only moments ago I called around to all my stores, talked to my guys, leaned a little, pushed a little, know what I mean?"

"Sure I do, Wacky. So you got anything for me?"

"Maybe I do, maybe I don't," Wacky said. "Though none of my guys will admit taking in any goods of a dubious nature, that tune may change after the seriousness of my displeasure over this situation becomes clear to my employees. But a thought occurred to me. Since I'm a modern professional businessman, I have videotape setups in all my stores. Take pictures of everybody who comes in, goes out, all the transactions that take place in my establishments. You want those tapes, I'll round them up for you to peruse at your leisure. After all, Mr. Zalman, I have my reputation to think of. I also intend to make some personal inquiries, speak with an acquaintance or two, but that could take time. Sometimes, after a robbery and a murder, people become close-mouthed and are often hard to find," Wacky said with professional delicacy.

"Hmm, videos, huh?" Zalman said thoughtfully. "Sounds like an interesting possibility. McCoy'll be around to collect 'em later this afternoon. Can you get 'em all together at the Santa Monica store?"

"For you, Mr. Zalman, it's a pleasure. I have a reputation to protect. I'm a man of honor," Wacky quacked, beginning his heartrending self-promotion speech. "In today's world . . ."

"Oh, wow," McCoy said.

Zalman turned and saw Mary Rose lugging a suitcase out of the bedroom. Her red hair was in pigtails, she was wearing faded skintight jeans and a red checked gingham shirt, and she seemed to be singing those I'm just a country girl lost in the big city blues. Triscuit was prancing happily around her feet; maybe there'd be a ride in the car.

"Ow," Mary Rose said as the suitcase tumbled over on its side and landed on her foot.

McCoy bounded over, grabbed the suitcase in one hand, and swept up Triscuit with the other.

"Triskie sure has taken to you, Mr. McCoy," Mary Rose said looking around the room. "Oh, my." She frowned. "Do you know a motel that takes poodles? Triskie's the only thing ah have, now that Happy's gone. Ah couldn't bear to be without Triskie."

"Ah have a lot of dogs mahself," McCoy said bashfully. "Maybe you'd like to come out to mah place in Newhall and see 'em? Ah've got plenty of room. It's kinda isolated, though. Kinda country out there, and mosta mah city friends don't like it. Too quiet for 'em. Peaceful. Most nights you can see the stars just like a big ol' canopy stretching over the earth, 'specially if there's a little bitty bit of cloud cover over the city lights."

Zalman stared at McCoy, dumbfounded. He couldn't believe what he was hearing. In the space of ten seconds flat, Doyle Dean McCoy had sprouted a full-blown southern drawl. But then, McCoy had no shame. Never had. He'd try any damn thing, even bashful, and for a big man, he did bashful pretty well. McCoy was video freak, and he'd spent long afternoons studying up on Gary Cooper's aw-shucks-ma'am attitude, and at last he was going to get some mileage out of it.

"That sounds so nice," Mary Rose said wistfully. "Ah'd just love to see your doggies. Bein' raised in the country, ah naturally love dogs, but in this little apartment ah can just have Triskie here. How many doggies do you have, Mr. McCoy?" she asked as she raised her blue eyes and smiled up at him. "There's another suitcase in the bedroom. Could you give me a hand with it? Ah'm afraid it's about as heavy as a hide-a-bed."

"Why sure ah will," McCoy said manfully as he followed her into the bedroom. "Well, ah got about fifteen Dobermans, coupla goats, a few ferrets, some chickens for eggs . . ."

Wacky Winger was whining in Zalman's ear like a midnight mosquito. Zalman grinned and went back to the phone. "Yeah, Wacky, I'm still here. Just watching the course of true love running smooth as creamy-style Skippy peanut butter. Tell you what. I'll send McCoy down to see you, get the tapes. Then he and this former lady friend of the late Mr. Henke can take a look at 'em, see if she recognizes anybody, okay?"

"A pleasure, Mr. Zalman," Wacky said. "You need anything else, see me first."

Zalman dropped McCoy, Mary Rose, Chester, and Triskie off at McCoy's truck. Mary Rose looked relaxed and almost happy as she settled into the front seat of his filthy pickup, Triscuit cuddled in her lap like a living dust bunny. McCoy's Doberman eyed Trisket hungrily.

"Why, this just reminds me of home, it sure does," Mary Rose said enthusiastically as she wrinkled her nose and took in the sweet aroma of gun oil and beer that lingered around Doyle Dean McCoy like aftershave.

McCoy raised his eyes to heaven, gunned the engine, and took off down Wilshire in a cloud of exhaust as Zalman headed home to shower and change.

When he had finally soaked off the sludge of the day, he called Marie at home.

"Hey, babe," he said when she answered. "Where you been all day? I tried you this morning, I tried you at the office . . ."

Marie giggled. "Howard took me over to this antique shop he knows out on Lankershim? I got an absolutely mint set of lobster claw salt and pepper shakers. With the original box!"

"Howard?" Zalman asked slowly. "Howard? Who the hell is Howard? Besides," he said suspiciously, "you already have lobster claw salt and peppers."

"No, I have clams."

"Lobsters."

"You're wrong, darling; it's clams I have. I bought them at the swap meet at the Blue Sky Drive-In on the way to Santa Barbara, remember? From the woman who started collecting in 1952? And it's Howard Yarrow."

"That pinhead!"

BLOODY MARY

"He isn't a pinhead, darling; he's just a little dull."

"Dull doesn't come close!" Zalman snapped. "Linoleum made in 1912 is dull. Yarrow is a pinhead! Besides, your father likes him and you know I can't like anybody your father likes. Therefore, by extension . . ."

"By extension, what, Jerry darling?" Marie purred.

Zalman knew he'd overplayed his hand. Marie was very feisty, and the minute he tried to tell her what to do, she'd do the exact opposite on principle.

"If you're going to say that I can't like anybody my father likes just because you don't, don't say it," Marie went on. "And I don't like the 'by extension' part, either. I'm nobody's extension, and you ought to know that pretty damn well by this time!"

"Honey, honey," Zalman backpedaled. "That wasn't what I meant at all! Not at all! It's just that I adore you and I don't like you hanging around with Yarrow, because your father thinks Howard the pinhead would be a swell Ozzie to your Harriet and I don't see it that way. I know you're nobody's extension. Who would know that better than me?" he soothed. "Besides, I thought you'd want to know how it went today, after all the fun and frolic we had at Le Croque last night."

"You're trying to soothe me," Marie said. "But I'm so thrilled about my lobster claws that I'll let it pass. Besides, I absolutely do want to know the gory details, so why don't you buy me a very expensive dinner and see if you can worm your way back into my good graces? Anywhere but Le Croque would be swell."

"That's the bad news. We gotta go to Le Croque. I gotta check up on Pete. He's worried his business is going down the tubes, and I swore he'd have a full house."

BLOODY MARY

"Honestly, Jerry! What if we get robbed again! Besides, if Pete sends over caviar, I'll barf. After last night I don't ever want to see caviar again in this lifetime."

"I'll forgive you about Howard the pinhead if you'll go to Le Croque with me," Zalman wheedled.

"Mmm," Marie grumbled.

"C'mon, don't you wanna hear what happened today? Doll, I swear this case has more wrinkles than six-week-old sheets in a sleazy motel. Besides, you can bring your new lobster claws and perform perverse acts on my body with them," Zalman said. "I know I'd love it."

"Okay," she said promptly. "You talked me into it."

"I knew I could," Zalman said.

Pete Marchetti was so happy he'd resumed his floating French cum Austro-Hungarian accent. "Ah, M'sieur Zalmannn," he said as Zalman and Marie fought their way through the standing room only crowd to the front of Le Croque.

"Don't start that with me, Pete," Zalman warned. "Besides, everybody in town heard you talk American last night, so you've blown the Prince Rudolf act."

"Aw, Jerry, this is L.A.!" Pete whined. "Nobody cares if I'm a phony as long as I'm good at it!"

"My point exactly," Zalman said. "Now, was I right or was I right? Is the joint jumping? You and White Asparagus are gonna make me a rich man, Pete, me boyo."

"You were right, Jer," Pete admitted. "Folks started lining up for dinner at happy hour. I made the front page of *Variety*. See the story?" He grinned. "At last I hit the big time!"

"You've got perspicacity, Pete."

"The hell I do! I'm very careful!"

"I'm hungry," Marie said. "I didn't get any dinner last night, and I was soooo busy all day today. Howard and I just had time for a hot dog in the Valley. Howard's soooo thoughtful."

"All right, all right, I get the message," Zalman said, kissing her on the neck. "I'll be more attentive, I'll be a better guy, I'll take Rutherford for walkies, if only you'll lay off about Howard the pinhead!"

"Okay." She grinned. "Feed me, Daddy."

"Gee, you kids are cute," Pete said as he led them to a table. "Let me order for you, okay? You won't regret it."

"Anything but caviar," Marie said.

"Or squid," Zalman added.

ZALMAN AND MARIE ORDERED CHAMPAGNE JUST FOR THE hell of it, and the pale gold glasses of liquid money improved their mood, as champagne always did. Zalman stopped feeling grumpy about Howard the pinhead and gave Marie a complete account of the news of the day, except for his encounter with the chilly lips of Annabelle Forrester. After all, why mention trifles?

"I knew Jason was up to no good," Marie said as she sipped her champagne and listened to Zalman recount his nephew's tale of woe. "The little wretch. He's going to be in big trouble if he doesn't straighten up, Jerry."

"I know, I know. And if Lucille finds out about this mess—"

"You mean when she finds out."

"She's going to have the kid's head on a plate, right next to mine. I'll help Brenda, but if Lucille finds out, I have to tell the truth. Don't I?" Zalman wondered, praying Marie would say no, it'd be fine to lie.

"Of course you have to tell the truth," Marie said, dashing his hopes.

"I was afraid you'd say that."

"It's Mary Rose who needs your help, poor thing."

"I'll take care of her," Zalman said. "Boy, you should have seen McCoy. His eyes lit up like a giant slot machine the minute they met. I thought he was going to heave her over his shoulder like a Continental soldier and ravish her in the condo."

"Sounds difficult," Marie said. "But romantic."

"M'sieur Zalmannn, zee appetizairs," Pete Marchetti announced with a theatrical flourish as a waiter brought forth a tray of pâté and pureed vegetables molded into the shape of fish.

"Let's eat!" Marie urged as she devoured a tiny cauliflower halibut with a parsley eye. "I'm starved!"

Next to appear was a Caesar salad, then chinook salmon grilled to perfection and served with a brilliant green tomato salsa. Zalman and Marie happily ate their way through Pete's creations, and though the noise in Le Croque was approaching the permanent auditory damage level, there were no unpleasant interruptions. No robbers, no dead jewelers, all was serenity. Until dessert.

Just as Zalman was forking into his Sacher torte, Pete skittered up to the table, a gold and white phone in his hand.

"It's for you, Jer," he said, breathing heavily as he

plugged in the phone at tableside. "Somebody's nervous."

Zalman frowned. "Terrific," he muttered.

Elaborately, Marie looked at her watch. "I wonder if Howard is on duty tonight," she said in a plaintive voice.

Zalman pinched her, but gently. "Jerry Zalman," he said as he picked up the phone.

"Yeah, Mr. Zalman," a woman's voice growled hoarsely. "It's Doris Henke. You want to come over to my place right away?" she said as she croaked out a Holmby Hills address. "I just shot somebody. Dead, I think." She hung up without another word.

"Really terrific," Zalman said, staring at the phone. "I need this like a frog needs a saxophone. Marie honey, I've got a great idea."

"What happened?" she said as she spooned up a healthy slug of strawberries Romanoff.

"Doris Henke shot somebody. Probably dead."

"Anybody we know?"

Zalman glared at her. "She hung up before I could ask, smarty-pants," he said. "I gotta go over there right away. You coming with me?"

Marie licked her spoon and stuck out a strawberry tongue. "Wouldn't miss it for all the cubic zirconias in Encino."

"Another emergency, Jer?" Pete whispered as he unplugged the phone. "No brandy? I got these little almond cakes to go with it."

"Sorry, Petey-pie, we gotta go," Zalman said as he stood up. "Talk to me later."

"Bye, Pete." Marie waved. "Great dinner."

"Nobody respects my efforts." Pete sighed. "All this work and they just eat and run. It's a crime!"

"You sure you don't want to get married?" Zalman asked Marie as they threaded their way through the crowded dining room. "It'd save a lot of driving back and forth."

"And be bored to death?" Marie laughed. "The minute we tied the knot you'd want me to pick up your laundry, take the car over to Art's to get the oil changed. You'd start working late; we'd eat at home all the time. Not a chance, darling. I'm a woman who wants romance, and if we got married how could you keep up the pace?"

"I could manage." Zalman grinned as they went out the front door and into the parking lot. "Believe it."

Zalman motioned for the car, and as they were standing around, the happy sound of the rich at play echoing from the restaurant, he took Marie in his arms and kissed her and thought about how much he loved feeling the warmth of her body. Plus, he loved how passionately she kissed him back. "Have I told you recently that I adore you?" he asked.

"Not often enough," Marie said.

"Consider yourself told. Doris Henke's call really cramped my style," Zalman admitted as he started to nibble her ear. "I was hoping we could drive up to Mulholland after dinner and listen to oldies on the radio. The stars are out, the moon is full, and I had big plans for a night of adolescent passion in the backseat of the car. Preferably to the accompaniment of the Teddy Bears singing 'To Know Him Is to Love Him.' "

"But there's a body waiting for us in Holmby Hills. Doesn't that excite you?" Marie asked.

"Yeah, but it's not quite the same."

The Henke estate was lit up like an old-time Hollywood premiere. Spotlights illuminated the weeping willows lining the sloping gravel driveway in front of the huge white Colonial house, and the willows were rustling like an audience anxious for the overture to end. Inside, every light was on, and golden squares shimmered out of the windowpanes and glinted off the chrome on the police car in the driveway.

A solitary cop in uniform was leaning up against one of the white pillars by the front door. His blue plastic name tag said Ed on it, and he was smoking a cigarette and staring pensively at the rose garden to one side of the house.

"I'm Jerry Zalman, Mrs. Henke's attorney," Zalman told Ed the cop.

Ed looked at him curiously, then gave Marie the once-over. "You Captain Thrasher's daughter?" he asked. "Don't see the resemblance," he said as he looked back at Zalman. "The captain's on his way over. He called in, said you was probably gonna show. Said the lady would probably be with you. Said he wants her to wait outside. Don't want her around the victim, 'swhat he said." Ed shrugged. He flicked his cigarette out into the driveway where it lay glowing on the gravel like a dying firefly. "Bad aphid damage," he observed, jerking a stubby finger at the roses. "Chewed 'em all the hell up. I got roses. I take care of 'em myself. Crime to let that kinda aphid damage go on."

"What do you use on them?" Marie asked curiously. "Orthonex?"

"Nah, I'm organic. I take garlic, onions, some red pepper, and a big handful of Bugler, that rolling tobacco comes in the blue can? I got a special blender I keep out in the shed. Whir it up with some Palmolive dish soap, shoot it on with a sprayer. No poison, no aphids," Ed said, proud of his handiwork.

"Gee, that's a good idea. I'm going to try it," Marie said. "I've got terrible aphids, and I hate spraying poison all over the yard. Bad for the birds."

"Dunno why God invented aphids," Ed said sadly. "Them and slugs."

"But aphids or no aphids, I'm going inside with Mr. Zalman," Marie told him. "I don't want to get you in trouble, Ed, but I haven't come all this way for nothing."

"Just telling you what the captain said," Ed replied. "Do what ya want. You ladies always do."

"You're a wise man, Ed," Zalman said to the cop as he opened the front door and stepped inside. "C'mon, babe, let's take a look around before your dad gets here."

Inside, another cop was standing guard at the closed living room door. "You the lawyer?" he asked.

Zalman nodded.

"Mrs. Henke's in there," the cop said laconically, pointing down the hall. "Study."

Zalman and Marie went down the hall and knocked on the study door.

"C'min," Doris Henke's hoarse voice croaked. "Oh, it's you, Mr. Zalman," she said as Zalman and Marie came in. "Good. You got here fast. I like that. Who's this?" she asked, eyeing Marie.

"I'm Marie Thrasher, a friend of Jerry's."

Doris Henke nodded absently. She looked tired and distracted, and without the careful makeup and elaborate hairstyle she'd worn in Zalman's office, her age was showing. She was wearing a strangely ratty pink terry-cloth bathrobe and fluffy pink slippers to match.

Only thing missing was a pair of bunny ears, Zalman thought, and she'd be all set to play Easter egg hunt. "You shot somebody?" he said.

Doris Henke smiled unpleasantly as she sat down in an armchair and curled her feet up under her like a teenager. "That's the way it looks."

"Tell me what happened before the homicide guys get here. We don't have long," Zalman pressed. "I have to warn you, the captain in charge is Miss Thrasher's father, and he's tough."

"You do get around," Doris Henke snorted, stretching out her trim legs in front of her. "Isn't that conflict of interest?"

"I'll be the judge of that," Marie replied sweetly.

"Just asking," Doris Henke said. "Anyway, it was all pretty cut and dried. My stepdaughter Brenda and I were alone in the house. I've let the live-in help go since they were all Happy's people," she explained. "I want to start fresh."

"Where's Annabelle?" Zalman asked.

"She's out with Bertie, that idiot boyfriend of hers. I phoned her, and they ought to be here any minute," Doris said.

"Who's Annabelle?" Marie asked.

"My daughter," Doris said. "Anyway, I was in bed, and Brenda's room is way down the hall from mine, so when I heard a noise downstairs I knew I had to look. I thought the men who robbed Happy had come to clean out the silverware drawer, and I can't afford any more losses! Happy kept a gun in the bedroom, and he taught me how to use it when we were first married."

"How romantic," Marie said sweetly.

Doris cocked an eyebrow and went on with her story. "It's a forty-five. I grabbed the gun, and when I went downstairs into the living room, a man in black jumped out, waving something at me. I thought he had a gun, so I shot the son of a bitch. Twice."

"Did you recognize him?" Zalman asked, wondering who the stiff in the living room was.

"Hell, no, I didn't! He was wearing a black mask. I still haven't seen his face and I don't want to. I wasn't about to play peekaboo with him or check his damn pulse, either! I'm a taxpayer. I called the cops! Let them look at him."

BLOODY MARY

"So you don't know who you shot?" Zalman asked. Some frigid fish, the widow Henke.

She shook her head emphatically.

"And where's your stepdaughter now?" Zalman said. So far, he hadn't mentioned his connection with Jason and Brenda, and he was hoping to keep it that way.

"In bed," Doris Henke said. "I don't want her involved in this. She's just a baby, and what with her father getting murdered last night . . ."

Some baby, Zalman thought, as the image of Brenda Henke and Jason Hanning decked out in their fancy duds shot through his head. How was he going to get out of this one? If there was any conflict of interest, it was between his various clients, or would-be clients, Zalman rationalized. After all, Doris Henke hadn't forked over a retainer, and neither had Failin' Phalen, the cheapskate. Jason and Brenda were clients on sufferance. Pete Marchetti paid in free lunches, and Mary Rose Peek was strictly a pity date.

All of a sudden, a bad feeling went crawling up the back of Zalman's neck like the itsy-bitsy spider, as it hit him that not one of his would-be clients was going to fork over cold cash. Except for five bucks from each of the kids and the piece of White Asparagus he'd wangled out of Pete Marchetti, this whole thing was on the cuff!

Zalman could see it coming, clear as a glass of Evian: he was going to get stiffed, and he didn't like it. Not that he minded giving to charity; every year at Christmas he gave a major chunk of change to the Motion Picture Relief Fund, but he did it anonymously because he didn't want anybody to find out he had a heart. Charity was okay. If a guy made a good living, he had a duty to give to charity. But this wasn't charity, this was freebie legal work! It chafed, it went against the grain, it rubbed him raw in all the wrong places!

The front door slammed and the floor shook as the sound of giant cop feet came pounding down the hallway. Then the study door opened and Captain Arnold Thrasher stood in the doorway, glowering at the assembled company, his fat face dark and angry.

"Here's where the going gets tough," Zalman said.

Thrasher stared wordlessly at Doris Henke, Zalman, and Marie.

"Hi, Daddy!" Marie chirped. Zalman wasn't looking at her, but he knew she was doing her fake Little Miss Perky act; he also knew it was a dead certainty she was wrinkling her nose.

Lieutenant Howard Yarrow loomed behind Thrasher in the doorway. He waved and smiled over Thrasher's shoulder at Marie. And then he winked.

Zalman was flabbergasted. He couldn't believe that a grown man would stoop to winking, but it was true. The guy actually winked! Yarrow did it again, and Zalman had a murderous urge to whack the dope over the head with a potted plant and push the body down the In-Sink-Er-Ator with a broom handle, but he stifled it.

Thrasher lumbered into the room with Yarrow right behind him, then hitched his bulky self up onto the back of the couch and took out a small blue spiralbound notebook and a Bic. Yarrow stood behind him at parade rest.

"Mrs. Henke," Thrasher said as he tapped his notebook with his Bic and smiled pleasantly. "I'm Captain Arnold Thrasher, and this is Lieutenant Yarrow. I assume Mr. Zalman is your attorney?"

Doris Henke nodded, pulling her pink robe close around her crepey neck.

"Who's the dead man?" Thrasher asked softly. He

wasn't doing his tough cop routine yet, and his manner with Doris Henke was surprisingly gentle.

"I don't know," Doris Henke said promptly as a door slammed in the hall. "I heard a noise, I came downstairs, he jumped out at me.... It was dark, he had something in his hand, and I thought it was a gun. Anyway, I was afraid he was going to kill me, so I shot him. Twice."

"Mother?" a woman's voice called.

"In here, darling," Doris answered as the door opened and Annabelle Forrester came into the room. A pale, thin young man without visible signs of a chin was at her heels like a Yorkie.

"What in God's name is going on?" Annabelle asked, irritation in her voice. "Sit down, Bertie, and stop hovering!"

Bertie the chinless wonder sat down.

"I'd better look at the body," Thrasher announced.

"The body!" Annabelle said. "Another one? Mother—"

"Come over here, dear, and sit by me," Doris told her daughter. "I'll explain it to you."

"Why don't you come with me, Zalman? Maybe the stiff is one of your pals and you can identify him for me. It'd be a big help." Thrasher smiled.

Zalman stood up, but before he could say anything to Marie, Arnie Thrasher moved in for the kill.

"Marie honey, I don't want you around this kind of thing," the big cop said, smiling with fatherly concern. "I've told you before, you shouldn't be around crime. Or criminals." He glanced at Zalman. "Lieutenant Yarrow will be glad to take—"

"The hell he will!" Zalman exploded. "I'm warning you, Arnie, you got away with that trick once, but not again! Keep your clone away from Marie or I'll bust his chops."

"You couldn't reach his chops!" Thrasher retorted.

BLOODY MARY

"And stop calling me Arnie. You wanna see the stiff or not?" he prodded.

"Yeah, I wanna see the stiff."

"I'll wait for you here, Jerry," Marie said. "With Mrs. Henke and Annabelle." Marie gave Annabelle a phony smile.

Zalman didn't like to leave Marie anywhere near Howard the winking pinhead, but he did want to find out who Doris Henke had shot, so he followed Arnie Thrasher out the door and down the hall.

The body was lying in the middle of the living room floor on a pale beige Oriental rug with a delicate tracery of raised blue flowers in the center. But now there was a creeping lake of dark blood oozing across the pretty flowers, and the rug was a dead loss. All the Woolite in the world wasn't going to foam away the deep, spreading bloodstain that was still seeping and changing like a deadly Rorschach blot.

Zalman peered carefully at the body. The man in black lay crumpled awkwardly on the floor, his left arm bent back in an odd, yogalike position that looked uncomfortable, but not as uncomfortable as the ragged hole in the middle of his chest. Doris Henke had shot him twice, all right, and she'd hit her target dead center both times. She'd learned Happy Henke's lessons with his bedside .45 very well.

The man had a ski mask pulled over his face, his right hand was outstretched, and he was clutching a heavy, ornately carved silver candelabrum. There was a leather bag lying on the floor next to him.

"Do the honors, Arnie," Zalman said as Thrasher crouched down next to the body, took the head in his hands, and gently eased off the black woolen ski mask.

It was Tony, Failin' Phalen's fish-faced assistant. His eyes were open, and he was wearing an aston-

BLOODY MARY

ished look that fit him like a baggy shirt. Like a lot of dead guys, he seemed surprised that his life had ended in the middle of somebody's living room rug.

Zalman didn't like it. Tony was just a dumb kid, a dumb kid who did errands, a dumb kid who went for sourdough, a dumb kid who had missed the demise of the late Mr. Henke but managed to be present for his own. No brains. No brains at all.

"Heeey," Thrasher said, the light of realization spreading over his face. "This is the kid from the other night!"

"Yeah," Zalman said shortly.

"He was gone when Henke got plugged!" Thrasher said triumphantly. "I love it! He goes out to the car, changes clothes, then comes back and robs the joint! Perfect!"

"Perfect," Zalman agreed.

"Whaddaya wanna bet . . ." Thrasher said slowly as he reached into his jacket pocket, pulled out his Bic, and gently teased open the mouth of the leather bag lying on the floor next to Tony's outstretched hand. "Hey there, hi there, ho there!" Thrasher cried happily. "I was right! I bet you a pepperoni pizza this comes from the Le Croque robbery," he said as a glittering stream of rings and bracelets spilled out onto the beige rug like a tiny freshet of spring water.

But there was no Picasso medallion in the pile of trinkets, Zalman noticed as Thrasher poked the jewelry with his pen. "No doubt about it," Zalman agreed. "That looks like the stuff from the robbery all right."

"It all fits," Thrasher said triumphantly. "This guy knows there's more jewelry here at the house so he comes back tonight, figuring he'll bag it all. But Mrs. Henke hears him and pop goes the weasel!"

"Pop goes the weasel," Zalman repeated. That bad feeling was starting to crawl up his neck again, but this time the itsy-bitsy spider was the size of a very hairy tarantula.

Zalman didn't like it. It was all too easy. This kid with the grouper's face wasn't smart enough to pull off a robbery-murder all by himself. Besides, there were two men at Le Croque. Sure, Tony could have been the tall guy in the Goofy mask, but who was the second man? Who was Shorty? Was he the brains of the outfit? And if Tony was at the Henke estate to pull off another robbery, why was he carrying the loot from Le Croque in his leather bag? It didn't make sense.

"Pop goes the weasel," Zalman muttered again. No use talking to Arnie Thrasher; might as well try reasoning with a stand of old-growth timber. Besides, it was too late in the day to make a decision. Zalman had learned long ago that one should never make a decision after three o'clock in the afternoon. There'd be plenty of time tomorrow to mull over murder. . . .

Moments later, Zalman and Arnie Thrasher left the living room and made way for the fingerprint guys, the photo guys, and the rest of Thrasher's merry minions, all of whom swarmed over Tony's bloody body like ants on Labor Day picnic burger.

Zalman walked slowly down the hall to rescue Marie from Yarrow's clutches; he doubted she'd want to drive up to Mulholland and neck after this. As a matter of fact, neither did he. He realized he was feeling a little queasy. Murder did that to you, he mused.

Part of it made sense, but part of it didn't. Why did Tony have the Le Croque loot on him? Who was Shorty and where was he?

So many questions and so few answers, Zalman thought. How long would he be able to keep Brenda and Jason out of trouble, Zalman wondered as he went back into the study. He hated to think of his sister's heart shattering into a thousand pieces, but would he be able to keep Jason Hanning out of the investigation? And, he wondered, since the Picasso medallion wasn't in the bag, where the hell was it? "Pop goes the weasel," he said as he opened the study door.

ANNABELLE FORRESTER AND BERTIE WERE LOUNGING on the couch, drinking martinis and listening to *Barry Manilow's Greatest Hits*. Doris Henke was leafing through *Vogue*, and Marie was staring grimly out the window into the night.

Ten centuries later Arnie Thrasher realized that he wasn't going to get anything new and exciting out of Doris Henke, just the same old song, so he grudgingly gave up and let everybody off the hook. Tony's body was tagged, zipped into a plastic body bag, heaved into a flesh pink coroner's wagon, and trucked off to the morgue.

Zalman and Marie weren't in the mood to drive up to Mulholland and neck under the stars, so when they got back to Zalman's house they jumped into the Jacuzzi, drank a few glasses of champagne, and soaked away the murderous aspects of the day in the warm, bubbling water.

Then they got into bed and made slow, tired love until the exhaustion of the day flared up into passion and finally smoldered down into exhaustion again.

But this time it was happy exhaustion, a warm, wrung-out sense of lassitude layered with joy that erased the dark ugliness they'd seen. Marie fell asleep in Zalman's arms, and before he fell asleep, he lay peacefully in the big bed watching her breathe. As he felt her breath on his cheek, he realized that despite Arnie Thrasher, despite two murders in two days, despite Jason and Brenda and Howard the pinhead, despite everything that was driving him crazy, he was happier than he'd ever been in his whole damn life.

But as Zalman strolled into the office the next morning, his balloon popped when he saw Captain Arnold Thrasher and Lieutenant Howard Yarrow perched on his waiting room couch. They looked like a pair of hawks swinging back and forth on a barbed-wire fence, waiting for a passing motorist to knock a juicy bit of road kill in their direction.

"These gentlemen are waiting for you, Mr. Zalman," Esther said in a nauseatingly professional tone that Zalman thought was too saucy by half.

"Thanks, Esther. Hold my calls," Zalman told her. "Nice tie, Arnie. Yellow clams make an interesting design statement, *n'est-ce pas?*"

"Don't ruin my day so fast, Zalman," Thrasher snarled as he and Yarrow followed Zalman into the office. The two cops sat down in the leather chairs, and the chairs groaned sadly. "I'm here to do you a favor, so don't start up with me," Thrasher said. "Me and Howard been up all night, making calls, asking questions, figuring this thing out, and I want you to be the first to know: you're in the clear, and so are all your dopey clients."

"Huh?" Zalman couldn't believe it. What did Thrasher say? Could hearing loss occur overnight? Was it time to plug in the old Miracle-Ear and settle down in the vibrating bed with a *Reader's Digest* condensed book? "In the clear?"

"That's right. Me and Howard here, we got the case practically closed."

"Practically closed?" Zalman knew it was one hundred percent impossible that Arnie Thrasher was correct, but he was crazy to hear the old wombat's story.

Thrasher held up his meaty hand. "I make a mistake, I admit it."

"And I admire you for it, Chief," Yarrow said smoothly. "Takes a big man to admit he's made a boo-boo."

"A boo-boo?" Zalman said slowly. First winking, now boo-boos. What could possibly come next?

"That's right," Thrasher said. "A boo-boo. See, after Mrs. Henke plugs that guy Tony last night— She ain't being charged on it, by the way. It's self-defense if I ever saw any. The guy was prowling through her living room; she was in fear of her life, so she's off the hook."

"Makes sense," Zalman admitted.

"Yeah, so anyway," Thrasher continued, "we have a little chat with Mr. Phalen this morning, and he tells us he's been going over his accounts and they look funny."

"Yeah, I know that," Zalman said impatiently. "So?"

"So as soon as Phalen hears Tony's been shot and that the kid had the Le Croque loot on him, Phalen says he's found out Tony was a heavy gambler and had big losses to cover. Phalen says it musta been Tony who was giving the books a fry job."

"Gambling, huh? Okay, it makes sense," Zalman said again.

Thrasher smiled happily. "That's what I thought. See, the way I figure it, Tony was stealing dough from the jewelry stores, but it wasn't enough, so he figures he'll rob all the richies at Le Croque and clean up. But when he sees how much loot he bags at the Le Croque robbery, he gets greedy. He knows Henke's wife has lots of real jewelry, not just those fake Diamettes and Emerelles Henke pitched on TV. Tony goes over to the Henke estate, but Mrs. Henke catches him in the act, and she plugs him. So we're square on the Le Croque robbery and the shooting last night," Thrasher said in triumph. "And you got nothing to worry about."

"Wait a minute, wait a minute," Zalman interrupted. "Okay, so Tony was one of the robbers at Le Croque, the guy in the Goofy mask. I'll buy that. But who was Shorty? It was Shorty who shot Happy Henke and conked Phalen over the head."

"Yeah, we know there was two guys. And all the Le Croque witnesses agree it was Shorty who killed Henke," Thrasher said, waving his hand impatiently. "Look, Zalman, it's only a matter of time before the rest of the loot starts showing up and I get Shorty. No killer's ever escaped me," Thrasher said proudly. "And Shorty ain't gonna be the first."

"No sirree bob," Yarrow said. "Me and the chief, we're cooking with gas. We'll bring the killer to justice."

No sirree bob, that's what was next. "Cooking with gas," Zalman repeated slowly. "That's great. But back to Tony. Don't you wonder why he was carrying some of the loot on him when he went to rob the Henke house? Why would he do that? Why carry a few pieces around with him? Why carry any? What did he think it was, a rabbit's foot and he was going to get lucky?"

"Hey, the criminal mind is like a river that runs deep and wide," Thrasher said mysteriously. "I been a cop a long time, and I still can't figure out the criminal mind. What are you bugging me for, Zalman?

I told you that you and your dopey clients are in the clear."

Jerry Zalman was rarely at a loss for words, but as he stared at Thrasher and Yarrow across his highly polished, very expensive desk, he felt like a housefly that had fallen into a pot of melted Velveeta and was frantically trying to do the backstroke. Everything about this case stank like last year's Limburger, but Zalman knew that if he continued to point out the irregularities to Arnie Thrasher, he'd only land himself, his nephew, and Brenda Henke deeper in the hot fondue.

"Uh-huh," he said noncommittally. "So what now, Arnie?"

"Well, I'm going home to bed, is what the hell now," Thrasher said. "Mrs. Henke's got no problem with me, and Tony's going nowhere, what with being dead. I'm gonna wait till Shorty tries to unload the rest of the Le Croque loot, then I pounce."

"Pounce, huh? Terrific, Arnie," Zalman said brightly. It was very hard to think of Arnie Thrasher pouncing. Lumbering, yes, but not pouncing. "I gotta hand it to you. As a detective, you're unbelievable."

Thrasher grinned as he hoisted himself out of his chair. "Nice of you to say so, Zalman. I still hate your guts, but I like to be magnanimous."

"You're a pip, Chief," Yarrow said.

Zalman looked at Yarrow. Was the sun glinting prisms off Yarrow's perfectly white teeth? "A pip," he echoed as he walked Thrasher and Yarrow to his office door. "A real pipperoo."

After he was sure they were gone, Zalman mixed a Bullshot and sat down at his desk to drink and think.

"Little Zalman, what now?" he asked himself.

"Did you say something, Mr. Z.?" Esther called.

"Just thinking aloud," he told her. "Helps me stay sane in a changing universe."

BLOODY MARY

Esther stuck her head in the door. "I love to verbalize, myself," she smiled. "By the way, I have to take an early lunch today. There's a new place over on El Camino where they scrub you with sea salt and hot herbs and then dunk you in lukewarm chamomile tea. I'm going for a facial and a full-body rubdown."

"Sounds like a laugh riot, Esther," Zalman said slowly. "Try McCoy for me, will you?"

Esther nodded and went back to her desk. "McCoy's on one," she said a minute later.

Zalman punched the speaker and leaned back in his chair. "Dean," he said as he clasped his hands behind his head and stared at the ceiling. "What ho, buddy?"

"This time it's for real," McCoy rhapsodized. "I know I've said it before, but at last it's the sweet mystery of love. And I haven't even kissed her. Yet." He emphasized the last word heavily.

"Oh, God," Zalman mumbled. "I ain't got time for Miss Lonelyhearts this morning. Did you see the news, Dean? You know Doris Henke plugged a guy last night?"

"Yeah, I saw it. Tony, Failin' Phalen's gofer."

"That's him. And listen to this, you'll love it. Arnie Thrasher and his male bimbo Yarrow just left my office. Thrasher claims everybody's off the hook, even yours truly. Says Tony had gambling debts, said he owed money all over town, and he was behind the whole deal. . . ."

"I was just gonna call you. Soon as I saw his picture on TV, I recognized him. Tony's the guy on the videotapes we got from Wacky," McCoy said. "Me and the southern belle cozied up last night and watched 'em. She made caramel corn with peanuts. She knew it was Tony right off. Positively. It's from a tape taken out at Wacky's Airport Wanch. Tony's got some jewelry in his hand and he's looking furtive.

BLOODY MARY

You can't make out what he's carrying on the tape, but I'm gonna buzz out to Wacky's and ask some questions as soon as Mary Rose is dressed."

"You two are still in your p.j.'s? It's eleven o'clock in the morning!"

"She made Belgian waffles," McCoy said. "She's a dream, Jer," he continued obliviously. "She loves dogs and she knows all the Presidents backwards and forwards. It's an amazing feat. You get her started, she can go from Washington right on down without missing a beat. Drove the dogs crazy. Chester and Millard wouldn't stop barking," McCoy said.

"That's a real thrill, Dean. More educational than ball scores, I'll bet."

"And she can cook."

"Belgian waffles and caramel corn with peanuts sounds like serious heartburn, Dean, but I'm glad love's in your corner. Look, first of all, this thing stinks, and second of all, I gotta find that medallion!"

"Give yourself a break, Jer! Thrasher's off your tush, so forget about it!"

"I can't, Dean! I'm in too deep. I can't punk out on my own nephew. If I flop now, my image is blown for life and the kid'll never respect me. He'll go bad! He's already got a father who's a yo-yo. If I can't get him and the girlfriend outta trouble, I'll just be another failed role model. Besides, I made him a promise."

"Break it. You've never been moral before. Why start now?"

"No, Dean," Zalman explained. "I cannot break a promise I made to my thirteen-year-old nephew and his twelve-year-old *chiquita*. I wouldn't be able to live with myself. Besides, if Marie found out, she'd kill me."

"Okay, that I believe." McCoy laughed. "That's a serious reason."

"Glad you see it my way at last."

"Jer, you're wrapped too tight on this. Look, me and Mary Rose'll drive in, we'll go over to Moe Zelnick's Dawg Haus and grab a chili dog. I'll bring the tape with me. But it's Tony all right; she lamped him right off."

Zalman sighed. In his continuing effort to promote himself as a private eye, McCoy had recently been reading detective fiction from the twenties, and his dialogue reflected it. On the other hand, he'd finally stopped saying "groovy" and "far out." But what the hell, Zelnick's sounded good. "C'mon over, Dean, we'll go for chili dogs."

" 'Bout an hour," McCoy said.

Zalman mixed himself a second Bullshot, returned to his desk, drank it off, and sat without moving for another fifteen minutes, mulling over the situation. Esther went off for her rubdown; he ignored a few calls and let the machine pick them up.

What was bugging him? Why didn't he believe it was case closed? Thrasher himself had announced that he was off the hook, it was no problem, it was ancient history. The mysterious Shorty would be caught—eventually—by L.A.'s finest, and then the Picasso medallion would be found. So why don't I believe it? Zalman wondered.

Was it possible that Thrasher was right? Was it conceivable? Could it happen on the face of the planet Earth?

No, Zalman decided, it wasn't possible, and that was the problem. Thrasher had never been right before, so why should he start now? Besides, Zalman thought slowly, as the full import of Thrasher's certainty hit him. If Arnie Thrasher was right . . .

Zalman heard the roar of McCoy's V8 engine blasting through the tranquillity of Beverly Drive, and as he jumped up from his desk, a new burst of adrenaline pumped through his veins. It wasn't the medallion, and it wasn't the kids; it was Arnie Thrasher. If Arnie Thrasher was right, then Jerry Zalman was wrong. . . .

"In two words, *im-possible!*" Zalman bellowed as he grabbed his jacket, slammed the office door, and ran down to the street.

Zalman squeezed into the cabin of McCoy's filthy Chevy truck next to Mary Rose Peek, who was wearing jeans, a cowboy shirt with scarlet and black sequined flowers on the yoke, and a big straw cowboy hat with a scarlet and black sequined band. She looked like an out-of-work country singer.

Chester, who was lounging in the bed of the truck on a ratty plaid blanket, began to bark at a passing poodle.

"Hi, Mr. Zalman!" Mary Rose said happily.

"Call me Jerry," he told her, "unless we go to court. Then call me Mr. Zalman. Dean, my friend, let's roll."

McCoy grunted as he gunned the pickup through Beverly Hills and made it over to Moe Zelnick's Dawg Haus in West L.A. in less than half an hour.

Zalman and Moe Zelnick went back a ways. They'd first met when Zalman was a kid and Zelnick had a Freezee Pop stand out in Mar Vista, where Zalman grew up. Zalman and his sister Lucille used to bike over to Zelnick's stand every Saturday afternoon, and Zelnick gave them all the Freezee Pops they could choke down. In return, they told him what horse their dad, Ernest, liked at Santa Anita or Hollywood Park.

One historic Saturday when Zalman was eleven, he gave Moe Zelnick a great tip on the three horse for the daily double, and Zelnick won five thousand bucks. In those days, five K was big money, and Zelnick bought the Dawg Haus, which he still owned, not to mention the real estate, which was worth more than a few million. Needless to say, Zalman never paid for another chili dog.

Zalman was always happy to see Moe Zelnick. He liked his food and he liked the Dawg Haus itself, which was shaped like a giant hot dog, complete with mustard and pickle relish dripping off the ends.

"Zally!" Moe Zelnick cried as he saw McCoy's truck pull up in front of the place. "It's a pleasure to see you."

"Zelly! It's a pleasure to be seen," Zalman replied as the three of them got out of the truck and took stools in front of the food stand, which fronted directly on the street. "You know Dean McCoy, and this is Mary Rose Peek," Zalman said.

Zelnick tipped his tall white chef's hat, wiped his hands on his apron, and shook hands with Mary Rose. "A pleasure, I'm sure."

"We're hungry, Zelly. We need egg creams all around, chili dogs with everything for the humans, and a pair of plain hot dogs for the dog," he said, jerking a thumb at Chester, who was still in the bed of the pickup. "No mustard for him; he's got a sensitive palate."

Zelnick handed the egg creams across the counter, and as they sipped the soda and watched him grilling the hot dogs, Zalman gave McCoy and Mary Rose a complete rundown on Thrasher's visit. "So now what?" he asked after he'd told all.

"Well, ah'm awfully sorry poor Tony got killed, 'cause he was nice to me when he was alive. But ah have to say good-bye to my old life, hello to my new life. That means ah have to find a place to live," Mary Rose said practically. "Dean's been ever so kind, and Triskie's just having the time of his little life out there with the rest of the doggies, but ah need a nest of my own. When we leave here, ah'm gonna rent a car and start looking."

"Stay with me as long as you like," McCoy said dreamily. "I'm crazy about your caramel corn."

Zalman put his head down on the counter. "Who's the second man? Where's the Picasso medallion?" he groaned hollowly. "I know I'm missing something. Arnie Thrasher can't be smarter than I am, Dean."

McCoy flashed an evil grin and nibbled a french fry. "Maybe that guy Yarrow's the brains of the operation. Maybe he's really an international spy and Arnie's fronting for him."

"Shut up, Dean," Zalman said. "Where's that damn medallion? Why did my sister have children? How did that rotten nephew of mine get me into this mess?"

AFTER THEY FINISHED THEIR CHILI DOGS, MCCOY AND Mary Rose drove to Westwood to rent her a car and Zalman went to Paramount Studios to calm the fears of a frightened young producer who was considering taking a low-money option on Huston's comeback opus, *The Southland Swelters*. The producer was nervous and wondered if Huston was honestly off the sauce and if he could deliver a sequel just in case they got lucky.

By the time Zalman was through cajoling the kid at Paramount, the traffic was clogged up worse than it was on Oscar night, so he skipped the office and drove straight home. His machine was blinking when he came through the door, but he called Marie first and let the message light blink.

Marie was in her office at Typeit. "Hon," she said as soon as she picked up the phone, "it's crisis time. Give me your instant opinion. I'm having some neon signs made for when I invade Bev Hills with my new branch of Typeit. Neon is so great looking at night, plus the guy who makes the signs told me there's something about the lead level in smog that makes the signs glimmer and look all shivery like flickering Christmas lights. So anyway, I'm thinking of changing the name to Print Now. In caps, hot blue neon, all scrolly. Do you think Print Now is more Nineties? Print Now," she added anxiously. "I have to decide yesterday."

"Great, do it. But put in an exclamation point," Zalman advised. "Make it Print Now exclamation point."

"Ooooh, you're right," Marie said thoughtfully. "I like it. Okay, I'll go for the hot blue and the exclamation point."

"C'mon over to my house when you're through and let's go eat," he said. "We'll drive out to the ocean, nosh fried clams, watch the midnight surf gods live it up under the California blue moon."

"Sounds great," she said. "I'll be there about seven-thirty."

Zalman forgot about the blinking message and took a nap, then showered and changed, so it wasn't until seven-thirty that Marie discovered the message on his machine when she let herself in.

"Jerry," she said as she came into the hall and dumped her purse on the table. "Do you know your machine is blinking?"

"No, hum a few bars," Zalman called as he padded out of the bedroom to meet her. Marie looked adorable, as always. She was wearing black toreador pants, an off-the-shoulder black and white zebra-striped spandex top, and dangling fish earrings. "Hi, doll," he said, kissing her shoulderblades hello. "Love the fish earrings," he said as he punched the machine and gave Marie another kiss.

The message was from Mary Rose. "Hi, Jerry," she said. "Ah rented a car, but when ah went back to the apartment there was a message from Doris Henke asking me to come over to her place. She was going through Happy's papers and guess what! She found a letter he left me, and Doris thinks there's a bequest for me in his will. Isn't that nice? Doris thought ah ought to have the letter right away. She said not to tell anyone just in case it didn't pan out, but ah thought ah'd better tell you. Ah'm going over there sevenish, and ah'll call you just as soon as ah know anythang. After ah know what's in the letter, ah mean. Bye-bye, now." There was a hollow clump as Mary Rose dropped the phone, retrieved it, and finally hung up.

"Great," Zalman said. "Let's go eat. I got a yen for fried clams and beer. Maybe there's something in Mary Rose's letter that'll help me find the damn medallion. It's driving me cra—"

Marie shook her head, her fish earrings bobbing up and down as if they were snapping at bait. "Wait a minute, wait a minute! What letter? There's no letter. If there's a letter I'll eat kibble for a week! If there was a letter, Doris Henke wouldn't give it to Mary Rose, she'd tear it up into tiny bits and give it the old flush-ho! But I'm positive there's no letter."

"What are you talking about, doll?" Zalman asked.

"Honestly, Jerry! Think about it for a second!" Marie said in exasperation. "Doris hates Mary Rose. If there was a letter, which I totally doubt, Doris would read it first and flush it second. She wouldn't give it to Mary Rose, and even if she did, she wouldn't give it to her unopened. And besides, what makes Doris think it's a bequest if she hasn't opened it in the first place? And if it is a bequest, maybe it's a zillion dollars in negotiable bonds, and Doris wouldn't give it to Mary Rose; she'd keep it herself! A letter, my foot! There's no letter," Marie said, shaking her head with absolute certainty.

"I hate to say it, but I think—"

"Anyway," Marie continued, without letting Zalman finish. "That Doris Henke is so mean, she wouldn't part with a ball of lint out of the dryer trap."

"Hmm," Zalman said. "Your syntax is out of whack, but I get the gist. I think you're right."

"You better believe I'm right!" Marie insisted. "Doris is getting Mary Rose over there on false pretenses, and we'd better run by the Henke place right now and see what's going on. Mary Rose is very sweet"—Marie grabbed her purse from the hall table—"but she can't protect herself, and she ain't too bright."

Traffic had lightened up a little, so Zalman made good time over to the Henke estate in Holmby Hills. But the minute he pulled into the driveway and saw the front door of the big white house standing wide open, Zalman had an eerie feeling. A bad feeling, that old ten-tons-of-trouble feeling knotting up in the pit of his stomach and screaming for Rolaids.

Zalman was irritated at himself. He knew Marie was right about Doris Henke. In her present incarnation, Doris Henke wouldn't do Mary Rose a favor unless there was a gun stuck in her ear. And he was mad at himself for not having checked his answering machine when he got home. He owed it to Mary Rose. Even though she was a pity date as a client she was on his caseload and he had to take care of her. Besides, he didn't have any choice.

As Zalman pulled into the Henke driveway and

killed the engine of the Mercedes he heard a terrible high-pitched wail rise up into the twilight and hover in the air around the house like a cloud of dusty pollen in summertime.

There was a moment of silence that seemed to shimmer like mint jelly; then the wail cascaded out of the open front door once again. Marie gasped and reached out for Zalman as the screaming continued, reverberating across the driveway. The harsh cry fell into a thick garbled mumble of horror and faded into the twilight. Four startled crows cawed angrily as they flew up and out of the willows surrounding the house and beat their dark wings back to the Valley where they belonged.

Then the scream changed and became a series of short blasts of raw pain that chopped up the serene wealth of the evening like a Cuisinart. Zalman and Marie looked at each other wordlessly, jumped out of the car, and ran up the broad steps to the house.

The screaming didn't stop. They followed the painful sound through the front hall and into the living room, the same room where Tony's body lay crumpled on the floor only a few hours ago.

Doris Henke was face down on the rug, a spreading lake of blood soaking into the carpet around her dumpy body, widening the rusty stain she'd made when she pumped a pair of bullets into Tony. Her little feet in their ankle strap heels were twisted awkwardly, and Zalman thought briefly of Dorothy's house crushing the Wicked Witch as it landed in Oz.

Mary Rose Peek was standing over Doris Henke's body, and her hands were like stretched claws covering her face as she screamed bloody murder. Mary Rose was wearing one of her southern-gal outfits, a pale pink cotton shift with trailing sleeves inset with lace, and the long, delicate sleeves were red and wet and heavy with Doris Henke's blood. The weight of the blood soaking into the wispy fabric dragged the long sleeves across Mary Rose's skirt, staining it dark red as well. But Mary Rose didn't know she was covered in blood. She simply stood in the middle of the room and screamed.

Quickly Zalman went over to Doris Henke and pressed his fingers into the warm, loose skin of her neck in search of a pulse. Nothing. He took a fast look around the Henke living room, but there was no one else there.

Mary Rose continued her rhythmic screaming, and the sound grated in Zalman's head like a bad rock band with too many amplifiers. "Marie," he said in desperation, "see what you can do with her, will you? Get her to stop. I gotta think for a minute. She's gotta stop screaming!"

"Sure," Marie said. "No problem." She walked up to Mary Rose and gave her a flat-hand slap across the face, hard. The crack of skin on skin echoed across the living room, and Mary Rose abruptly stopped screaming and looked around, uncomprehending. Her blue eyes fastened on Doris Henke, and then she began to cry as she stared at the crumpled mess on the floor in front of her.

"Thank God you did that," Zalman said with relief. "I'd never have the guts to slap a lady."

"I was a Girl Scout," Marie said. "Besides, it takes a lady to slap a lady. I'm sorry, Mary Rose," she told the weeping redhead. "I had to do it. Come over here, sit down, and tell us what happened. Better make it fast."

"Ah don't knowww." Mary Rose sobbed convulsively, rubbing her eyes. "Nothing happened," she wailed. "Doris called me, told me she had a letter from Happy for me, a bequest or something, and she asked me to come over and pick it up. Ah thought ah ought to, 'specially as Doris was being so nice about it."

BLOODY MARY

"Yeah, we know all that," Zalman said impatiently. "I got your message on my machine. Just tell us what happened when you got here, okay?"

"Nothing!" Mary Rose howled. "When ah came in here, she was lying on the floor, but she was still alive, ah swear it. At first ah thought she'd had a heart attack and maybe she needed CPR. So ah bent down over her and that's when ah saw the blood," Mary Rose said as she finally focused on her blood-stained dress. "And then she made this terrible noise, this sound way down deep in her throat. It was the same sound my dog made after he got hit by a truck when I was little and my daddy had to shoot him. Oh, God," Mary Rose said, trembling. "Ah'll never forget it as long as ah live! Ah can still hear it! Ah didn't want to touch her, but ah took first aid back in school, so ah thought ah better do the best ah could. Then it hit me; ah realized that somebody had killed her. Ah couldn't help it, Mr. Zalman, ah just started in screaming! She was all covered in blood, and now ah got it all over me," Mary Rose moaned as she plucked at her wet sleeves. "What's gonna happen to me now, Mr. Zalman? Ah think ah'm gonna be sick."

"Hello? Doris? Anybody home?" a man's voice called from the hall.

"Great. Just what we need," Zalman said angrily. "A kibbitzer." He stuck his head out into the hall to see who it was.

Failin' Phalen was standing at the open front doorway, looking around. He was wearing a white sport coat and gray slacks, and he looked unpleasantly chipper. "Hello?" he called. "Doris?"

"Whaddaya want, Phalen?" Zalman snapped.

"Hey, Jer. Great to see you," Phalen said in surprise. "I didn't know you was gonna be here. I thought it was just me and Doris. She told me . . ."

"Doris told you what?"

BLOODY MARY

Phalen frowned and looked past Zalman and into the living room without answering. "Is that Doris?" he said, his voice shaking. "What happened?" he asked as he pushed past Zalman, went into the living room, and stared down at Doris Henke's body. "Doris?" he asked tentatively.

"That's her," Zalman said shortly.

Failin' Phalen turned away from the body and looked at Mary Rose Peek, her dress bloody, her red hair disheveled. "What did you do?" he asked the redhead. "You killed her!"

Mary Rose widened her eyes. "Me?" she said, backing up. "Ah didn't."

Phalen paid no attention. "Poor Doris," he moaned. "What a tragedy."

"C'mon, Phalen," Zalman said roughly. "We gotta call the cops, pronto! Tell me what you're doing here, last chance for gas."

"Me? I ain't doing nothing! Doris wanted me to come over. She called me," Failin' Phalen said, glancing apprehensively at Mary Rose and then at Doris Henke's sprawled body. "She told me she'd figured out how to clean up the mess at the jewelry stores in a way that would leave us both in a solid financial position."

"She tell you what she had in mind?" Zalman probed.

"No dammit! Wish she had," Phalen said mournfully. "Now she's dead, and I'm still floating face down in the money soup. She says come on over, we'll talk about it. That's it, that's all I know."

"That's it? She says all your worries are over and that's it? Nothing about how she was gonna straighten you out?"

"Not a word," Failin' Phalen said piously, his hand over his heart. "If I'm lyin', I'm dyin'. Uh," he added as he glanced at Doris Henke's body huddled on the floor. "Bad choice of words, I guess."

Zalman didn't like it. Doris Henke, a woman not known for her kind and gentle nature, had called Mary Rose and Failin' Phalen and asked them to come to her house. She'd given them vague reasons, reasons she knew would bring them both running. Were her reasons real? Or did Doris Henke have something else in mind? Then, bingo-bango-bongo, Doris Henke dies.

Zalman shook his head. "Too damn coincidental, too damn simple," he mumbled. "And life just ain't like that. This stinks like ten-day-old whitefish."

"You're telling me," Phalen whined. "The worst part is, I talk to my insurance guy this morning, he tells me that cheapskate Happy never took out an employee dishonesty policy. It's optional, it only woulda cost a little more, and the cheap schmo didn't go for it. I'm screwed," he moaned as he buried his head in his hands. "All the dough Tony siphoned off the company, down the drain, gone! I'll never recoup a dime."

"Okay, Phalen, enough with the display of emotional grief," Zalman snapped. "I can see you're torn up that Doris Henke's dead, but we can hold a wake later. Marie, go call the cops and then take Mary Rose outside and wait by the car. By the car," he stressed. "I don't want blood all over my new seats. Phalen, you stay here with the body."

"Me! Why me?" Phalen cried. "I don't want to stay with the body. You're an attorney; you stay with the body."

"I gotta go find Brenda Henke," Zalman snapped. "Somebody's gotta tell the kid she's an orphan, and unless you want to do it, it looks like I'm elected."

"Okay, I'll stay with the body," Phalen said promptly.

"I thought you'd see it my way," Zalman said as he left the room and went slowly up the broad staircase to the second floor of the Henke house. He didn't want to do it, but he looked carefully in all the rooms along the long hallway, shuddering at the overblown decor favored by the late Mrs. Henke.

It was the kind of interior decoration that gave Beverly Hills a bad name. Gilt, flocked red velvet wallpaper, and heavy maroon damask draperies shot with thick gold thread gave every room a dark, oppressive air. Hothouse rooms nobody lived in, stilted rooms nobody used. Each room was perfect in its empty ugliness and untouched by any sign of human life.

He found Annabelle Forrester's small suite of rooms and took a fast look around. She wasn't there, but the piles of clothes scattered on every chair and the messy pink ruffled dressing table covered with a huge assortment of makeup and crystal perfume bottles made him think she had a hot date with Bertie the chinless wonder. Absently, Zalman wondered if Bertie had a string of polo ponies and lots of inherited money or if he was just another wealthy wannabe.

Zalman continued his search, and finally, at the far end of the hall, he opened the door to Brenda Henke's two-room suite and stuck his head inside.

The room was empty, but unlike Annabelle's morass of studied femininity, it was obvious that the person who lived here was a kid. There were posters of Guns 'n' Roses and Bon Jovi thumbtacked to the wall over a computer station. Zalman smiled when he saw the pile of blue Achenbach tests stacked up next to it, waiting to be scored. That Jason, he thought, thirteen years old and in business for himself.

Zalman looked around. There was a huge entertainment system along one side of the room, and CDs were scattered on the floor like rice at a church wedding. In the bedroom, clothes were piled up on the couch, the closet doors were standing open, and the bed was unmade.

Zalman looked at Brenda's dressing table and recognized the purse she'd been carrying when she came into his office. He opened it up and looked inside. Full. A set of keys on a silver Tiffany ingot ring, lip gloss, a half-empty pack of Black Jack gum, the little lace-edged handkerchief she'd carried. . . .

Zalman frowned. He didn't like finding the purse here. Not at all. He'd been married twice, he had a sister and a true love, and he'd never known a lady of any age to go anywhere without her purse. He closed the door to Brenda's room and slowly retraced his steps, looking carefully into each room on the second floor one more time. No Brenda Henke. Finally he quit looking and yelled for Brenda a few times, but she didn't show up. He went back downstairs to the kitchen, then out the back door to the pool house. Zip. No Brenda.

Curiouser and curiouser, Zalman thought as he walked through the big backyard toward the Henke house. Where was Brenda Henke? Maybe she was with Jason, but that still left the worrisome purse. Zalman heard the wail of approaching sirens and knew he wouldn't have a chance to call Jason until much, much later. Anyway, he didn't want Jason involved with the cops, especially Captain Arnie Thrasher. Zalman shivered. No use stirring up that particular hornet's nest unless absolutely necessary.

Step by step, Zalman thought as he got ready to face the cops. There would be plenty of time to panic later.

Twenty minutes later the Henke estate looked like all three rings of Ringling Brothers Barnum and Bailey at a Madison Square Garden Saturday matinee. The next-door neighbors gawked through the hedge as a chopper hovered overhead like a brilliant Mothra on patrol. The chopper trained its spotlight on the ground until the paramedics arrived; then it buzzed off to a fresh disaster on the other side of town. A harried pair of paramedics rushed out of the ambulance and into the house, leaving their radio squawking into the night like a love-crazed mallard.

As soon as all the action broke loose outside, Mary Rose Peek collapsed in a frail heap. She began to weep uncontrollably, deep sobs racking her body like a fever. Zalman told Marie to take her back inside the house and stash her in the study with Failin' Phalen. At least that way, she'd be out of the immediate line of fire.

Just as Marie came back outside, Lieutenant Howard Yarrow squealed into the driveway in a plainwrap Plymouth and jumped out of the car. He grinned like a predatory Bucky Beaver when he saw Marie standing next to the Mercedes.

"Hi, Marie." Yarrow waved happily as he jogged over to her side, ignoring Zalman. He was wearing a multihued plaid sport coat of the variety favored by local TV weather guys at very small stations. "Your dad's on his way. I just talked to him. On my radio."

"Gee, that's great," Marie said without visible enthusiasm. "He'll just love this, I know."

Yarrow turned to Zalman. "You here again, Mr. Zalman?" he said. "How convenient."

Zalman stared up at Yarrow and momentarily thought about belting him in his handsome kisser and causing him to undergo quite a bit of expensive dental work, but he knew it would be a wrong move. The problem with throwing a punch into a guy is that all too often the puncher looks dumber than the punched. Besides, Zalman was wise enough to know that cop socky wasn't a bright move under any circumstances.

"The body's on the floor in the living room," Zalman said, trying for a professionally neutral tone of voice. "Miss Peek discovered it, and she's in the study with Mr. Phalen."

"Same gang we had the other night, huh?" Yarrow smiled happily. "I'm getting used to running into you at murder scenes, Mr. Zalman. Kinda habitual. Well, I'd love to stay and chat, but I think I'd better go inside and check out the crime scene before Captain Thrasher shows up."

"You do that," Zalman said.

Yarrow paused and squinted down the driveway. "Say," he said, pointing. "What the hell's that?" He was staring over Zalman's shoulder at an approaching car.

Zalman turned, looked, and groaned.

Jason Hanning's pink Caddy squealed into the driveway, the petulant Tyrone in his black leather jacket hunched over the wheel.

"Kids. What a wacky town. I love L.A." Yarrow snickered as he went into the house.

"What's going on?" Jason called as he jumped out of the car and surveyed the mob scene nervously. He was wearing his usual snappy Italian suit, and he was twiddling a licorice stick between manicured fingers.

BLOODY MARY

"What the hell are you doing here, Jason?" Zalman groaned.

"I have a date with Brenda, no big deal!" Jason said, anxiety creeping into his voice as he looked around the Henke driveway at all the cars. "What happened? Where's Brenda?"

"C'mere!" Zalman growled as he grabbed his nephew by his well-tailored shoulder and dragged him behind the Mercedes. "No screwing around, Jason. Doris Henke's been killed."

"No shit?" Jason said in amazement, his eyes the size of dinner plates.

"No shit. You know where Brenda is?"

"She's not here?" Jason asked slowly, pocketing his licorice stick. "No screwing around, Uncle Jerry, I don't know where she is."

"Oh, boy, we're in top trouble," Zalman said as he looked back at Marie.

Lieutenant Yarrow came out of the house and trotted down the steps to Marie's side, grinning like a lovesick fool.

"Look at that reptile, would ya?" Zalman demanded. "I could get a big-time hate on for him real easy."

"Where did he get that jacket?" Jason asked, awestruck. "That's positively the worst sport coat I've ever seen in my life!"

"Never mind the sartorial splendor of L.A.'s finest, just tell me . . ." Zalman began but he stopped as another plain-wrap Plymouth pulled in.

Captain Arnie Thrasher got out of the car and stared angrily across the driveway. "Zalman!" he screamed, his anger reverberating across the length and breadth of Holmby Hills.

"Who's that guy?" Jason asked.

"Marie's father."

"Tell you the truth, I don't see the resemblance. What an oinker!"

"Zalman!" Thrasher screamed.

"Yeah, and that's the good news," Zalman told the kid, ignoring Thrasher. "The bad news is he hates anybody named Zalman, he's in charge of the investigation, and Brenda's disappeared."

"Brenda? Disappeared?"

"Gone. And sooner or later, your mom's gonna find out about this whole mess, and she'll probably bury you up to your neck in a red anthill until you're twenty-one, right next to me. I hate to ask you this, Jason, but is there any chance Brenda stood you up?"

"Zalman!" Thrasher screamed again.

Jason shook his head disdainfully. "Me? Not a chance. Brenda and I had important business to discuss about the Achenbach tests she's doing. Besides, we're crazy about each other."

"Zalman!" Thrasher's howl cut through the night like a Ginsu.

"Gimme a minute, will you, Arnie?" Zalman yelled. "Look," he said, turning back to Jason. "I dunno where Brenda is. I searched the house right after Marie and I got here, but I didn't have much time. Is it possible she's at a friend's house?"

Jason shrugged. "Possible? Sure."

"But not probable. We gotta check it out anyway. Maybe she's hiding. You and Tyrone know some nooks, a few crannies in this joint? Go over the house, top to bottom, while I deal with Thrasher. Anybody asks you anything, act like a pair of stupid kids."

"Zalllmannnn!"

"Piece of cake," Jason said. "Being a kid is a great cover." He went over to the Caddy and mumbled to Tyrone; then the two kids sauntered around the back of the house, looking wide-eyed.

Zalman walked slowly over to Thrasher. "Hi,

Arnie." He smiled brightly as he put his arm around Marie.

"About time! Who's the kid?" Thrasher demanded. "And where'd he go?"

"He's my nephew, Jason Hanning. He's doing some research for a school project," Zalman improvised.

"Jason's planning to be an FBI agent when he grows up," Marie said helpfully.

"If he grows up," Zalman stressed.

"Another one of your crazy family?" Thrasher groaned, slapping himself too hard on the forehead. "Ouch! How many Zalmans can there be in this part of the country? I can't take any more of you," Thrasher warned.

Luckily for Zalman, Thrasher's rage was deflected when he saw a tall, excessively rumpled fellow climbing out of a well-dented yellow Volkswagen beetle with a crumpled right fender. "Aw, no! It's Dickie Willet! How'd he get here so fast? I hate that guy!"

"The reporter from the *L.A. Zone*?" Zalman asked. "Just what I need."

Willet sauntered over to the steps and fished in his pockets for a smoke. He was wearing a dirty raincoat, heavy horn-rimmed glasses, and a brown fedora pushed back on his head like an aging Jimmy Olson. He had a camera bag and several Nikons over one shoulder, and he obviously took his costume for his part as a boy reporter very seriously. Or maybe one of the studios was doing yet another remake of *The Front Page* and Willet was up for a part.

"What's the word, hummingbird?" Willet said as he lit a Marlboro, inhaled deeply, and began to cough.

Zalman knew all about Dickie Willet. The so-called reporter covered crime for the *L.A. Zone*, a sleazy rag that specialized in hot gossip, cold comfort, scuttlebutt, cheap shots, and thinly disguised tabloid trash, which Willet claimed was sharp investigative reporting and penetrating journalism of the highest order. Everybody else knew the *Zone* was utter garbage but lots and lots of fun to read.

"How'd you find out about this, Willet?" Thrasher demanded.

"Just good luck," Willet replied, coughing. "Seems the kid in the mansion next door was out by the pool shooting a video for his girlfriend's band. They heard all the action and had the presence of mind to call the *Zone* with a Newshound Poop Scoop. We pay a hundred bucks cash money for a good Poop Scoop, y'know. Now the *Zone* is on the spot, and you can be sure no news will escape Dickie Willet!" He leered as the odor of three-day-old bourbon and dead gym towels oozed out of his pores and into the night air. "Say," Willet said slowly, "I know who you are. You're Jerry Zalman, right?"

"Right," Zalman admitted.

"I heard a lot about you," Willet said, offering Zalman a dirty hand. "How'd that killing over at the Magic Cavern turn out, anyway?"

Zalman ignored both the question and the hand. "C'mon over to my office tomorrow," Zalman said as he gave Dickie Willet his card. "Be there, I'll give you the whole story."

"I want an exclusive!" the reporter demanded. "C'mon you guys, lemme interview somebody before the TV crews get all the good stuff, will ya? Print is a tough racket!"

"I'm giving you nothing!" Thrasher snorted. "You're not a legitimate journalist, you're a sleazy hack!"

"Everybody's a critic," Willet sighed as he watched Thrasher stalk into the house.

A cherry red Corvette pulled into the driveway, and Willet turned to look at it. "Boy, I could go for her in a big way," the reporter breathed heavily.

"Get real, Willet," Zalman told him as he walked

over to the car. "You can look, but you'll never touch."

"What's going on here, Mr. Zalman?" Annabelle Forrester said coolly as she swung a perfect leg out of the driver's seat and got out of the car.

Bertie was sitting next to her in the passenger seat, pale and blond and twittery. He was drumming his fingers to the light jazz on the car radio.

Zalman took a closer look at him. He hadn't really noticed it before, but Bertie was the embodiment of a Monty Python reject. He had a faint mustache, and he looked as if he was wearing a caterpillar on his lip. Bertie switched off the radio, got out of the car, and walked slowly over to Annabelle's side.

"Hey! How 'bout an interview at my place, baby!" Willet shouted at Annabelle.

Annabelle Forrester wasn't fazed by Willet. Bertie sighed but said nothing. "What's all this?" Annabelle frowned as Zalman walked over to her. "Is something the matter?"

Zalman shook hands with Bertie. His hand was soft, damp, and cold. "Bad news, Miss Forrester," Zalman said as gently as possible.

"Call me Annabelle," she said, laying a ringed hand on Zalman's chest.

Zalman could feel Marie's eyes drilling into his back as he inched away from the suggestive touch. "I'm afraid your mother's been killed," Zalman said. "I'm sorry."

"My mother?" Annabelle asked in amazement. "You can't be serious."

"I'm afraid I am."

Annabelle's sapphire eyes fluttered briefly as she leaned back against the door of the red Corvette. "Are the police here?" she asked.

"Plain wraps," Zalman said, pointing at the Plymouths. "Captain Thrasher just arrived. He's inside."

"I'd better go and talk to him," Annabelle said slowly.

"Miss Forrester?" Zalman asked.

"You'll never call me Annabelle, will you?" she said, her voice soft and breathy.

"Not now," Zalman said. He remembered the Snow Queen, a scary fairy story he'd heard as a kid, and thought that Miss Annabelle Forrester could be the Snow Queen's stunt double. "Do you know where your sister is?" he asked.

"What sister? I don't have . . . Oh, you mean Brenda. Haven't the vaguest. Why? Is she lost? Stay here, Bertie. I'll be back for you."

"What's going on, Mr. Zalman?" Bertie the chinless wonder said.

"Murder, kidnapping, robbery. Par for the course in this town," Zalman answered. "You're not from around here, are you, Bertie?"

"How'd you guess?" Bertie asked in surprise as he watched Annabelle's taffy blond hair swinging back and forth when she walked across the driveway.

"You've got that pale, hungry look they get on the East Coast," Zalman told him. "Too much fluorescent lighting and pasta."

"How 'bout an interview with Beauty, Zalman?" Willet shouted from the other side of the wide driveway as Annabelle's tiny heels clicked up the steps. "C'mon, it won't hurt you and it'll do me a lot of good."

"I gotta go, Bertie. Talk to me tomorrow, Willet," Zalman stalled as he walked back to Marie.

Marie smiled very, very sweetly as Annabelle Forrester disappeared into the white house.

"Don't start," Zalman warned.

"I wouldn't dream of starting," Marie replied. "She is pretty, though. Awfully pretty. Wouldn't you agree, Jerry, darling?"

BLOODY MARY

"Agree with what?"

"Wouldn't you agree that she's awfully, awfully pretty?"

"Marie, let me tell you how much I care about Annabelle Forrester."

"Oh, please do," Marie said.

"I think that if you and I captured the Snow Queen and Howard the pinhead Yarrow and drilled some little tiny holes in the top of their heads, they'd make a great pair of salt and pepper shakers for your collection. Do I make myself reasonably clear?"

"I'd love to drill a few holes in her head." Marie smiled dreamily. "Big, painful holes."

"I see we understand each other perfectly," Zalman said.

"How 'bout it, Zalman?" Willet shouted again.

"Buzz off," Zalman snapped as he and Marie followed Annabelle Forrester into the house, leaving Willet standing sullenly in the driveway.

"You'll be soorrry," the reporter called.

"I'm sorry now, Willet!" Zalman mumbled. "You don't know how sorry I am."

Inside, Lieutenant Howard Yarrow and Captain Arnold Thrasher were standing near the living room door. Yarrow was beaming, and he had the proud air of a young matador who had just conquered his first dangerous bull.

"I can give you the whole rundown, Chief," he said to Thrasher. "Right after I got here I had a little chat with a Miss Mary Rose Peek. She's the one who found the body. She claims that she—"

"Hold it, hold it," Thrasher said as he saw Zalman. "Not in front of the civilians. And especially not in front of him!" Thrasher said, pointing at Zalman. "C'mon, let's go get a geeze at the stiff and you can tell me everything you know."

"That won't take long," Zalman said.

BLOODY MARY

"Honestly, Daddy. What language," Marie teased.

"You've been hanging around with Zalman too much," Thrasher said sadly. "You're getting a fresh mouth, just like him." The two cops went thudding into the living room to look at the body, and Zalman and Marie went into the study to talk to Mary Rose.

The redhead was lying on the couch with a cold compress on her pale forehead, and Failin' Phalen was slumped in a nearby chair. Annabelle Forrester wasn't in the room.

"This is awful," Phalen moaned as soon as he saw Zalman. "A nightmare. First Happy, then Tony, now Doris. This is a murder epidemic! A slaughter plague! Poor old Doris, she never hurt a flea in her life!"

"Ha!" Marie snorted. "I bet she hurt plenty of fleas."

Mary Rose moaned as she took the compress off her head and looked at Zalman with the eyes of a squished kitty. "What's going happen to me now, Mr. Zalman?"

"My business! What's gonna happen to my business! I had such hopes, such plans for the future of Henke's Hideaway," Phalen sobbed. "A Christmas catalog of faux jewelry in the shape of ornaments! A line of faux dog collars! Now, poof! Murder, theft, it's all gone. Life is so unfair!"

"Quit whining, will you, Phalen?" Zalman told him. "You got no problem here."

"Easy for you to say," Phalen whined. "You got money in the bank. I sank every dime I had left in Henke's Hideaway. Between Happy's death and Tony's embezzling, I'm flat broke, and I'd call that a big problem, especially in this town."

"I'm afraid, Mr. Zalman," Mary Rose sniffled.

"Don't worry, Mary Rose. Nothing bad will—"

"That's what you say, Zalman. I say different," Arnie Thrasher said triumphantly as he barged into the room, Yarrow panting at his heels. "Miss Peek, you're under arrest for the murder of Doris Henke. You have the right to—"

"But I didn't kill her," Mary Rose cried. "Mr. Zalman, make him stop!"

"You can't make it stick, Arnie," Zalman shouted.

"The hell you say!" Thrasher sneered. "She had the motive and the means, and God knows she had the opportunity. She's covered with blood, and you found her standing over the body, right?"

"Welll," Zalman hedged.

"Right. Besides, Yarrow here found the gun outside in the rosebushes, and I'll bet you it's been wiped clean of prints."

"So what does that prove? Anybody can wipe a gun clean. Any killer would've—"

"Yeah, but I think she did it. I think she shot Mrs. Henke, wiped the gun, threw it outside, then came on with this bozo story about how Mrs. Henke asked her over and then she found the body and got blood on her dress when she gave Mrs. Henke CPR. You saw the body, Zalman. Would you try CPR with a stiff like that?"

"No, but I'm smarter than she is," Zalman said.

"Jerry! I'm shocked. What a terrible thing to say," Marie said primly.

"Come along, Miss Peek," Thrasher said firmly.

Mary Rose sat up and dropped her compress on the floor. She started to cry again, large round droplets cascading down her cheeks like a trickle of perfect Diamettes. "Why is this happening to me? Ah didn't do anything wrong! Ah wouldn't! Ah couldn't!"

"It's all a terrible mistake," Marie said as she sat down on the couch next to Mary Rose and tried to comfort her. "Jerry will help you, won't you, Jerry?"

"Yeah, sure," Zalman said. "Saint Zalman of Beverly Hills, that's me. You can't get away with this, Thrasher! You got nothing on my client!"

"You oughta get a better class of clients, Zalman! And stay away from my daughter!"

"Don't get personal!"

"Why not? She's my daughter and I don't want her hanging around with an ambulance-chasing shrimp like you!"

"That's a dirty crack, Thrasher!"

"Which one, Zalman?"

Ten minutes later, when Thrasher triumphantly led a handcuffed Mary Rose down the steps in her blood-stained dress, Dickie Willet had his revenge. The boozy *Zone* reporter got the whole sequence on film, including Mary Rose crying bitterly, Jerry Zalman red in the face as he screamed assorted invectives at Thrasher, Yarrow showing a large mouthful of white teeth as he grinned, and Marie Thrasher angrily stamping her foot at her father.

NEXT MORNING WHEN ZALMAN STORMED INTO HIS OFfice, the first thing he saw was Esther Wong staring at the front page of the *L.A. Zone*.

"Have you seen this?" Esther asked as she held up the newspaper. "Not a very flattering picture of you, Mr. Z."

On the *Zone*'s front page was a full-color shot of Mary Rose in her bloody dress with Zalman by her side, a bulldog look in his eye as he snarled angrily at the photographer. The headline screamed BLOODY MARY, SHE KILLS 'EM! in garish red letters, and some wag in the art department had decorated the lettering with little droplets meant to suggest splattered blood.

Zalman stared at it, scowling. "Marie says I look cute when I snarl," he said. "Me, I think I just look feral."

On the inside pages of the *Zone*, Dickie Willet had done his worst. Why not? It was a story too good to resist. It had everything—love, sex, death, a woman scorned, and lots and lots and lots of lovely money to wonder about.

Mary Rose Peek was cast as the Other Woman who, abandoned by her murdered lover, kills the grieving widow in revenge. Who cared if it wasn't true? Who cared if it bent the facts? It was juicy, it was yummy, it was a fun murder, and Willet was clearly out to milk the story dry.

Zalman knew the Henke killing was bound to be the talk of the town. L.A. hadn't seen a murder quite like it since the time a fading movie star's husband caught her in the sack with a local TV film critic. The husband tossed the star off the top of the Bonaventure Hotel in downtown L.A., and the movie star landed splat in the middle of a hot tub in the back of a white stretch limo. The murderous husband went to jail for five to ten, and the film critic moved to France where he was planning to write a coffee table book as a tribute to his dead lady love.

"Esther," Zalman said, "forget that rag. This is an emergency."

"Oh, goody, I was getting bored all by myself," Esther said, tossing the *Zone* on the floor. "What do you want me to do?"

"I want McCoy and Jason in here as soon as possible. Tell Jason to make sure Tyrone is here, too. At least he can drive Jason around, even if he doesn't talk much. Call Marie, too. I need somebody with brains and common sense, and Marie's in charge of that department. We have two big problems, and we're going to need all the help we can get," Zalman said. "Then I want you to write a press release. That weasel Dickie Willet is gonna show up any minute, and I want to be ready for him."

"Is he cute?" Esther wondered hopefully.

"Not in my opinion. I want to put out our side of the story, got it? It doesn't have to be long, just a page, page and a half."

"Me? A press release? I don't know how to write a press release!" Esther protested.

"Fake it. Write about a page of jive saying how innocent victim Mary Rose Peek will be set free in a matter of hours and it's all a miscarriage of justice and blah, blah, blah. It doesn't have to say anything; it just has to sound like it says something. Pad it, pretend it's your résumé."

"Oh, I get it, Mr. Z. I'll give it a shot," Esther said. "But do you think Dickie Willet will dare come over here after writing those lies?" she asked, pointing at the *L.A. Zone,* which she'd tossed on the floor.

"You bet he will," Zalman snapped. "He's a reporter, or so he says. He's gonna need some fresh dirt to shovel for the next edition."

"Hmm," Esther said. "Should we have hors d'oeuvres?"

"This is a murder investigation, Esther, not a cocktail party!"

"Might soothe the savage press," Esther said delicately.

"Maybe you've got a point," Zalman conceded. "Get Pete Marchetti to send a few trays over."

"I love his shrimp rolls," Esther mused. "And maybe some of those crab timbales . . ."

"Matter of fact, get a temporary secretary in here to answer the phone while you work on the press release. Use my office. You know," Zalman said thoughtfully as he looked at the crumpled *Zone* on the floor. "All of a sudden I have a great idea. I'm betting Mary Rose is innocent. If I'm right, and we both know I usually am, and we milk this thing for all the publicity we can squeeze out of it, I might be able to pitch it as a TV movie to that kid over at Paramount."

"Bernadette Peters as Mary Rose," Esther said promptly. "Who for you?"

Zalman laughed as he went into his office. "Me for me, Esther. Who else has the savoir faire?"

"Okay, gang, listen up!" Zalman snapped as he leaned back in his chair, blew a double smoke ring, and watched it float into the small crowd he'd assembled in his office.

"Oui, mon capitaine," Marie said.

"Tell you the truth, I could get used to having troops to command," Zalman said approvingly as he looked at his audience. "Too bad I missed my chance, never went to West Point and became an officer."

McCoy shifted unhappily on the couch and fired up a Lucky. He gulped the bottle of Tuborg and thoughtfully gave Chester the villainous Doberman the remaining backwash. "Zally, we gotta get Mary Rose out of jail," he said, puffing nervous clouds of smoke into the air. "She's helpless. Why, Mary Rose is so peaceful, she don't even force bulbs. Okay, she can recite the Presidents backwards and forwards, but she can't stand up to Arnie Thrasher. No offense, Marie, but Arnie's gonna chain-saw right through that poor girl."

"Daddy's very sweet once you get to know him," Marie insisted in a weak attempt to defend her father. "It's just that he has a hate thing about Jerry. And you, Dean."

BLOODY MARY

McCoy shook his big head. "I don't care how he feels about me, Marie; it's Mary Rose I'm worried about. He'll keep on drilling her, questioning her, he'll drive her crazy! He'll try to bend her to his will, break her free-spirited southern heart! She didn't kill Doris Henke," McCoy said as he slumped back on the couch. Chester burped, snuggled up to McCoy's boots, and slurped longingly at the empty beer bottle.

"I'll get her out," Zalman told his pal. "Jeez, Dean, you're hurting my feelings here!"

"What feelings?" McCoy cracked sadly.

Zalman ignored him. "We've known each other all these years and you still don't trust me to get the babe outta jail. Believe me, I'll handle it."

"You'da been a great general, Jerry," McCoy said morosely.

"General Jerry, I like it," Zalman said, a dreamy note in his voice.

"I think I'll call you General Jerry. But not till an opportune moment presents itself." Marie giggled. "I'm sure one will."

Zalman waved a mocking fist at her. "One of these days, Alice," he Gleasoned. "Okay, enough idle banter, gang. We gotta diversify. Divide and conquer, believe and achieve! McCoy, go downtown and post the bond for Mary Rose."

"Great, but who's gonna pay?" McCoy asked.

"I hate to do this—it goes against every principle I learned as a toddler at my father's knee—but I'll pay," Zalman offered.

"What?" McCoy asked in amazement. "You will?"

"Jerry, are you feeling okay?" Marie asked. "Not running a temperature, are we?"

"Lay off, you two! Somebody's gotta get Mary Rose outta jail, and I don't see anybody else in this room with capital."

"I resent that," Marie said. "I've got a Gold Card, and I'm as solvent as you are."

"Besides," Zalman continued, "if the gods decide to smile on me, I'm going to hawk the life story of Ms. Mary Rose Peek to that boy producer over at Paramount."

Marie laughed. "Jerry, you're impossible."

"True. But I think we have a shot at a two-parter."

"How about Bernadette Peters for Mary Rose?" Esther put in.

Zalman grinned wolfishly. "I'll take a handsome percentage, of course, and Mary Rose will walk away with enough dough to start a new life in the city of her choice. Get it?"

"You devil. It's a great angle. Okay, cut me in for half of your action," Marie said promptly. "I'll front the bucks for the bail."

"Done deal," Zalman told her. "I knew I had a good reason for loving you, and I just remembered what it is: you're beautiful, you're generous, and you've got a six-figure income to back it up. Dean, work out the details, then bop downtown and pick up Mary Rose."

"You got it," McCoy said.

"Next case. Marie, call Saks or Neiman's and buy Mary Rose a normal outfit. Conservative. A nice navy blue suit, medium-length skirt. No pink, no red, no magenta, nothing that has a bloody hue. Get me?" Zalman said, stabbing the air with his cigar.

"I gotcha, General Jerry."

"Yeah, I like it. General Jerry. Marie, keep that up and you can be a colonel in my private army. I bet you'd look great in the right uniform. Bring Mary Rose back here so's I can have a little talk with her. Esther's writing a press release and I'm going to bombard that slime ball Dickie Willet with our version of the story. You're on track, Esther?"

Esther flipped a snappy salute. "I'm working on it now. This is so much fun, Mr. Z. I think we should do more murders, not just those boring divorces and palimonies."

Zalman frowned and wagged a warning finger at her. "Bite your tongue, Esther. Never forget that in Beverly Hills, divorce not only pays the rent, it also buys the Mercedes. Okay. Next case. You two," he said, turning to Jason Hanning and Tyrone.

Tyrone slouched down in the armchair, his studded black leather outfit squeaking in protest. "What am I s'posed to do?" He scowled defiantly, a toothpick hanging out of the corner of his mouth.

"You're s'posed to do exactly what I tell you to do," Zalman stressed.

Tyrone shifted the toothpick to the other side of his mouth, sighed heavily, and rattled his silver bracelets like the Ghost of Christmas Past come to settle up.

"Get over to the Henke joint and go through it room by room," Zalman said as he spun his chair around angrily and stared down at Beverly Drive. All of a sudden he thought he saw somebody in a trench coat duck into the boutique across the street. Was Dickie Willet watching his office? Zalman took a closer look, but there was no one there.

"Aw, Uncle Jerry, we did that last night," Jason Hanning moaned. "I don't wanna go back there for nothing! Brenda isn't at the house."

Zalman spun around again and turned the brunt of his legal attention on his recalcitrant nephew.

The kid looked terrible. His hair was messed up, he had dark circles under his eyes, his suit needed a good pressing, and he'd even loosened his tie.

"Jason, close your yap and attend to the voice of wisdom. I know Brenda isn't in the house," Zalman said, keeping a firm grip on his thinning patience.

"Yeah, yeah, yeah . . ."

BLOODY MARY

"You've called every human being she knows, and she's nowhere. Gone, disappeared, poof! Right?"

"Yeah, yeah, yeah . . ."

"Hey, don't yeah-yeah-yeah me when I'm trying to teach you something, Jason! Just because you're thirteen, it doesn't mean you know everything since Moses handed down the tablets," Zalman told the kid as he leaned forward across his desk and stared at him harshly. "I want you to look for something that'll help me figure out where Brenda is or who's got her or why they've got her. Look, last night when Doris Henke got popped, Brenda Henke saw the murderer, right?"

Jason nodded slowly. "Got to be," he agreed.

"And now the killer's got her. So, my smart nephew, we're looking for a clue to Brenda's whereabouts. Or a clue that'll tell us who Brenda saw. Are the dots beginning to connect in your brilliant head?"

Jason nodded thoughtfully. "Yeah, yeah, yeah . . ."

Zalman blew a cloud of smoke across the desk. "Good. I'm sending you because you and Tyrone know the intricacies of her wily little preteen mind. I'm betting there's something in that house that you and you alone might recognize. It's a long shot, but it's the long shots that pay off big. Get it?"

Jason straightened up in his chair. "I get it," he said slowly.

"So you two mugs go through the house. I want you to become one with Brenda."

"Huh?" Tyrone asked slowly as he put his spent toothpick in an ashtray and leaned forward, looking puzzled. "Become one? Whazzat?"

"You know," Zalman said impatiently. "Try to think like Brenda. Put yourself in her place."

"I don't get it," Tyrone said.

"Tyrone," Marie said. "Did you ever see the 'Star Trek' episode with the big monster called the Horta who can eat rock and she's killing all the miners on the planet?"

"My second favorite episode," Tyrone said. "After 'The Trouble with Tribbles.' "

"Remember at the end of the story when Mr. Spock does the Vulcan mind meld with the Horta?"

"Sure!" Tyrone said, a smile of understanding spreading over his face. "She's the mother of her race, and the miners are killing her eggs. That's why she's killing the miners. She's really quite gentle."

"Mr. Zalman wants you to do a Vulcan mind meld with Brenda."

"Be like Mr. Spock?" Tyrone said happily. "Why dint you say so?"

Zalman rolled his eyes skyward. "You media brats kill me. You only understand something if you've seen it on TV. Go. Have a Vulcan mind meld. Just remember that whoever bagged Brenda can't possibly be smarter than all of us."

Jason jumped out of his chair and knotted his tie. "That's right, Uncle Jerry," he said, his voice invigorated, his face shining with strength. "Let's go do it to it, Tyrone."

"On track, troops?" Zalman asked as he pushed back his chair and stood behind his desk with his cigar clamped between his teeth.

There was a chorus of yesses and a nodding of heads and a faint ruff from Chester.

"Hey, wait a minute, wait a minute," Marie said suspiciously. "We know what we're supposed to do, but what are you supposed to do, General Jerry?"

Zalman grinned happily and stubbed out his cigar. "Me? I'm a general. My job is to stimulate and motivate. Once you get Mary Rose out of the pokey, that's when I go to work."

* * *

Zalman played phone tag for an hour, then went across the street The 24-Hour Diner for lunch. When he finished his pastrami he asked them to send over an assortment of sandwiches for the troops, since Pete Marchetti's hors d'oeuvre trays tended to be more decorative than filling.

As he was coming out of The Diner, he thought he saw a flash of trench coat disappearing around the corner, but when he looked, there was nobody there.

He wandered casually down the street and pretended he was window-shopping, but he still didn't see anybody behind him, so he went to the Liquor Stall and ordered Diet Coke for Marie and Esther, beer for McCoy, and Dr Pepper for Jason and Tyrone.

When Zalman opened the office door at three-thirty there was a temporary secretary sitting at Esther's desk, the phone stuck to his ear.

"He's not in right now, Mr. Huston," the young man said, eyeing Zalman suspiciously. He was wearing a green Hawaiian shirt decorated with pineapples, chinos, and sunglasses on a green cord around his neck, and he had a weird chopped haircut. "But I'll give him your message. May I help you, sir?" the young man said as he hung up.

"Probably. I'm Jerry Zalman."

"Oh, hel-lo, Mr. Zalman! I'm Albert Moreau from TempTyme? Miss Wong brought me in for the day. She said you were having a big rush and needed extra help," he said, settling his sunglasses on top of his head.

"True enough, Albert," Zalman said as he went into his office. He was about to throw his briefcase across the room, but Esther had taken up residence on the couch and had stacks of paper spread in long rows up and down the cushions.

"Hi, Mr. Z.," she mumbled. Her long black hair was piled up on top of her head, and she was wearing her glasses—very unusual, for Esther. She had a pencil stuck behind one ear and a stapler in her hand. "Don't make me lose my place. I'm collating."

"Esther, what the hell have you written?" Zalman said as he looked at the stacks of papers. "I asked for a press release, dear. It wasn't necessary to turn it into a miniseries."

"If I'm going to write a press release, I want to do my best work," she said primly as she stapled three heavy cream-colored pages together and handed them to Zalman. "There, doesn't that look professional?"

Zalman scanned the pages briefly. "Yup. I have to admit it does," he told her as he read it over. "I'm impressed, Esther. You've made Bloody Mary Rose shine like a lily. You oughta try writing a bodice ripper. I particularly like the element of romantic tension you gave to Mary Rose's description, not to mention the nuances. But is she really a wronged heroine for the ages cloaked in a sheath of soured love? Makes her sound like a bad beef Stroganoff."

"I thought it gave her an air of defiant victory," Esther huffed.

"You did a great job, dear. Now, get young Albert in here. I'm going to give him a pep talk."

"He's very sweet, Mr. Z. Don't yell at him," she warned. "He's from out of state, and I think he gets frightened easily."

"I won't yell at him! I just want to make sure he can handle whatever's coming down the freeway at him this afternoon. Albert!" Zalman bellowed. "C'mere a minute."

Albert Moreau stuck his head in the door. "Yes, Mr. Zalman?" he said softly. He had a green steno pad in his hand and looked expectant.

"Siddown over there, Albert," Zalman said, motioning to the leather chair. "You're just a temp, but—"

"We at TempTyme pride ourselves on being able to step into any milieu," Albert said happily.

"Never mind the milieu, Moreau. Any minute now this place is going to look like the Wild Animal Park at the San Diego Zoo, so get ready for trouble. Luckily, you don't know anything, so you can't give anything away. If that geek reporter Willet gives you any gas or tries to frighten you, send him to me. I'll take care of him."

"Don't you worry yourself. I can handle it," Albert said as he got up. "I hate a run-of-the-mill job."

"Great. Go back to your desk and pretend like I'm Dick Nixon and you're Rosemary Woods."

"Who?"

Zalman stared at him. "Why am I starting to feel old?" he mumbled. "Never happened before. Back to your post, Albert."

"You can depend on me, Mr. Zalman," Albert said happily as he leaned in the doorway, tapping his steno pad. "I just moved to L.A. from Michigan and I love it. It's wonderful to live smack-dab on the cutting edge of celebrityhood. Every morning when I get up I think to myself, Albert, today's the day you could be on TV!" he said as he went back to his desk.

Zalman stared silently at Albert's retreating back. "Esther, after this war is over, remind me to go to Switzerland and take the sleep cure."

A HALF HOUR LATER ZALMAN WAS ON THE PHONE WITH Huston, trying to persuade the writer that changing the main characters in *The Southland Swelters* from a pair of dedicated social workers in the barrio to a pair of hard-boiled cops in Manhattan wouldn't make an iota of difference to the overall integrity of the piece, when Albert signaled that there was a call waiting on the other line.

Impatiently, Zalman punched the button. "Zalman," he snapped.

"I've got the girl," a falsetto voice shrilled. "Bring the formula for the Rubyola to the deli counter at Gelsons Market in Century City in an hour and I'll give her to you unharmed."

"Forget it," Zalman told the falsetto. "The deli counter at Gelsons is a nightmare at lunch."

"Don't kid me," the voice squealed. "Write the formula on a piece of yellow legal paper, hold it in your hand, and belly up to the counter, right in front of the Chinese chicken salad!"

"How do I know Brenda's okay?" Zalman demanded. "Put her on."

"No dice," the voice said. "I gave her sleeping pills. She's okay, and if you want her to stay okay, bring the formula for the Rubyola to Gelsons!"

"How'll I know you?" Zalman asked.

"I'll know you. Don't try anything or I'll kill the

girl!" the falsetto squealed, and then the kidnapper slammed the phone down before Zalman could argue any further.

Zalman got up out of his chair, went over to the bar, and made himself a Bullshot. "Damn," he said to himself. "I don't have the Rubyola formula. Now what am I gonna do?"

Thoughtfully, he walked back to his desk and went over things for a half an hour, until a sneaky little idea began to form in the back of his brain.

"You want the Rubyola, I'll give you the Rubyola. *Albert!*" Zalman yelled. "C'mere, I got a job for you."

While he was waiting for Albert to finish, Zalman spun around in his chair and took a fast look at Beverly Drive. There was a sudden furtive movement as a trench coat disappeared into the boutique.

"Whoever you are, I saw you that time, sucker," Zalman muttered. "I see you, but who the hell are you?"

Zalman pulled the Mercedes into the parking garage beneath Century City, stashed the car in a loading zone, and grabbed the yellow legal tablet. He ripped off the top sheet of paper and took the escalator up into the light.

Century City was alive with awed tourists gawking at the pricey goods in the fancy shops and wealthy locals genuflecting before the revered god of retail enshrined in the hallowed mall.

Zalman cut through the heavy foot traffic to Gelsons Market and went inside. The big grocery store was teeming with shoppers as the best of Beverly Hills fought for truffles and Brie, snarling and snapping over exotic delights like a pack of hungry stoats. Zalman thought he saw Zsa Zsa by the grapes, but he wasn't sure.

BLOODY MARY

Zalman took a number and pushed his way up to the Chinese chicken salad end of the busy deli counter, prominently waving the sheet of yellow legal paper like a fan. The deli counter was packed three deep with hungry young brokers grabbing a fast lunch and expensively dressed hausfraus picking up microwaveable dinners. Tanned, lean bodies pressed all around him, pushing him forward against the glass. He felt like a herring. A crushed herring.

Suddenly Zalman felt something small and hard being jammed into his back.

"Don't turn around," the falsetto shrilled softly.

The counterman called Zalman's number.

"A pound of Chinese chicken salad," Zalman blurted, waving his number over his head.

"Never mind that! I got a gun in my pocket and I'm serious." The gun dug deeper into Zalman's back.

Zalman held the sheet of paper over his shoulder. The falsetto's hand snaked around, tugging at the paper but Zalman wouldn't let go as the counterman dug out a pound of Chinese chicken salad and slapped it into a plastic container.

"Where's Brenda?" Zalman said as he took the container from the counterman.

"Give me the formula first. Is this it?"

"You bet," Zalman said. "Take a look." He waved the paper and tried to turn around at the same time so he could get a glimpse of the kidnapper, but the crowd on either side had him pinned.

"I trust you," the falsetto sneered. "Just like you trust me. Leggo, will ya? The girl's in the trunk of a tan Chrysler on level three in the garage."

Zalman let the paper slip out of his hand.

"Don't try to follow me," the falsetto voice whispered. "I got guys watching you."

The owner of the falsetto gave Zalman a sharp push

forward, and he stumbled into a fiftyish blonde in tennis clothes.

"Watch it, bud," she said angrily.

Zalman righted himself and tried to look around. He knew the falsetto was getting away, fading into the hungry throng, and once the squeaky kidnapper slipped away . . . He thought he saw a flash of pale blue behind him, but he couldn't move; he was trapped at the deli counter.

Quickly, Zalman dumped the plastic container of Chinese chicken salad on the floor, spreading it as wide as he could. He made sure to slop some on the snarky tennis hen.

The crowd around the counter squealed and backed off. The blonde gave him a sharp poke with her elbow.

"You jerk," she said disdainfully.

A clear space opened up as the crowd tried to avoid the greasy mess on the floor, and Zalman whipped around, broad-jumped over the chicken salad, and ran out the door.

At first he didn't see anything, but as he desperately scanned the front of Gelsons he caught a flash of blue as a tall figure in a jogging suit bolted into the parking garage.

Zalman ran for the garage as fast as he could, hurdling a pair of twins in a stroller. Inside the gloomy garage he tore quickly up and down the rows of cars. Nothing. Not a sign. Finally he got a bright idea, ducked down, and looked along the floor underneath the cars. At the end of a row, he saw a man in pale blue crouching behind a tire, his back to Zalman.

Zalman ran across the rows of cars as quietly as he could in his Gucci loafers. The man was still there, hiding.

Zalman came up behind him and popped him one on the back of the head. "Okay, pal, where's Brenda?" he growled as he popped the guy in blue a second time.

BLOODY MARY

"Ow-ow-ow," the guy moaned when he saw Zalman standing over him. "Oh, damn it all to hell!"

It was chinless Bertie, Annabelle Forrester's weak-link boyfriend.

"You heard me, tough guy, where's the girl?" Zalman snapped as he drew back his fist to give Bertie another well-deserved punch.

Bertie cowered on the floor, his hands over his head. "Okay, okay, please don't hit me again, Mr. Zalman! I'm sorry! I didn't mean it!"

"You didn't mean it! You didn't mean to kidnap a twelve-year-old girl? You didn't mean to follow me around, hiding in doorways like a junior high school pimp? I oughta—" Zalman cuffed him again.

"I wasn't following you, and I didn't kidnap Brenda," Bertie whined miserably. "It was all a lie. I don't have her, I never did."

"C'mon . . ."

"It's the truth, Mr. Zalman, swear to God! After Doris was murdered, Annabelle and I were talking, and she said Doris must have given you the Rubyola formula for safekeeping. Doris trusted you; at least, that's what Annabelle thought."

"Annabelle planned this?" Zalman asked slowly.

"No, no, it was all my idea. Annabelle doesn't know, I swear it! I did it on my own. I figured if I could get the secret formula for the Rubyola, I'd be rich and then Annabelle would like me better. She just goes out with me because she thinks I'm harmless," Bertie said sadly. "I'm a real man, I have feelings, but she doesn't take me seriously. I don't have Brenda. I don't have anything. I'm a zero, a nothing, a cipher, a hopeless case. . . ."

"Get up, you idiot, and stop sniveling!" Zalman snapped. "Stop feeling sorry for yourself." He reached into Bertie's pocket, took out the sheet of yellow legal paper, and tore it up. "There, that make you feel better?"

"But that's . . ." Bertie said, his eyes following the scraps of paper floating to the oily floor of the garage.

"That's a bunch of high school chemistry crapola my secretary scribbled down," Zalman said. "You don't have Brenda, I don't have the secret of the Rubyola, so we're even. Now, get out of here, kid. You bother me."

"I can go? Really? You're letting me go?"

"Who wants you, idiot? Beat it before I lose my temper," Zalman barked. "And you want some free advice? Forget about Annabelle. You two ain't fated to be mated."

Bertie scrambled up off the floor and backed away, then turned and ran like hell away from Jerry Zalman and out of Century City.

Zalman stood in the gloom and watched Bertie run. "If you weren't following me, then who the hell's been hanging around outside my office in a trench coat?" Zalman mumbled thoughtfully as he went to the Mercedes.

ZALMAN DROVE BACK TO THE OFFICE, CLEANED UP, AND drank a glass of mineral water. He was just sitting down at his desk when Jason Hanning burst into the office, frantically waving a sheaf of blue paper.

"Well?" Zalman asked. "What's up?"

Tyrone slouched in behind Jason and threw himself in the leather chair, an evil grin lurking behind his toothpick. "I melded," he said. "It was great."

"I got it," Jason said, fanning the blue pages on Zalman's desk like a winning hand at a hot Vegas table.

"Then you're supposed to say 'Eureka.' " Zalman scowled. "So? Don't keep it a secret, laddie buck. What have you got?"

Jason stared down at the blue pages on Zalman's desk. "I've got something, but I'm not quite sure what it is," he admitted. "I haven't had a real chance to look at it yet, Uncle Jerry. I just figured out on the way over that it was a clue."

Zalman looked at the papers. "My brilliant legal mind tells me these are the fabled Achenbach tests," he said.

"Brenda was going to score these. It's a fresh batch we collected from Dr. Pud last Friday. Brenda took 'em home and she had 'em stacked up by her computer."

"I remember," Zalman said. "I saw them when I went through her room right after Doris Henke got killed. So?"

"So when me and Tyrone were cruising for clues I saw the Achenbachs and thought, hey, better take these home with me and do 'em myself. Get 'em back to Dr. Pud as soon as possible. I got a business to run, and with Brenda out of commission, I'm losing money hand over fist," Jason said sadly. "But I looked at 'em in the car on the way over, and I think there's something funny going on. Something's weird about one of these tests."

Zalman took a closer look at the pile of Achenbachs. The front page was a list of questions that demanded written answers. He opened one of the Achenbachs and looked at the second page. Inside, the questions were multiple choice, requiring only that the parent choose zero, one, or two.

"Weird? Like what's weird?" Zalman asked. "By the way, you guys have any trouble getting into the Henke house?" he asked. "Didn't Thrasher have the place roped off?"

"Sure, he did." Jason grinned, nodding at Tyrone. "Ty, give Uncle Jerry the souvenir you picked up for him."

Tyrone lurched out of the chair, dug deep into the zippered pocket of his black leathers, pulled out a carefully folded strip of yellow plastic, and gleefully waved it over his head like a flag. It said CRIME SCENE —DO NOT ENTER in heavy black letters.

"Got this fuh you," Tyrone grunted as he flapped the yellow and black strip in the air.

"Sorry I asked." Zalman laughed, shaking his head. "Save it for Marie; she likes collectible stuff. Okay, so you got into the house and you bagged these Achenbachs. Show me what's weird about 'em."

Jason bent over the Achenbachs on Zalman's desk. "Look at this," he said slowly as he pointed at the double folded blue paper. "Inside is this checklist? The parent is supposed to rate the kid on a scale of zero to two by answering these questions."

Zalman leaned over Jason's shoulder and looked carefully at the Achenbach. " 'Confused or in a fog,' " he read. "Hell, I feel like that all the time."

"It's the stress of the modern world," Jason said. "But look here." He pointed at one of the tests. "This one was on the top of the pile, catty-corner and upside down. I think Brenda put it that way on purpose."

"What makes you think that, Jason? Sounds a little thin to me," Zalman said doubtfully.

"Uh-uh," Jason said with certainty. "Not if you knew Brenda like I know Brenda. She's very neat, orderly. Everything in her room has to be at right angles."

"Her room was messy when I was in it," Zalman said slowly. "There were CDs all over the floor."

"Right! Right!" Jason said. "That's not like her, either. She's compulsive, and compulsive people have to have things in a particular order. Brenda has to have everything at right angles. She'd never leave a piece of paper catty-corner. It'd be an impossibility for her. She's been working on her klepto traits with Dr. Pud, but very often, when you begin to control one compulsion, the anxiety spills out into another area. See, the feelings of early loss and abandonment have to go somewhere and—"

"Never mind the ten-cent analysis, save it for a term paper. Just tell me what's funny about this Achenbach, will ya? I'm losing patience in a big way."

"I'm getting to it," Jason said. "The parent circled these numbers here, you can see that. But what about this? These circled letters in the copy aren't part of the test. Besides, the parent's answers are in number two lead pencil, and these circled letters are in pen. Brenda circled these letters, then left the Achenbach in a weird position for me to find. I know she did."

"Great, suppose it is a message. What does it mean? Do we have to send for a decoder ring? Soak this in lemon juice overnight? Hot vinegar? What, Jason? Tell Uncle Jerry, okay?" Zalman said.

"I don't know yet," Jason said impatiently. "The circled letters are B and A and L. It's a message from Brenda, I'm sure of it, but I don't know what it is. What do you think, Uncle Jerry? What does B-A-L mean?" Jason asked.

Zalman shrugged. "Doesn't mean a thing to me. B-A-L, huh?" He peered down at the circled letters.

"You guys got it all wrong," Tyrone advised from the depths of his chair. "Turn it around. Sherlock

Holmes did that in 'The Secret Weapon' and it worked for him."

"That's Marie's favorite story," Zalman said as he turned the letters over in his mind. "About Dr. Tobel and the bombsight. BAL, BLA, ALB, LAB . . ."

"Lab? Lab, like laboratory?" Jason asked slowly. "You think . . ."

"Sure," Zalman reasoned. "Has to be. Happy Henke was a chemist, an inventor, so he had some place where he did his inventing, right? Lots of retorts and vials and electric sparks and arcing—"

" 'It's alive! It's alive!' " Tyrone howled in a pretty good Dr. Frankenstein imitation.

Zalman winced and looked at his watch. "Marie and McCoy oughta be back any minute now with Bloody Mary. We can ask her what she knows about Happy's lab. But meanwhile, I gotta take care of the paying customers. *Albert!*" he yelled.

Albert Moreau stuck his head meekly into the office. "Yes, Mr. Zalman?" he asked.

"This is your lucky day, my son," Zalman informed the temp benignly. "Get on the horn and call Mr. Huston back, the writer I was just talking to? Tell him I'll straighten out the mess at Paramount first thing in the morning. If he's still unhappy, soothe him. You know how to soothe, don't you, Albert?"

Albert smiled knowingly. "Sure, I do. Just put your lips together and lie," he said.

"Very good, Albert. You'll go far in this town. Tell him you saw his last picture, it was great, he's always been your favorite writer, and he's underrated. Unsuccessful writers love to hear that they're underrated. Get it?"

"I sure do, Mr. Zalman." Albert Moreau smiled. "Ego massage is my speciality. Anything else you want me to do, just ask," he said as he went back to his desk. "This is so exciting, Mr. Zalman! I just love it here!"

Zalman heard Albert pick up the phone and start chattering away as if he'd been born to schmooze.

Zalman lay back in his chair and stared at the ceiling. He was beginning to get an idea, he could feel it reaching for him with damp, unpleasant tentacles, but his reverie was interrupted a few minutes later when Dickie Willet, the rumpled reporter from the *L.A. Zone*, floated into the office on an alcoholic cloud.

Willet looked as if he'd been slept in. He was wearing a Burberry raincoat that had seen better days in early 1958, torn jeans, and dirty Nikes.

"So, Mr. Zalman? You got a story for the press?" Willet said, pushing his stingy-brimmed fedora back on his head as if Perry White had sent him after a hot lead for the *Daily Planet*. "You running a day-care center now?" He grinned blearily, waving at Jason and Tyrone. "Your business dropping off since the murder?"

Tyrone let out a very low but very distinct growl.

"Never mind about my business dropping off, Willet. My business is none of your business," Zalman snapped. "And what the hell are you dressed up for? The high school play? Get out of my office. *Albert!* Give Willet a press release. That's it for you, Willet. Out," he said.

"C'mon, Zalman, you gotta gimme a break!" Willet whined. "Those TV guys get all the good stuff first!"

"Hey! Did you give my client a break with the Bloody Mary tag you hung on her?" Zalman snarled. "Poor girl, she's in jail; you're breaking her heart. Bloody Mary—you think she's ever gonna live that down?"

"Some guy in the art department put in the drops of blood; it wasn't me," Willet claimed.

"You're a lying weasel, Willet," Zalman said. "But what can I do? Y'know, it ain't the freedom of the press that bothers me; it's the improvisation of the press. Have a drink. You look like you could use one," he told the reporter, waving at the bar.

"Hey, Zalman, you're okay," Willet said as he stalked over to the bar and poured himself a double shot of Johnnie Walker Black. "Brrrrr!" he said as he chugged it down. "Need a little pick-me-up. Late night hanging around the jail. Gimme her story straight, I'll do right by the little lady. It's a slow news day, so if you got something hot, give it to me first. I'll turn Bloody Mary Rose into Snow flippin' White." He grinned, pouring himself another shot. "Believe you me."

Zalman was about to say something rude to Dickie Willet when he heard the door to the outer office open. Rutherford and Chester bounded in, barking and snapping playfully at each other's tails. They quickly gave the room a good nosing, then settled down on the couch and began to groom each other. Marie, McCoy, and Mary Rose followed the dogs into the room and flopped down wherever they could find a seat.

Mary Rose perched on the arm of the couch. She looked pale, but she was demurely dressed in the navy blue suit and pearls Zalman had specified.

"You like the outfit?" Marie asked. "I tried to imagine what Harriet Nelson would wear if she were playing the Nuremberg trials."

"That's off the record, Willet," Zalman snapped. "Out, out, out! Grab another drink and go wait with young Albert," he said.

"C'mon, lemme interview her," Willet said, leering at Mary Rose. "It's my job!"

"And my job is to keep you away from her, especially after what happened last night," Zalman said. "Albert," he called. "What's up?"

"The guy at Paramount's still at lunch," Albert complained. "I've left word and I'm on hold for Mr. Huston."

Zalman couldn't remember telling Albert to call the kid at Paramount, but what the hell. He was showing initiative. "Terrific. Where's Esther, anyway?"

"She went to pick up a snack tray from Le Croque," Albert said. "And it sounds delicious! But don't worry, I'm holding down the fort."

"Thank God, food," Willet mumbled. "I haven't eaten in days. . . ."

"There's some sandwiches over there, Willet," Zalman said, pointing at the bag The Diner had delivered. Despite himself, he felt sorry for the reporter, though he couldn't figure out why. Dickie Willet was a no-talent loser and a complete yold. "Whatsamatter, don't they pay you at the *Zone*? Eat something and stop moaning, for God's sake. Just get out of my office."

Willet pounced on the sack of sandwiches and fled into the outer office, mumbling hungrily to himself.

Zalman slammed the door behind him. "All right, kiddies," he said as he went back behind his desk and surveyed his assembled troops. "We don't have much time. Tyrone. Get up and give Mary Rose a seat."

Grudgingly, Tyrone gave his seat to Mary Rose, then sat down on the floor.

Mary Rose took the chair and crossed her long legs carefully. "Ah'm so humiliated," she said, twining a long strand of red hair in her fingers. "Jail! Ah'll never live it down, never!"

"Trust me," Zalman told her. "If I have my way, you'll be a heroine. Plus, I may be able to make you some money."

"Marie told me about the TV movie idea," Mary

Rose said. "Ah think Bernadette Peters would be perfect for me. We have the same hair."

"Never mind that right now," Zalman told her. "I got other fish to fry with you. First, I want you to answer some questions. And another thing, I got Willet off your back this time, but sooner or later you're going to have to face the press—cameras, lights, microphones—so get ready for it."

"The press? Ah hadn't thought of that," she moaned. "This is awful!"

"Be brave. Remember, if we're gonna sell your story as a TV movie, you'll have to come across as the wronged woman, the tragic heroine. Read Esther's press release so you can get your character straight. Be vulnerable, be sincere, and keep your mouth shut. Now attend to my words. Did Happy Henke have a secret office? A lab? Some little room somewhere?"

Mary Rose began to cry. "Oh, Happy," she said. "How could you be dead? You were so full of life!"

"Mary Rose, there's no time for eulogies," Zalman said firmly. "What about the lab? Huh?"

Mary Rose stared off through the window as if Beverly Drive had been magically transformed into a picture window into the past. "Ah thought Happy loved me, but now ah know he loved his work more. Dean helped me to see that."

Zalman glowered at McCoy who elaborately stared off into a corner of the room, whistling soundlessly. "How noble. Mary Rose, every second counts. A young girl's life is at stake."

"Good dialogue, Jerry," Marie snorted.

Zalman glared at her, hoping Mary Rose would cut to the chase. But no luck. Mary Rose continued her aimless nattering.

"He said he'd divorce Doris," the redhead cried. "But he lied to me. He never meant to divorce her; it was all a cruel deception. All he really wanted was to make his gems. It was the Rubyola he cared about, not me," she said, fingering her long red hair. "He used to stare at my hair for hours. He took hundreds of pictures of my hair! Hundreds! At first ah thought it was kinky, but Happy told me my hair was exactly the color he wanted for the Rubyola. Ah don't think he loved me at all! Just my hair! He just wanted to create the perfect faux gemstone, and that's all he dreamed of, day and night. He'd invented the Diamette and the Emerelle, and they were the most important faux gems since the zircon! Once he'd created the Rubyola, the perfect stone that would be affordable to women everywhere, his place in faux gem history would be assured! That's what he used to tell me."

Zalman couldn't take it any more. "The lab! What about the lab?" he yelled. "Tell me about the lab!"

Mary Rose was startled into a momentary silence. "He had a lab in a warehouse downtown," she said softly. "Nobody knew about it but Happy and me."

"Nobody?" Zalman asked slowly. There was that idea again, wrapping its arms around his brain.... "You sure?"

"Well, ah don't think anybody else knew," Mary Rose said. "Happy said it was our secret."

"I bet he lied," McCoy said jealously.

"We'd meet there sometimes when Happy was too busy to come to my place," Mary Rose said sadly. "Happy! How could you lie to me?" She started to cry again.

"Mary Rose, Mary Rose, where is the lab?" Zalman prompted. "C'mon dear, this is important. It could mean Brenda Henke's life!"

"Don't badger the poor girl," Marie said, trying to comfort Mary Rose.

"Well, downtown, like ah said." Mary Rose snuffled. "It's in a big warehouse around the corner from that new Museum of Contemporary Art on Grand. It's tucked away back there, but it's got this big old balcony running along it. Happy had a lab on the third floor, and ah guess he still does, because ah don't think Doris could've found out about it before she died. If that's the lab you're talking about, that's where it is.''

Marie jumped up out of her chair like a jill-in-the-box. "Let's go!" she said, her eyes bright in anticipation of the chase. "C'mon guys, let's beat it downtown. This is the good part!"

"Siddown, siddown. Not a chance," Zalman told her gruffly. "Me and McCoy work the danger side of the street. This could be rough going. I don't want a hair of your pretty little head—"

"What? I'll pop you one right in the snout, Jerry Zalman!" Marie said angrily. "Who fronted the bail money? Who did the legwork? I'm not gonna miss out on the fun after I've done all the shopping!"

"I'm telling you, you're not going downtown, and that's a fact! It's too dangerous for you! Matter of fact, it's too dangerous for me, but I don't have a choice. There's not a chance in this lifetime I'm letting you go with me and that's it," Zalman fired back.

ZALMAN PULLED THE MERCEDES OUT OF HIS PARKING space in the lot next door to his office and onto Beverly Drive. Traffic was fierce, and the post-shopping crush was a monstrous snarl of angry, sweating motorists.

Zalman sighed and pounded the steering wheel helplessly. In the City of Angels, rush hour never ended, and it was an aggravating tick buried deep in the hide of longtime Angelenos who could still recall the city's salad days, that receding piece of the past before L.A. became a megalopolis.

Every street strained under the weight of the ever-increasing inhuman traffic, and Zalman figured that if you stacked up all the cars in L.A. they'd probably reach Neptune. Maybe Pluto.

"Hoo, boy," McCoy hooted as Zalman rammed the Mercedes down Wilshire Boulevard through the packed streets toward downtown L.A. "I don't think I've ever seen Marie so mad before, have you, Jer?"

Zalman said nothing.

"Boy, it's pretty amazing she can yell so loud, don't you think, Jer?"

Zalman said nothing.

"I mean, being as she's such a little person and all. Got some bellow on her, I'll say that. Guess she gets it from her father, huh, Jer? Wouldn't you say yelling loud is probably an inherited trait, like brown eyes?"

"Don't push your luck, Dean," Zalman told him. "I'm not letting Marie get in any danger. I love her too much for that. Besides, this is man's work, right?"

McCoy said nothing.

"Look," Zalman reasoned. "There's only one way it can be. Annabelle Forrester disguised herself as a man, robbed Le Croque with Tony, and killed Happy Henke. Doris killed Tony to protect her daughter. Then Bertie killed Doris."

"Why?" McCoy asked.

"Look, the guy's a total idiot, but he's in love with Annabelle. Doris wanted Annabelle to hook up with Prince Charles."

"He's taken."

"Don't quibble, McCoy. Bertie wanted Doris out of the way. There's another possibility, too," Zalman said. "It's possible Annabelle killed Doris."

"You think she'd kill her own mother?" McCoy asked.

"It's a cold world out there, and a cold lady like Annabelle can do without a pain-in-the-ass mother like Doris, but she can't do without money."

"Sad but true," McCoy agreed. "Still . . ."

"I'm telling you, McCoy, she's mean. Annabelle Forrester has a beautiful face, but there's a black hole where her heart oughta be. She's empty inside."

"How do you know?" McCoy asked curiously.

"I'll tell you how I know. She kissed me. That's how I know."

"Did you tell Marie?"

"Of course I didn't tell Marie! Do you think I'm an idiot?"

"So tell me about the kiss," McCoy asked with interest.

"In all modesty, I admit I've kissed a few girls in my career," Zalman said. "And even though Annabelle Forrester is as pretty as they come, kissing her was like—"

"C'mon, Jer. Just between us boys."

"It was like kissing a 'sixty-two Buick," Zalman said. "Annabelle's got a heart like an engine block and lips to match. She's a tough muffin, Dean. There's a big estate involved, and Brenda Henke is standing square in the middle, right between Annabelle Forrester and all those buckeroos. I'm betting that Brenda knows where Happy hid the formula for the Rubyola, but there's another point: if Brenda dies, Annabelle's bound to inherit. She'll be the only one left!"

"Especially if she's killed everybody else," McCoy pointed out.

"Look, Dean, there'll be a few unpleasant moments at the lab, but we can handle it. We have to get Brenda away from Annabelle in one piece," Zalman said as he shook his head in disbelief. "A twelve-year-old girl who thinks she's Mary Astor! That's gonna be hard enough. I can't have Marie to worry about."

McCoy said nothing.

"Look at it my way," Zalman said in a plea for understanding. "I couldn't let Marie come with us. She'd just get in the way."

"Maybe so," McCoy agreed mildly. "But you shouldn't have told her that, Jer. That's why she was yelling so loud." McCoy poked his ear with an exploratory finger. "I think my eardrum is bustovated."

Zalman pounded the steering wheel in frustration. "I'm serious, Dean! There's a killer on the loose, and let's not underestimate her just because she's a beautiful woman. We're supposed to be brave, resourceful. All that silly rough-and-ready stuff. And the most important thing of all, we got our reputations to protect."

McCoy shifted uncomfortably in the passenger seat. "Speak for yourself, Jer. I got no reputation. But I agree with you about Marie. That lab is no place for a woman. If Annabelle's as mean as you think she is—"

"If only we could trust Thrasher to handle it," Zalman said. "We might have to face tough stuff!"

"I hate tough stuff," McCoy said. "But you know Thrasher won't believe you. Besides, the old weasel figures he's got Mary Rose nailed."

"Why does he hate me? I make a good living, I'm a nice guy," Zalman wondered as he barreled through a yellow light. Yellow lights didn't count in L.A.

"He hates you because he's Marie's father and she loves you. You oughta watch more talk shows, Jer. Find out about psychology. Hey, we can handle it, right?"

"Right," Zalman said.

"Piece of cake. Still, I wish you'da let me bring Chester," McCoy said. "Chester just loves to bite people. He thinks it's his duty as a Doberman."

"I've had enough drool to last me a lifetime, Dean. I can't take any more. Besides, I told you what these seats cost. Goddamn Rutherford ripped them all to hell with his claws the day we took the goddamn monkey to the goddamn airport. That's seven hundred bucks you're sitting on, and I'm not ready to try for double or nothing!"

"What are you gonna do, take Wilshire all the way downtown?" McCoy asked, ignoring Zalman's complaints. "It'll take forever."

"Do I have a choice? If we get stuck on the freeway at this time of the day, we'll orbit the city forever, like a failing sputnik," Zalman said. "Brenda'll die of old age."

"They still call 'em sputniks, Jer?"

"Figure of speech, Dean."

Thirty minutes later Zalman pulled up in front of the grungy warehouse Mary Rose had described and surveyed the decrepit building with unadulterated dismay.

It was a sad six-story structure stained with a few peeling egg-shaped splotches that used to be paint, and it looked as if it housed runaways, sweatshops, the odd drug dealer, and a struggling artist or two.

A chipped iron balcony ran along the length of the second floor, but it was much too high to grab on to without a ladder. The ambience was strictly steerage.

"This looks pretty slimy," Zalman observed. "Just the way for a bon vivant like *moi* to pass a pleasant evening."

"It'll be dark soon," McCoy pointed out helpfully. "I told you we shoulda brought Chester. At least we coulda left him to guard the car."

"Too late now. Let's take a walk around the building," Zalman said as he got out of the Mercedes and stared at the ugly streets apprehensively. "Reconnoiter."

"We better figure out how we're gonna get in, too," McCoy said, staring up at the iron balcony. "That puppy's way too high to grab."

"I didn't think about that," Zalman admitted. "Also, I didn't think about the fact that it's nasty downtown after dark."

"That's my department." McCoy grinned, pulling open his Levi jacket to reveal a stainless-steel .38 tucked in his waistband. "I brought a friend, just in case."

"Jesus, Dean!" Zalman snapped, looking around to see if anyone had noticed McCoy's flash of weaponry. "That's illegal! That's a concealed weapon!"

"Damn right it's concealed," McCoy said. "What the hell good is a weapon if you don't conceal it? If everybody knows you got a gun, you lose the element of surprise, Jer."

"Thrasher catches you with that, you're in the soup, pal."

"I got a sharp lawyer," McCoy said. "He'll get me off." He twirled the pistol on his forefinger like Roy Rogers. "Nice, huh? It's a Smith Chief's Model. Just got it."

Zalman shook his head. "It's a wonder you've survived this long, Dean. You're ready for the nineties, all right. The eighteen-nineties. Put it away."

McCoy tucked the gun back in his waistband, and slowly they walked around the big warehouse.

It was an anonymous building with dirty windows like vacant eyes staring out of the upper floors at the glitz and glass going up across town. The warehouse took up most of a city block. There was a front entrance next to a grimy alleyway, but the door was padlocked. There was a pair of roll-up garage doors at the front and another pair at the back, but both of them were made of heavy steel plates, and they were padlocked as well.

Zalman stared at the streets around him. It was getting late, and the office workers who inhabited the high-rises during the day were hitting the high road back to the West Side, back to the San Fernando Valley, abandoning the dark, downtown city to the homeless, the illegals, the bombed, the crazed, the victims, the wacked, the winos, and the rest of the tattered leftovers who crawled out every night and made their way to the corner of Jesus Saves and Open All Night for a hot cuppa charity soup and a stale bologna sandwich.

"Every city is two cities," Zalman said as he watched the cars rocketing through the streets, windows up, doors locked, solitary drivers tense and tight-lipped in the harsh glare of the sodium streetlights.

McCoy snorted in agreement. "Peel back the rug, you see a lotta people get swept under every morning and scurry out every night," he said absently as he looked at the building. "Well, there ain't no open doors, so the first thing we gotta do is get inside. Front entrance is locked, so the way I see it, we can break down one of those steel doors," he said, pointing down the street toward the roll-up garage doors. "Or we can figure out something else."

"We can't break down the doors," Zalman said, "unless we nuke 'em or ram 'em with a moving van. Got any other ideas?"

"Yup," McCoy said. "Follow me."

McCoy led Zalman back around the side of the building into the fetid alleyway by the barred front entrance. The alley smelled of cold grease, old sneakers, and years of broken wine bottles.

McCoy stood quietly for a moment until his eyes adjusted to the darkness, and then he peered into the gloom. "Say, pal," he said. He studied a pile of cardboard scattered on the ground next to a row of trash cans, then gave it a gentle nudge with the silver toe of his boot. "Anybody home?"

The dank pile of cardboard shifted, and a dirt-covered face that looked a lot like a fist stared out at them with undisguised anger. "Piss off," the face said delicately and disappeared back underneath its shelter of Lady Kenmore cardboard and assorted burlap bags.

"You wanna make ten bucks?"

The cardboard shifted again. "I wanna win the lottery and retire to the Riviera is what the hell I want," it said hollowly from deep within its shelter. "I wanna weekend in sunny Spain with a famous movie star. I want—"

"Okay, okay, we get the picture. But do you wanna make ten bucks? That's the sixty-four-dollar question," McCoy said again.

The face popped out, shiny brown eyes blinking like a clever rat's. "Sure I do. I'm a wage slave just like everybody else. But I got standards. What do gotta do for it?" the voice croaked with the lustrous patina of a million packs of unfiltered Camels. "Nothing naughty."

"Perish the thought," Zalman said.

"Two things," McCoy began.

"Two things, twenty bucks. One thing, ten bucks. Take yer pick."

"Everybody's a negotiator these days," McCoy said. "Okay, okay. First. You know a way into this building?"

"Mebbe I know someone who does. What's number two?" A hand popped out of the mass of cardboard and snapped its nicotine-stained fingers impatiently. "Pay as you go, pardner. No VISA, no MasterCard, and we don't take American Express."

Zalman peeled off a ten and extended it warily toward the hand. The hand snapped up the bill like a peckish 'gator and stuffed it under the mound of burlap and into the lower depths of its garments.

"Number two is you gotta watch for the cops once me and my pal here get inside," McCoy said.

"I don't know about that. We better wait for Pokey," the voice said craftily. "Mebbe Pokey knows how to get inside. But if you wanna talk to Pokey, it's gonna cost you extra."

"Somehow I already knew that," Zalman said. "Tell you what, sport, this is your lucky day. Help us out here and you'll be rewarded handsomely."

"The hell with that, I want cash!"

Zalman peeled off a twenty. "Help us out, make yourself useful, and there's another twenty in it for you when we're through."

The cardboard and burlap shifted quickly, and a woman of about fifty scrambled up off the ground, her monkey-face grin as wide as Niagara Falls, her black hair as spiky as a petulant Medusa's. "It's a deal, buster," she said. "Name's Edna Cudahay. You want to get into that building, you want to be talking to Pokey. Be along any minute now," Edna said. "Got a smoke?"

McCoy forked over a pack of Luckies, and a few minutes later another woman came marching into the alleyway, a pair of galvanized buckets rattling in her hands. She stopped dead when she saw that Edna had company. "Whatcha got here, Edna?" she asked suspiciously, staring back and forth between Zalman and McCoy.

"Pokey, it's our lucky night. We got a pair of gentlemen what's got folding money," Edna Cudahay told her partner. "Gimme the buckets, I'll go water 'em down."

"What's in the buckets?" Zalman asked curiously as Pokey handed them to Edna.

"Good haul," Edna observed as she took the buckets over to a faucet in the wall and sprayed them with water.

"Pokey's my name, snails're my game. I'm Pokey Snails." The woman grinned. "I'm a snail rancher."

Zalman looked at McCoy and shrugged. "Snail rancher?"

"Escargot, the food of the nineties! *Helix aspera*. Snails! Just like you got in the garden, just like you pay twenty bucks a plate for in a fancy-schmancy restaurant. I collect 'em off the freeway median strips, under the bridges, in front of them snitzy apartment buildings around Bunker Hill. Flush 'em out good for a month with cornmeal, sell 'em to fancy-shmancy restaurants."

"Snails? Yuck," McCoy said with a shiver. "I'd never eat a damn snail. Only a damn fool would eat a damn snail."

"Rich people like to eat weird food. They think it's classy," Pokey Snails observed. "Now me, I couldn't agree with you more. They taste like a steel-belted

Goodyear radial. Besides, they're my pals. But it's a living."

"Bucket of snails is what we got here." Edna laughed, rattling the buckets.

"Lay off, Edna," Pokey said sharply. "Don't you crack them shells! Them's prime eating snails, but not with no cracked shells. Now, what's the deal here, mister?" she asked Zalman.

"These two wanna get into the warehouse. They got cash," Edna said, pulling another Lucky from McCoy's pack.

Pokey Snails stared doubtfully at Zalman. "I dunno about that. I got my snail ranch in there," she said. "Hidden in a crawl space. Anything goes wrong and I lose the ranch, me and Edna are in deep poop. So you want in, it's gonna cost you."

"Let me put it this way, Pokey," Zalman told her. "Money is not a problem here. Getting into the warehouse, that's the only problem we have right now, okay? You got any ideas?"

Pokey Snails frowned. "Mebbe I do. Me, I slip in through a vent and wiggle into the crawl space where I got the snails. I'm smaller than I look. You could fit," she told Zalman, looking him up and down. "But not him. He's too big."

"He's gotta go, too," Zalman said. "He's the muscle."

"That's what I thought. Well, tell you what. I just happen to know where there's a Dipsy Dumpster ain't been locked down tonight. You guys push it over to the balcony, hop up on top, and go in through a window. Won't even get that pretty jacket dirty," Pokey said, fingering Zalman's lapel. "But you want in, it'll cost you a hundred now, a hundred later."

Zalman sighed and reached for his money clip.

Ten minutes later, Zalman, McCoy, and Edna were rolling the half-empty Dumpster up the street toward the alley next to the warehouse. The noise was tremendous, the steel wheels grinding on the pavement with the explosive crash of ten sticks of dynamite. Pokey Snails had refused to push and was standing to one side guarding her precious buckets of snails and watching the show.

"When this is over, I'm going back to grad school, make a mid-life career switch," Zalman puffed as he heaved his shoulder into the filthy steel Dumpster. "I can't take the glamour of the legal profession much longer. The high life is starting to wear me down."

"I know what you mean, Jer," McCoy said. "You thought it was all going to be sunglasses and martinis, didn't you? Long summer days reading scripts by the pool. And now all of a sudden you find out life is just a—"

"Bucket of snails," Zalman panted.

"You two guys complain too much," Edna told them. "You don't stop sniveling, I'm upping my price to three hundred smackerrooskis."

"Just an observation, Edna. Nothing personal," Zalman told her, grunting.

But as they approached the corner, the huge Dumpster swiveled and threatened to roll away from them, back down Grand and, with any luck, all the way through the orchestra section of the Music Center and out the other side into Chinatown.

"Hey!" Edna yelled sharply as she struggled to control her end of the Dumpster. "Put your damn shoulder into it, will ya? Pair a goddamn shirkers is what we got here, Pokey."

Pokey Snails coughed out a laugh as the Dumpster bucked like a mule and started to roll back down the street again. "Grab it, cowboys!" she yelled.

Zalman was hanging on by his fingernails. "It's getting away from me!" he groaned. "Dean, push dammit!"

BLOODY MARY

"I got it, I got it," McCoy puffed as he muscled the Dumpster back on the right track. "Say, Edna, what's a nice girl like you . . ."

Edna groaned and rolled her eyes. "My first husband—that was Timmy—he put the skids on my life," she said. "He was a big guy, just like you. Always wore lotsa fancy cowboy junk, too," she said pointedly as she stared down at McCoy's silver-toed boots. "Just like you. I was just a slip of a girl in Sunday school. One night after organ practice he—"

"Okay, okay, I'm sorry I asked," McCoy said as they painfully shoved the Dumpster into position in the alley. "Now, Edna," he said. "Me and Jerry gotta go inside. This is where you and Pokey get to be the lookouts."

"Lookouts, my aunt Fanny," Edna said, her eyes glittering like steelies. "You guys gonna boost something, me and Pokey want a fair cut. Just what's fair is all I ask. Nothing more, nothing less. Me and Pokey got our living to make." Her mouth was set in a stern line as she folded her arms underneath her burlap shawl. It was clear that Edna Cudahay would not be denied.

"Be reasonable, Edna," Zalman begged. "We're not thieves! Far from it!"

"How far?" Edna asked. "I just want what's fair, what's coming to me. My second husband—that was Billy—he always told me to get what's fair. You guys gonna boost something, we want a fair cut. Otherwise, we're gone."

"Okay," Zalman capitulated. He had no choice. He knew if he didn't soothe Edna, they'd never get inside. He remembered what Albert Moreau had said about soothing: "Just put your lips together and lie."

"You're right, Edna," Zalman said. "We are gonna boost something. It's a jewel heist, see. We're after the most famous gem of the Orient, the Sultan's Eye.

It's the fifth largest ruby in the world, and it lies hidden within these very walls."

'But it's got a curse on it," McCoy improvised. "And a woman's life is in danger."

"And if we don't recapture the Sultan's Eye and return it to— "

"—to the sultan's beautiful daughter—" McCoy said, warming to the theme.

"Yeah, that's right. If we don't return it to the sultan's beautiful daughter, she'll die and we'll all be doomed. You, too, ladies."

"Me!" Edna squawked. "What do I got to do with the Sultan's Eyeball?"

"We didn't do nothing!" Pokey said. "Just tending our snails."

"Guilt by association, Cudahay," Zalman said wisely. "So you and Pokey'll get what's fair, but you gotta be the lookouts."

"Or you're doomed," McCoy added.

"I wish we'd never met you guys," Edna said. "I think you're a pair of wacko shirkers. But I don't wanna get involved with no Sultan's Eyeball curse," she said thoughtfully. "That's for damn sure. Okay, me and Pokey'll stay here and be the lookouts. But it'll cost you."

"I knew it would," Zalman said. "We pay another two bills on the way out, take it or leave it."

"It's took," Edna said.

"I knew we could depend on you."

"You mess with my snails and I'll kill you," Pokey Snails warned. "I got over five thousand head jammed into that crawl space, and I got my living to make."

"We won't hurt your snails," Zalman promised.

"Better damn not," Pokey mumbled.

McCoy climbed up on the lid of the Dumpster and gave Zalman a hand up. "Okay, Jer. You get up on my shoulders."

"Oh, God, I hate this. . . ."

"C'mon, it's a lead-pipe cinch. If you stand on my shoulders, you can reach the bottom of that balcony, easy. You worm up there, then give me a hand up, and we're in. Edna, you and Pokey stay here. You see the cops, you see anything that looks weirder than usual, bang that garbage can lid on the Dumpster good and hard. We'll hear it."

"I hope we do," Zalman said as he struggled up onto McCoy's shoulders. "Otherwise, we're all doomed."

IT WAS A STRUGGLE, BUT THEY MADE IT ONTO THE BALCONY. Zalman had a tough time giving McCoy a hand up; McCoy was twice Zalman's height and a lot heavier. But those endless boring laps Zalman did in his pool finally paid off, and he yanked his pal up onto the second floor balcony without dislocating either of his shoulders.

"There's gotta be an easier way to make a living," Zalman said as they cautiously worked their way around the building on the rickety balcony until McCoy found a half-open window. "This is not my idea of fun. We get caught, we're going to jail, Dean."

"You can handle it, Jer. You're as tough as they come. That's what you keep telling me," McCoy said absently as he searched through his pockets.

"I can't be trusted. I lie a lot. On the other hand,

maybe the cops'll shoot us in the back and we'll die in agony. Or maybe this balcony will collapse and we'll swan-dive into the concrete."

"I bet our heads'll pop like rotten grapes when we hit the pavement." McCoy grinned wickedly. *"Splat!"* he said as he searched for the folding buck knife he always carried.

"Hurry up, will you, Dean?"

McCoy found his knife. "Gimme a minute and we'll be in," he said as he pried at the window frame, thick with fifty years of gummy paint. "Jer, you worry too much. We go in, bag Annabelle, and we're out." He popped open the window and stuck a long leg inside. "You're wrapped tighter'n a mummy. Lemme worry about the muscle part, okay? You're always telling me you're the brains of the outfit, so quit worrying and think," McCoy said as he disappeared inside. "Make a plan. Scheme. Tell me who's gonna take the Super Bowl. Do something constructive with all that brain power."

Zalman glowered and stuck an unlit cigar in his mouth so he'd have something to chew on. "You in?" he asked.

"In," McCoy said. "And the coast is clear. Follow me, Jer."

Zalman and McCoy made their way carefully through the second floor. They were in a sweatshop, and there were rows of sewing machines waiting peacefully for morning. Piles of cut garments were loaded on battered worktables; racks of finished clothing were shoved up against the walls.

"Mary Rose said it was on the third floor," Zalman told McCoy as they came to the fire door. They slipped silently up the staircase, dark and dirty and smelling of stale cigarette smoke and yesterday's lunch.

One flight up on the landing outside the door, McCoy put his finger to his lips and knelt down to peer through the crack underneath the door. He got up, opened the door slowly, and they went in.

They were in an artist's studio. On a low platform in the center of the room there was a gigantic set of concrete lawn furniture splattered with Day-Glo paint, and a pair of soft-sculpture dummies lounged on huge concrete chairs. The dummies were happily toasting a rubber dachshund on a long fork over a paper mâché barbecue complete with licking paper flames. They were wearing Bermuda shorts and beer-can hats and they had their heads thrown back and their mouths open, as if they were laughing.

"Fun in the sun?" McCoy whispered.

Zalman shook his head. "Hot dog," he suggested.

Zalman and McCoy slipped past the dummies, through the studio, and out the door at the other end of the room. Zalman tapped McCoy on the shoulder and pointed. There was a bright white light shining through a wall of glass bricks right in front of them.

"Let's go around the other way," McCoy said softly. "Maybe we'll be able to see something from the other side."

Zalman nodded, and they backtracked through the artist's studio, out the door, and down a long hallway.

At the end of the hallway there was a wide double door big enough to drive a VW bug through, but the door was closed. Zalman and McCoy crept closer to it, and as they approached, they could hear voices coming through the open transom over the big door.

"No, no, *no!*" Brenda Henke's voice said decisively. "I won't, won't, *won't!*"

There was a mumbled reply that Zalman couldn't understand.

"No, no, no!" Brenda snapped, her voice as clear and as sharp as a shard of glass slicing through a brand-new tire. "Not even if you . . ."

More indistinct mumbling.

"What do I get out of it?" Brenda asked craftily.

Zalman looked at McCoy. "It's Brenda, all right. You can take the girl out of Beverly Hills . . ." he whispered. "Twelve years old and she wants to make a deal with a killer."

"She should be running a network," McCoy whispered. He pointed at the open transom. "Climb on my shoulders, Zally. You can see what Annabelle's doing; then we burst in and make with the hero routine." McCoy knelt down on the floor and gestured to his shoulders. "Climb up, pal. I won't drop you."

"I wanted to be an acrobat, I woulda joined Circus Vargas," Zalman complained quietly as he clambered onto McCoy's shoulders. "But not me, I was too smart. I hadda go to law school."

"Quiet down," McCoy whispered as he clamped his big hands firmly around Zalman's ankles. Carefully balancing Zalman on his shoulders, McCoy stood up very, very slowly so Zalman could get a good look through the open transom.

Zalman peeked through a corner of the window. He could see Brenda Henke tied to a straight-backed chair in the middle of the room. She was wearing jeans and a Camp Beverly Hills sweat shirt, and her blond hair was no longer carefully marcelled. For the first time since she'd flounced into his office, Brenda Henke looked like a twelve-year-old kid, but she sure didn't sound like one.

"No, no, no!" Brenda shrilled at someone lurking in the shadows, someone wearing a long white coat. "I won't tell you and you can't make me! Nyah, nyah, nyah!"

Zalman looked around. It was Happy Henke's laboratory, all right. There was a long, scarred wooden worktable cluttered with vials and beakers, and there were shelves against one wall littered with glittering bottles of varicolored chemicals and soft, glowing powders. Another wall was lined with glass shelves on which brilliant gem specimens were displayed. Green malachite and royal purple amethyst, quartz crystals and endless varieties of beryl, turquoise, peridot, jasper, each one different but each one hot with the internal blush of rich, pure, perfect color.

The funny thing, Zalman realized, was that he had no idea if the gems on display were real or the product of Happy Henke's experiments in faux gemology. Were those diamonds or Diamettes? Emeralds or Emerelles? And was the secret of the precious Rubyola hidden in this room? The finest faux gem ever created? The faux gem that would glow with inner fires and yet would be affordable to women everywhere?

At the far end of the room there was a huge furnace with the name Verneuil stamped over its mouth in Art Nouveau letters. The furnace was alive with flames, a million bright sparks snapping like tiny snakes of fire, and alongside it lay a pile of chair legs and broken furniture that someone was using for kindling. Next to the furnace stood a metal table laden with thick ceramic rods.

"No! No! No!" Brenda cried at her captor. "It's not fair! I'm so bored here. I hate this place! I always hated this place," the girl wailed. "These dumb ropes are cutting me!"

"Quit complaining," a man's voice roared. "I haven't hurt you!"

Brenda shook her blond head, whipping her hair from side to side. "I'm not telling you where it is! I hate you! Meany!"

The man stepped out of the shadows, a look of supreme agony plastered across his face. "I can't stand it anymore!" Failin' Phalen shrieked, shaking his fist at Brenda. "You're driving me crazy!!

"Oops," Zalman said quietly. "I think we goofed, Dean."

"What do you mean, 'we'?" McCoy asked.

"I don't care!" Brenda said, struggling against her ropes. "I hate you! I hate you to bits!"

"Shut up, for God's sake," Phalen cried again, his doughy face twisted in pain. "I gotta think!"

"I want my kitty," Brenda cried. "Who's feeding my kitty? She's all alone at the house, my kitty. I want my kitty. I hate these clothes; they're all icky! I never wear sloppy stuff. I hate ugly clothes. I hate them! Hate, hate, hate them!"

"Tell me where the notes are!" Failin' Phalen cried. "I'll let you go, I swear it. All I want is the Rubyola! Tell me where Happy's notes are and I'll let you go."

Brenda shook her head back and forth, back and forth, back and forth, back and . . . "I won't, I won't, I won't!"

"Yaaagghh! I can't stand it! The notes, I gotta have the notes, you little monster."

"Won't, won't, won't! I hate you! It's because of you I'm an orphan!"

"You're better off!" Phalen cried in desperation. "You monster, I did you a big favor and this is how you repay me! You could be the richest little girl in Beverly Hills! Have anything you want! Tell me where the notes are; then I can make the Rubyola myself. C'mon, Brenda, don't make me hurt you!"

"You wouldn't dare," Brenda said emphatically. "Daddy always said you were a pipsqueak. Pipsqueak, pipsqueak, pipsqueak, pipsqueak . . ."

"Cut out that pipsqueak stuff!" Phalen howled. "I'm no—"

". . . pipsqueak, pipsqueak . . ."

"I don't blame him. I'm gonna kill her myself if she doesn't shut up," Zalman said.

"Who's in there?" McCoy whispered urgently. "Where's Annabelle? What's going on?"

BLOODY MARY

"It's not Anna . . . You're wiggling me. Quit that goddamn wiggling!" Zalman snapped.

"Not Annabelle? Who is it?" McCoy asked.

"It's Failin' Phalen."

"Phalen? That—"

"Pipsqueak! Neener, neener, neener!" Brenda screamed at her captor. "Neener, neener, neener, you pipsqueak!"

"I'm gonna kill you, honest to God!" Phalen howled.

"Hold on to my legs, goddammit, Dean, will you?" Zalman said as he felt himself start to fall. He tried to stay upright, but he couldn't hang on. Zalman teetered wildly on his precarious perch on top of McCoy, and as he began to fall forward he instinctively grabbed the transom for support.

Too late. His valiant efforts didn't help. Zalman lost his balance completely, and his legs thunked on the wooden door as McCoy made a last futile effort to steady him.

"What the hell's that?" Phalen howled from inside the room. "Who's there?"

Zalman lost his fingernail hold on the open transom, dropped on top of McCoy, and they both collapsed on the floor in a tangled heap.

"Ow!" McCoy said. "That hurt!"

Zalman struggled to get up as Failin' Phalen pulled open the door, but he got his head caught in McCoy's foot and they both fell down again.

"Oh, no," Phalen moaned. "Zalman! This is awful. Get up, will ya?"

"I'm trying," Zalman said, hoping to recapture his lost dignity. "Dean, get the hell off me!"

"I'm trying!" McCoy said.

Phalen yanked a .32 automatic out of the pocket of his white coat. "Now!" he yelled. "Do it now!"

McCoy got his boot out of Zalman's face, and the two men scrambled to their feet.

"Inside," Phalen said, waving the gun. "You're an attorney. Maybe you can get the little monster to shut up."

Zalman and McCoy trudged sheepishly into Happy Henke's lab.

"Ha!" Brenda said derisively. "Some big rescue."

"Shut up!" Failin' Phalen snarled.

"Yeah, shut up," McCoy said.

"I'd listen to them, if I was you," Zalman told her.

Brenda stuck her tongue out.

"You see what I have to put up with?" Phalen cried. "She's driving me crazy. The notes, kid, all I want is Happy's notes," he moaned. "I don't want to hurt you."

Brenda Bronx-cheered him.

Failin' Phalen couldn't take it anymore. Brenda's endless whining and shrill complaints had driven the entrepreneur over the edge of sanity and into a pit of madness known only by parents of preteen tykes. Phalen's eyes bugged out like those of a hyperthyroid frog. "I'll shut you up!" he howled as he swiveled his blue steel automatic toward Brenda.

"You wouldn't dare," she sneered as he raised the gun.

Zalman and McCoy realized that Brenda was wrong. Failin' Phalen would dare. Brenda had driven him to desperation, and unless they got the gun, little Miss Brenda was going to be plugged full of holes.

McCoy jumped for Phalen, and the two men scuffled briefly for the gun. McCoy knocked it out of Phalen's hand, and the gun went skittering across the floor and clunked hollowly against the wall.

"Get the kid, Jerry," McCoy cried as he dove headlong across the floor after Phalen's gun. "I'll take care of this."

But Doyle Dean McCoy was wrong. As he scrabbled for the gun on the floor, Failin' Phalen quickly wheeled around, grabbed a gigantic crystal from the worktable, jumped on McCoy, and slammed him over the head with it as hard as he could.

McCoy groaned heavily. The sound was thick and hard, and Zalman knew from the dull thunk of the rock on McCoy's noggin that his old pal was going down for the count. Worse, he'd be completely useless. McCoy slumped to the floor, his mouth open in surprise.

Failin' Phalen grabbed the gun off the floor and aimed it at Zalman's heart.

Zalman looked around the room. He'd figured that Annabelle Forrester kidnapped Brenda but he'd figured wrong. With McCoy out of the picture and Failin' Phalen holding a gun on him, Zalman wished he hadn't been so damn brave. Why me? Zalman asked himself. Why do these things always happen to me?

Failin' Phalen didn't waste any time. Like Zalman, he knew from the sound of the rock on McCoy's skull that the big lug wouldn't be cracking wise any time in the foreseeable future.

Brenda Henke was shrieking in the high-pitched howl of a bat in pain.

"Shut up!" Phalen roared in desperation. He fired off a round at the ceiling, but Brenda only yelled louder. "Shut her up," Phalen said, his face contorted in pain, "or I'm gonna kill her!"

Zalman held up a placating hand. "No problem, Maxie," he said jovially. He smiled again, showing Phalen lots of teeth. "Belt up, Brenda. Phalen's serious, and he's got a gun."

Brenda shook her head. "I won't, I won't, I—"

Zalman shrugged philosophically, yanked his handkerchief out of his pocket, and gagged Brenda with it. "It's for your own good," he told her. "Believe me."

"Thank God," Failin' Phalen sighed as Brenda's

deafening shrieks were muffled by Zalman's gag. "I couldn't take the noise. You have kids?"

"Not a chance," Zalman said.

"Me neither. Now I know why."

"Maxie, what're we gonna do about this?" Zalman asked, waving around the room. "Looks like we're in trouble. Got big problems."

Zalman thought he'd emphasize the "we" part of the setup. With McCoy and his strong-arm tactics temporarily out of the picture, Zalman knew that the next best thing was to get Failin' Phalen talking and keep him talking. Enter into prolonged negotiations.

Zalman wondered if Phalen was stupid enough to believe that this encounter fell under the umbrella of privileged communication, but it was his best shot. If he could play for time, cajole Failin' Phalen, maybe McCoy would wake up. Or maybe Phalen would do something stupid and Zalman could leap on him and get the gun. Zalman smiled again, hoping he looked friendly and professional, like a lawyer, not like a prisoner.

"I'm glad I found you, Maxie," Zalman said pleasantly as he searched in his pockets for his cigar case. He'd had one in his mouth a while ago, but it disappeared when he was rolling around on the floor with McCoy. Shame to waste a good cigar, he thought.

"Hey!" Failin' Phalen said sharply. "Hands out of your pockets, Zalman."

"Just looking for my cigars . . . Ah, here's my case," Zalman said, as if vying for the Mr. Congeniality title. "Have one?" he asked Phalen as he lit up.

"No, thanks," Phalen said disconsolately, staring down at McCoy. "Damn. This is a helluva mess."

"I thought we'd better talk," Zalman said smoothly. "That's why I'm here."

"Am I still your client?" Failin' Phalen said, a little peevishly.

"Maxie! What a question," Zalman sidestepped. "You know my reputation."

"Yeah. That's why I thought I'd better ask," Phalen said.

Zalman frowned. Why did guys always think he was drifty? He didn't understand it. He never did anything illegal, if he could help it. He paid his taxes, he was kind to his family and friends, so why did drifty jerks like Failin' Phalen think he was drifty, too? Was it an image problem? Zalman wondered.

It was a worrisome subject, but this wasn't the time to delve into it. This was the time to get the hell out of Happy Henke's laboratory in one piece, along with McCoy and Brenda, Zalman thought as he looked over at the girl.

Brenda Henke was wiggling madly and making snorting sounds in her hankie gag like an overheated pony at an alimony park kiddie ride. Zalman realized that he was the guy in charge. After all, he was the only sane adult left in the room. Maybe in the world.

He turned back to Failin' Phalen. "Maxie," Zalman began reasonably, puffing on his cigar. "Tell me the whole story, pal, I have to know. I never guessed it was you. Never."

"Yeah?" Failin' Phalen said, a tinge of pride in his voice. "Who'd you think it was?"

"Annabelle Forrester," Zalman said sheepishly.

"Really? Gee, I'm smarter than I thought!"

"You sure are. C'mon, I'm your attorney; you can tell me. It'll make you feel better. I never expected to find you here. After all, you were sitting right next to me at the Le Croque robbery, so I never thought you were in on it. After Doris got killed, I figured the second robber at Le Croque had to be Annabelle dressed as a man. I kept thinking about those little feet," Zalman said slowly. "Boy, I'll bet that took some brilliant planning, huh?"

Phalen smiled happily. "Well, yes," he began modestly. "But Annabelle had nothing to do with it. At first I didn't have a plan. At first I improvised," he said airily. "Step by step. Slowly, it fell into place and turned into the masterpiece you see here today."

"You're a regular Lee Strasberg," Zalman told him. He wished he could get Phalen to put the gun down so he could leap on the loony entrepreneur and murder him personally. "Improvisation? Fantastic."

"I've always been creative," Phalen confided. "I take after my mother. But maybe it's my creativity that's kept me from hooking into anything big," he said, sighing. "Maybe my dreams have been too complex. Always on the fringe, always on the edge of the really big deals. I know guys around town call me Failin' Phalen, and don't think that doesn't hurt. Guys laughing at me behind my back. I don't understand why. I'm smart," he said defensively. "Smart as anybody else. But I've never connected with the right thing, the right project."

"Guys're gonna envy you now," Zalman told him.

"I hope so," Phalen went on. "All the time I see guys who aren't any smarter than me riding around in limos, beautiful girls next to 'em. Why not me? Why haven't I found success? I've taken all the courses, gone to so many seminars . . . Real estate investment, government auctions, multilevel marketing." He sighed wistfully. "I've always been able to raise money, but my deals work for a while and then they go bad. Just when I think I've got a deal going, it collapses on top of me."

"You gotta stick to it, Maxie," Zalman advised. "Follow through. It's not just the conception of an idea, it's the follow-through."

"I know, I know! When I got into the jewelry

stores with Happy, may he rest in peace, I thought I had the perfect deal. Happy was a worldwide guy—he had a big reputation; everybody respected him. I put up every dime I'd made on the Dinky Rinks to get us going, but I always knew Happy was the brains. Okay, I was the junior partner. I knew that going in, and I could live with it. But I couldn't hold up my end, just like always," Failin' Phalen said, misery splashed across his face like sweat. "Other guys get all the breaks, and I get the hole in the doughnut."

"Timing is everything," Zalman said, leaning on the worktable a tad closer to Phalen. "What happened after you and Happy became partners?"

Phalen's eyes lit up. "At first it was great. The honeymoon phase," he said. "But Happy was used to having lots of bucks, and it was hard for me to keep up. You know how it is, Jerry. A guy takes you out to dinner in an expensive joint, you got to reciprocate or you look like a jerk. And Happy lived high, Happy did. You saw his house?"

Zalman nodded. "Very . . . palatial."

"Happy thought of himself as a king, didn't he, sweetheart?" Phalen asked Brenda.

Brenda grunted and stamped her foot.

"Quit that, now," Phalen warned kindly, waving the gun at her. "He always said you were his little princess. I'd hate to kill you, sweetheart, I really would," Phalen told her, turning his attention back to Zalman. "So I started to siphon a little cash out of the stores for expenses. Chump change, nothing I couldn't blame on somebody else. I only needed another five, six hundred bucks a week," Phalen said sadly. "To keep up appearances. But cash money is hard to come by. Everybody's got their finger in your pocket all the time. The government takes a slice up front, I got a greedy ex-wife . . . Jerry, you probably know this better'n anybody else, but a guy's gotta maintain an illusion of big money in this town. The right house, sharp clothes, Mercedes . . . It all takes money. Boy, tips alone . . ." Phalen shook his head.

"It's an expensive town," Zalman agreed.

"And in order to be in business with Happy, I had to keep up with his life-style. Couldn't let him think I was a poverty guy. Happy wouldn't want a guy for a partner who looked second string. Know what I mean?" Phalen said beseechingly.

"Sure, sure," Zalman said. "Guy like Happy Henke doesn't like to make mistakes."

"Happy never made mistakes. Well, maybe Doris. Doris was his only mistake."

"Ah, Doris . . ." Zalman said noncommittally.

Brenda made a glug noise and started stamping her foot again. Zalman tossed her a dark frown so she'd stop that damn stamping before Phalen went nuts and shot her. Either Brenda got the message or her foot got tired, because she quit it.

"He thought Doris was a class act when he married her, thought she was a society type and her influence would be good for Brenda." Phalen smiled at the girl. "That's right, sweetheart, he was only thinking of you. That's the kind of guy Happy was, always thinking of somebody else. He thought Doris was real hoity-toity. Turned out she was strictly from Hicksville. Just put up a good front. So he took up with Mary Rose. But Doris didn't like to be forgotten. Besides, she had passions, she had needs, and when Doris gave me the eye, I stepped in."

"You were both lonely. . . ." Zalman smiled paternally. "These things happen."

"She was a bitch!" Phalen said, shaking his head. "Brrr! Ice cube city! But was she mad at Happy! She couldn't believe he'd drop her for a dingbat like Mary Rose who, we both know, is a lovely girl but not too bright." Phalen tapped his skull meaningfully. "Nothing upstairs."

Zalman puffed his cigar and tried to look therapeutic. He had to keep Phalen talking until he could jump for the gun. It was his only option.

McCoy moaned and Zalman had a brief flare-up of hope. Maybe McCoy would wake up and kill Failin' Phalen, and they'd all have a good laugh over dinner at Chinois. But no luck. The big lug was still unconscious. Zalman glanced at Brenda, tied to the chair. At least she'd settled down. She was sitting quietly, her blue eyes staring angrily at Phalen.

Was the cavalry going to come riding in over the hill? Not likely, Zalman thought as he edged closer to Phalen. It was all up to him. He had to jump for the gun, and Zalman hated jumping on guys who had guns; he just hated it!

Zalman casually edged toward Failin' Phalen, smiling pleasantly.

"I realized Doris found me attractive," Phalen continued, looking thoughtful. "I realized she was lonely. I'm the kind of guy who notices these things."

"You're a sensitive guy. It's a quality women appreciate," Zalman said.

"It wasn't hard to persuade her that I was crazy about her. Doris was lonely, and she craved emotional understanding. But you know what happened? After Doris and I got together, my financial situation got worse! Doris cost me a fortune," Phalen said. "I thought that since Doris had dough, she'd pick up the tab once in a while, but noooo! She wanted presents all the time, she wanted romantic interludes. . . ." He shook his head, groaning.

Brenda rolled her eyes.

"You don't think about this angle going in," Phalen went on. "But when you're fooling around with another guy's wife, it costs big money. It's just like being a kid again, except you've got your own apartment so you figure you won't have to spring for a motel." Phalen conked himself on the forehead dramatically. "Except Doris wants afternoon assignations at the Beverly Wilshire, champagne on ice, the whole shebang. She wants me to bring her little love tokens. Gold, I might add. Nothing but the best for Doris. All of a sudden my finances are blacker than ever. Imagine the picture of Dorian Gray in a bad mood."

"Tragic tale," Zalman told him. "A lotta guys could learn from your story, Maxie. Ever thought of writing your autobiography?"

Phalen ignored him. "I start draining more dough off the stores. Too much. It was only a matter of time before Happy found out, so I took the plunge and told Doris what I was doing. I said we were through, I couldn't afford it any more."

"How'd she take it?"

Phalen groaned. "It was a nightmare. Here I thought she'd let me off the hook and she started threatening me. She said I had to figure out a way to get the money back without Happy finding out about the losses. She knew that if Happy went down the drain, she'd go with him."

"Then what happened?" Zalman asked.

A bright fervor flamed in Failin' Phalen's eyes. "That's when my life changed for the better. When I developed my Master Plan for Positive Power," Phalen said dreamily. "Picture this. One night, it's late. I'm flipping through the channels, and for some reason—it must have been ordained—I start watching this motivation guy. He's on one of those weird cable channels; he's on all the time. Big guy, white hair, he calls himself the Coach. You musta seen him. Everybody's seen the Coach."

"The Coach? I'm not sure," Zalman said slowly.

"There's so many guys on late night TV." He felt a little apologetic that he hadn't seen the Coach. Whoever he was, he was important to Failin' Phalen.

"Jeez, Jerry. You oughta watch the Coach," Phalen advised. "Make a big, big difference to your life if you can develop a Master Plan for Positive Power. The Coach is a guy about fifty. White hair. You ever play football in high school?" Phalen asked, casting a critical eye at Zalman. "Guess not. Too small. But he looks just like what you figure a high school football coach would look like. Fatherly, an older guy who knows what life's all about. You woulda respected him," Phalen said. "So I'm watching his show and the way the Coach gives his delivery, he's looking straight at the camera all the time. And as I watched, I realized the Coach was talking to me. Directly to me, looking straight into my heart right through the screen. I knew that I was the only man in L.A. capable of receiving the Coach's message. I, Maxie Phalen, had to develop a Master Plan for Positive Power."

"Positive Power?" Uh-oh, Zalman thought. Now we're getting into the serious lunacy. "Go on, Maxie." He smiled.

Phalen shook his head, resting the gun barrel lightly on the edge of the table next to him. "So I'm listening to the Coach, and the Coach says that in order to attain Positive Power, you have to be in charge of your own destiny. The Coach says, 'Circumstances beyond your control mean you have to take control of your circumstances.' And he says it right to me! The message was for me! It was a revelation, a bolt from the blue. I, Maxie Phalen, was in charge of my own circumstances, my own destiny. I could win with Positive Power! I felt that the Coach was directing his energy directly through my TV right at me. It was part of the Master Plan."

"Yes?" Zalman said. He moved closer, blowing a

cloud of smoke into the air that looked like swarming bees. Only a minute more and he'd leap on this lunatic and rip his damn crazy head off. What was Failin' Phalen talking about? The Coach, Positive Power, energy coming through the TV set? The guy was bonkers. Zalman smiled like Sincere was going out of style.

"That's when I conceived my Master Plan for Positive Power. I could see my future like it was laid out on a crystal chessboard. The Coach says you gotta have a Master Plan for Positive Power in your life. So I conceived it. I go back to Doris and I tell her that the only thing standing between us and true love for the ages was Happy. And money, of course. My first step is that I persuade Doris to get that dumb kid, Tony, on the string. I told her she had to romance him, get him going."

"Tony? And she went for it?" Zalman asked curiously. "You asked her to seduce Tony and she went for it?"

"Like a ton of gold bricks," Phalen said smugly. "Doris was a little kinky, and Tony loved the older woman bit. I told Doris I was going to hide in the closet and watch, and—"

"Okay, okay, don't tell me any more. I get the picture. Then what happened?" Zalman asked. He felt like a kid hearing a naughty bedtime story.

"So Doris and Tony start fooling around. Then I take the next step toward achieving my Master Plan for Positive Power. I told Doris she had to persuade Tony to rob Le Croque with her. No one would suspect me."

"Doris," Zalman said. "Damn. It was Doris in those little shoes."

"Great idea, huh? At first I figured that after I sold the loot from the robbery, I could reimburse the stores for the dough I'd embezzled, and no one would be the wiser. No one would know I was the mastermind behind it all. Get it?"

"You bet I do."

"I'd have the perfect alibi. I'd be sitting there with Happy, see, and Doris and Tony would burst in, all dressed up with masks. . . ."

"It was the mother, not the daughter," Zalman mused sadly.

"Yeah, sure it was Doris! She disguised her voice, stuffed cotton in her cheeks. Doris loved to play dress-up. Drag just killed her."

"I'll be damned," Zalman said.

"So in they go. That's when things went wrong. First, Tony conked me hard on the head," Phalen said, rubbing his head. "Hurt like hell, I wanna tell you. And then, when Happy wouldn't fork over the diamond pinky ring and that stupid medallion, Doris got overexcited and plugged him."

"Overexcited, hm? How much did Tony know?" Zalman asked.

"Not much, like I said. Never knew about me, never knew about my Master Plan. He thought it was going to be him and Doris right down the line. Schmuck. So the plan is, they'll strip all the jewelry from the ladies at Le Croque, and then I'll turn around and sell it."

"Very neat, Maxie. But once Doris killed Happy—"

"Yeah. That's when things went wrong. Y'know," Phalen said confidentially, "I think she was planning to kill him all along. She'd talked about it in quiet moments. She said he had it coming, cheating on her with Mary Rose. Still, I didn't exactly know she was going to do it," Failin' Phalen said. "But after it happened I figured, hey, I had the Coach, I had my Master Plan for Positive Power. I could handle it," Phalen said. "That Dor-Dor, she was tough."

"Dor-Dor?" Zalman said weakly.

Brenda squinched her eyes shut very tight and made a noise that sounded like "yunk." It was probably "yuck," but "yunk" was close enough.

"She liked baby talk," Phalen said. "Dor-Dor." He shivered. "Disgusting, the things a man has to do to make a living."

'So why did you come to me? Why did Doris?" Zalman asked. "Why did you want me to represent you?"

"I thought it was a smart move. Phil Hanning told me your girlfriend's father was the cop in charge, and I thought you'd have an in."

"Some in," Zalman said. "Thrasher hates my guts."

"I didn't know that at the time!" Phalen said, aggrieved. "I thought you'd be a funnel of information."

"You didn't think much of me, did you?" Zalman said quietly.

"No offense, Jerry," Failin' Phalen said. "You gotta reputation as a fixer, but you're also Phil Hanning's brother-in-law, and Phil said you were a brilliant legal mind. Since Phil said you were a smart guy, I figured you had to be an idiot. No offense," he said again.

Zalman couldn't believe it. Hanning again, always Hanning, causing him endless torment. Hanning, stirring up trouble. Hanning, the albatross of Jerry Zalman's existence on the planet Earth.

"THINGS WERE STARTING TO BREAK MY WAY AT LAST," Failin' Phalen continued, the fevered light of unreality burning in his eyes. "When I discovered the Coach and developed my Master Plan for Positive Power, I had a new lease on life, a shot at success in a big way."

"Success in business?" Zalman asked.

"No, success in crime," Phalen said promptly. "Okay, I couldn't make it in business, even though I had genius ideas. Genius ideas! Jerry, I ask you. Tell me that the Great Dictators of the World Chess Set wasn't a brilliant stroke. Solid pewter statuettes of all the big killers! Stalin, Hitler, Genghis Khan . . . all the greats. Woulda made a swell gift for the little ones at home, clustered around the fire in their jammies on Christmas morning. After all, chess is educational, nontoxic, and fun for kids of all ages. But it stiffed. I'll never understand it. Where did I go wrong?" he said moodily.

"Great idea, Maxie," Zalman told him. "Maybe a tad out of step with the times."

Angrily, Phalen jabbed the gun at the ceiling. "So, forget business. I saw that my Master Plan for Positive Power was to become a master criminal. Great, huh? Another stroke of genius by yours truly."

"Terrific, Maxie," Zalman said. "You're a real Moriarty."

"Who's he, famous gangster?"

"Sort of," Zalman told him.

"He alive or dead?"

"Oh, dead. Very dead."

"You know," Phalen said, frowning thoughtfully. "After I take care of a few little details, I'm going to disappear, start a new life in one of those warm countries down south."

"Montevideo?"

"Someplace where there's a lot of fruit. Maybe I'll change my name to Moriarty. I'm tired of people calling me Failin' Phalen. It irks me. Maxie Moriarty isn't a bad name. Anyway," the new Moriarty said, "you want to hear the rest of the story?"

"Absolutely," Zalman said smoothly. Just a little closer and maybe he could jump for the gun.

"I thought you'd appreciate it. Jerry, I'm sorry I underestimated you. No offense."

"No offense," Zalman said.

"But now I had another problem," Phalen said. "Tony. He knew too much and he was in my way. So I got Dor-Dor to set him up. She told him she needed cash and he had to hock some of the jewelry from the robbery. I figured somebody would remember him, tag him for the Le Croque job. Nobody'd come looking for me in a million years."

"Wacky Winger had videotapes of Tony trying to unload a few of the trinkets," Zalman said. "I wondered why he did it."

"You know Wacky Winger? No kidding?" Phalen laughed, shaking his head.

"We're old friends." Zalman edged closer to Failin' Phalen.

Phalen held the gun loosely in his hand, barely resting the barrel on the table. "Funny world. Poor Tony just did what he was told. He was a modern boy, real passive, Jell-O for brains. He liked Doris ordering him around. Then Dor-Dor told him they were gonna play jewel thief and the lady. She told him to wear his mask, sneak into her bedroom, tie her up, and—"

"I get the idea," Zalman said prudishly.

"Tony thought it was a sex game. Anyway, he did whatever Dor-Dor wanted. He never figured she'd kill him, even after he saw her pop Happy. But she did. I thought it was a little cold."

"She really had a taste for murder, didn't she?"

"Bloodthirsty wench." Phalen grinned. "Yeah, she shot Tony—what? Twice? Right in the pump. Brrrr! I told you she was ice cube city. By the time I told her we'd have to kill Mary Rose, Dor-Dor was raring to go. See, after she shot Tony, I knew I'd have to get rid of her before she killed me. Her or me, that's the way I saw it. So I told her to get Mary Rose over to the house and then kill her. But I killed Dor-Dor first and framed Mary Rose. Neat, huh?"

"Geometric," Zalman said.

"It's a shame Dor-Dor didn't get to kill Mary Rose. She was looking forward to it," Phalen said sentimentally. "She liked seeing people suffer."

"Maxie," Zalman said. "Listen to me. Take my advice as an attorney. You've made a mistake. You killed Doris and you'll have to pay for it, but you don't have to fry for it. We can get you off. Okay, maybe you'll have to spend a few years in the rubber room, but—"

"No can do, Jer." Phalen held up his hand, and a sad expression flickered briefly over his face. "It's too late. I have to kill you. Her, too, I'm afraid." He pointed the gun at Brenda. "I don't wanna do it. Doris liked killing, not me. Well, actually, I didn't mind killing Doris. It was easy. God, she was a pain! But it's just that . . . that . . ." Phalen screwed up his face like a toddler who'd just realized there was no

Santy. "My Master Plan's gone wrong, and I gotta improvise. You and the kid are the only people who know I killed Doris. So I guess you're next."

Zalman realized the conversation was taking a negative turn. "Doris killed Tony. Then you killed Doris and set up Mary Rose to take the fall?" he said thoughtfully, pretending he hadn't heard Phalen's threat. "Is that it?" Zalman asked, playing for time.

"You bet. I was just gonna kill Dor-Dor and split, but then this little beast walked in on us, so I had to kidnap her."

"Another improvisation?"

"Yeah," Phalen said enthusiastically, momentarily diverted by another chance to illuminate his own brilliance. "I'm in the clear on the murders, but I need money. Brenda knows where Happy hid his notes, and if I can glom on to the secret formula for the Rubyola, I'll be set for life."

"Dor-Dor didn't have the notes?" It really gagged Zalman to call anybody Dor-Dor, but he thought he'd better act friendly, seeing as how Phalen was planning on killing him.

Phalen shook his head. "I kept asking her, but she said she didn't know where they were. Then, after I killed Doris, I figured that Brenda had the notes. I knew how Hap felt about the little monster, so I thought maybe . . . But the little beast wouldn't tell me doodly squat, would you, sweetheart? Bad Brenda. Very bad. I'm gonna have to do something painful to you, honey," Phalen said slowly. "I've had it with penny-pinching. Everyone else has dough, why not me? I'm hip, I'm modern! I want a new life! This life stinks! And in order to live my new life in a sultry climate, I need the Rubyola. It's a question of leverage. I don't want to hurt her," he said, appealing to Zalman. "Honestly. Pain makes me nauseated, and it would be a desecration of Happy's memory. But I have no choice."

"There's always a choice," Zalman said quietly.

"Don't be so existential," Phalen snapped. "I've got to have dough, so Brenda has to tell me where Happy's notes are. Then you both gotta die."

"C'mon Phalen, she's only twelve."

"Life's unfair," Phalen said smugly, "but I promise it'll be fast. You won't feel a thing. I've got the whole building wired and the charge'll go off in a few minutes. You see, I've gotta get rid of the evidence, and you're it, sweetheart," Phalen told Brenda. "You too, Zalman. So you all gotta die. But I'll give you two choices: the fast way or the slow way."

"Neither, thanks," Zalman said as he whipped out his right hand and tossed a beaker full of green sludge across the room at Failin' Phalen. The beaker broke at Phalen's feet, splattering oily green slime all over his legs. Phalen jumped back, losing his tentative hold on the gun and sending it skittering under a table.

Zalman dropped to the floor and scuttled around the end of the big worktable, as far away from Phalen as he could get.

"C'mon, Jerry! That wasn't nice!" Phalen said unhappily, slipping and sliding in the green goo at his feet as he tried to grab the gun. "I don't want to kill you! I'm a victim of circumstances beyond my control! Like the Coach says, now I gotta take control of my circumstances. Killing you is taking control, don't you see that?" he said.

"This is goddamn ridiculous, Maxie!" Zalman yelled. He felt like an idiot, crouched under a table, a twelve-year-old girl tied to a chair between him and certain death.

But in that moment, Zalman realized that the Coach was right. He, too, was a victim of circumstances beyond his control. He was trapped in an empty warehouse with an unconscious pal and a helpless child, and if he wanted to escape before the big explosion he had to take control. He knew he could do it. Jerry Zalman was a guy who believed in maintaining a positive mental attitude, and if he didn't put his attitude to work, his lovely life was going right down the tubes.

No more dinner at Le Croque at Pete Marchetti's expense. No more rides in the Mercedes. No more snuggling with Marie. . . . He was having a great life, and dying would be a terrible waste of time.

Besides, Zalman reasoned, he had to get out of this or his reputation would crumble like dry toast. Guys would laugh at him. Nobody would ever take him seriously again. Killed by Failin' Phalen—it was embarrassing! He'd never live it down even if he was dead. The ignominy of it all! Dying like a schmo crouched under a table. No way was this the end of Jerry Zalman, he thought as he looked around for a weapon.

"Improvise, huh?" Zalman mumbled as an idea hit him. "The Coach said to improvise. Okay, I'll give you improvise."

Zalman edged around the table, over to McCoy's inert body, and pulled the stainless-steel .38 out of his pal's waistband. He couldn't bring himself to shoot Phalen, so he fired a round into the air, then leapt up and ran full tilt at him waving the gun and howling like a werewolf.

But as Zalman rushed across the room, Phalen instinctively jumped toward him.

Startled, Zalman slipped on the oily green slime and lost his hold on McCoy's gun. As he cartwheeled madly, struggling for traction in the grease, the .38 fell into the green slop, skittered across the floor, and lodged in a corner.

"What the hell!" Phalen exploded. "What's the matter with you?" He was still searching for the gun he'd lost under the table.

Zalman got up and kept coming. He could almost feel Failin' Phalen's throat in his hands. . . .

"Are you crazy?" Phalen yelled, slipping, sliding, and retreating all at the same time. "I'm gonna kill you." Finally he found the gun and fired off another wild round at Zalman. But the gun was slippery from the grease on the floor, and Phalen lost control of it again. The gun fell out of his hand and clonked up against the wall as he teetered wildly.

Zalman began to throw things at Failin' Phalen, vials and beakers and sacks and bags of crushed powder that exploded into a fine mist of multi-colored dust as they broke open on the floor.

Phalen got halfway to his feet and tried to lunge forward, but he slipped on the oily green slime and fell back to the floor.

Jerry Zalman and Failin' Phalen had precisely the same idea at the same moment. They both threw themselves at the gun and collided headlong on the floor in the sloppy green mess. Zalman got his hand on the gun; he could feel the cold metal in his hand, his fingers gripping the . . . but he lost it.

Phalen grabbed a jagged crystal mineral specimen from the litter on the floor and caught Zalman a solid thump on the side of his head.

Zalman felt all the blood in his body sink to his feet. His head was empty, hollow, and he felt himself falling, dropping down into a great black hole, like a runaway elevator taking that long nosedive from the fiftieth floor straight into a flat black slab of asphalt. Down, down, down he went, straight down into the abyss. . . .

When he woke up a few minutes later, he was tied to a chair. Brenda Henke was staring him right in the face, her hankie gag hanging loose around her neck like a bandanna. Zalman's head hurt like hell, and he could feel caked blood stiffening up on one side of his face. His whole body felt like an overstarched shirt.

"Oh, well," Brenda said. "You tried."

" 'Tried' doesn't quite make it," Zalman said sadly, "under the circumstances. Sorry, Brenda. I had to improvise, and I'm a guy who likes a solid plan."

"You awake, Jer?" Phalen said cheerfully. He was at the far end of the room, stoking the big Verneuil furnace with chunks of wood. He'd broken up most of the tables and was busily stuffing the pieces into the open mouth of the furnace. He was humming "Whistle While You Work" as he tossed the wood into the fire.

Zalman didn't like the look of things. Not at all. "Maxie," he said, figuring it was time to begin some serious negotiations. "Tell you what, pal," he began.

"No way," Phalen said, a grim look spreading over his face as he turned away from the roaring fire and walked over to Zalman and Brenda. "I'll tell *you* what, pal," he said, stabbing a finger at Zalman. "Time to die. End of the line, bud. I'm gonna stuff you into the fire and watch you burn. I'm thinkin, maybe if she sees you fry, little Brenda here will be persuaded to give me the secret of the Rubyola. Think that's possible, sweetheart?" Failin' Phalen said.

Brenda set her mouth in an ugly snarl, but Zalman could see that her lips were trembling. Matter of fact, so were his.

"Maxie—" Zalman began, but Phalen cut him off.

"No more!" Phalen said. "Now Phalen take command!"

The madman grabbed the back of Zalman's wooden chair and dragged him across the floor toward the gaping mouth of the Verneuil furnace. Flames were leaping and spitting, and the dry chunks of wood and

The chair legs were crackling fiercely, throwing jagged Halloween shadows across the room.

"What the hell's wrong with you, Phalen?" Zalman shouted desperately. "You can't do this to me!"

"The hell you say," Phalen said, yanking on the chair. "I can, I will, and I'm gonna! Another magnificent improvisation by Maxie Phalen! The Coach would be proud of me!"

The chair legs squealed sharply on the concrete floor like a teacher's nails on the blackboard "Ouch, I hate it when that happens!" Phalen shuddered. But the high-pitched noise didn't stop him, and he kept dragging Zalman across the floor, closer to the roaring furnace.

Zalman looked around helplessly. Phalen was going to toss him in the cooker, no doubt about it. Brenda and the unconscious McCoy would be the next to fry. A helluva bad way to die, Zalman thought grimly. He could feel the heat of the flames scorching his face as Phalen started to lift him up bodily.

But the combo of chair and Zalman was too heavy for Failin' Phalen. He lost his grip, and Zalman fell over sideways, searing his arm on a corner of the white-hot furnace.

"Ow, damn! That hurts!" Zalman yelped as he desperately tried to wriggle away from the harsh pain biting into his arm.

Phalen grunted, tugged at the chair, and lost control completely. Zalman thudded onto his back on the floor with his legs up in the air like an embarrassed turtle.

Brenda screamed and Zalman helplessly lashed out at Phalen with one Guccied foot, but he couldn't connect with the crazed entrepreneur. Phalen got a better hold on the chair and wrestled Zalman up off the floor and toward the grinning mouth of the furnace once again.

BLOODY MARY

Zalman couldn't believe it. He'd been in some tough spots in his life, but this was the worst. McCoy was useless hunk of meat, and Brenda Henke wasn't any help either. It looked as if Jerry Zalman was going to be a flame-broiled Whopper.

"Hold it right there, buddy!" a woman yelled.

Zalman whipped his head around. It was Marie, determined look on her face, a snub-nose .38 in one hand and Rutherford straining and panting on a short leash in the other.

"What took you so long?" Zalman asked weakly.

"What the hell's the matter with you, Phalen?" Marie snapped, her auburn hair glowing in the flickering light of the furnace. "You think you can cook my fiancé? Think again, buddy. I've got my own plans for him."

"Are we engaged?" Zalman croaked. "I'm so glad to hear it."

Phalen stared at Marie, uncomprehending. "Noooo!" he howled as he realized that once again, he was failin'. "Not again! I can't stand it!"

"Tough noogies, pal," Marie said firmly, aiming the .38 at his heart. "You blew it. Untie him, and the girl, too. I mean now!"

"It's not fair! It's not fair!" Phalen shrieked, his eyes glittering wildly in the snapping light. He gave Zalman a hearty shove with his foot and Zalman fell over, clonking his sore head on the concrete.

"Ow! That hurts!" Zalman moaned again.

"Shuddup!" Phalen said.

Brenda started to whimper. "I wanna go home, I wanna go home, I wanna go home. . . ."

"Untie 'em," Marie said, cold as a ten-karat diamond. "Untie 'em both or I'm gonna drill you."

"You wouldn't dare." Phalen sneered.

"Yes, she would," Zalman warned him. "She's tough. Very tough."

BLOODY MARY

As usual, Failin' Phalen didn't know what was good for him. Quickly he jammed his hand into his pocket and pulled out his gun.

But Marie saw it coming. She dropped Rutherford's leash and brought her left hand up to the gun and crouched, all in one smooth, fluid daughter-of-a-cop motion. She fired and caught Phalen in the left shoulder.

"Uhhh," he moaned, clutching his wound. But Failin' Phalen wasn't going down without a fight. He brought his gun up in his right hand and aimed.

Zalman knew Phalen had Marie dead center in the crosshairs, but Phalen hadn't reckoned on the love of a good dog.

Rutherford saw the gun in Phalen's hand and knew his adored mistress was in danger. He went tearing across the room, his rubbery lips peeled back in anger, his short leash trailing on the floor behind him. Halfway across the room, the snarling Doberman made a mighty leap and hurled himself through the air at Failin' Phalen.

Snarling, Rutherford hit Failin' Phalen full in the chest, and the crazed entrepreneur bounced back and slammed into the open mouth of the roaring Verneuil furnace. Rutherford ricocheted off Phalen and onto the floor.

There was a momentary hiss as Failin' Phalen's entire body trembled and caught fire instantaneously. He was briefly outlined in flame, his hair standing straight out from his head, a thousand hungry tongues licking greedily at his body. His mouth was open in horror, and then he was completely consumed in hissing flames.

Zalman looked away. He didn't want to see any more, but he knew the fat was in the fire. He could smell it.

Unhurt, Rutherford skittered across the floor, his

sharp nails scrabbling for traction on the cold concrete. He righted himself and scampered back to Marie's side, nudging her legs with his moist snout and whimpering for approval.

"Gooood boy," she said, stroking his head. "What a good oootsie-wootsie woojie kills 'um bad guy. Hmmmm? Isn't hims a goooooood booooooy...."

"Honey, please!" Zalman yelled, thrashing around wildly on the floor. "Later! Positive reinforcement later! Untie me now!"

Marie straightened up and gave McCoy a sharp jab with her foot. "Get up, Dean, you no-good lug. I can't carry all of you guys."

McCoy moaned and she kicked him again.

"Marie, the building's going to explode!" Zalman hollered. "Hurry! Get McCoy's buck knife out of his pocket," he said, wiggling in his chair.

Marie bent down and searched McCoy's pocket for the knife.

"Hurry up," Zalman called anxiously.

"I *am* hurrying," Marie said angrily as she finally found McCoy's knife. She gave McCoy another poke for good measure. "Get up, Dean," she warned as she ran over to Zalman. "I told you I ought to come along."

"You were right! I'll never doubt you again! Just cut me loose, will you?" Zalman yelled. "I'm telling you, Phalen wired the building and it's gonna explode any minute."

"What?" Marie cried as she opened the knife and sawed through the ropes that tied Zalman to the chair. "Blow me up? Not a chance!" she said as she ran to Brenda and cut her free.

The minute she was cut loose, Brenda ran over to one of the worktables and rummaged around furiously. "Got it!" she cried gleefully, holding up handful of jewelry in one hand and the Picasso medallion in the other.

"Never mind that, Brenda. Give me a hand with McCoy!" Marie yelled.

Zalman tried to sit up, but it was tough going. Every inch of him was cracking in pain. His clonked head hurt, his burned arm was killing him, and worst of all, he had a very bad bruise on his ego.

Marie and Brenda were yanking at McCoy's inert body, trying desperately to pull him to his feet. "Honey, come on!" Marie yelled at Zalman. "Help me with McCoy. He's out cold and he weighs a ton!"

Rutherford nuzzled Zalman and licked him on the lips.

"Yecch!" Zalman said as he staggered to his feet and ran over to McCoy. "Not on the lips!"

Marie and Brenda took one of McCoy's booted feet, and Zalman latched on to the other. Together, the three of them managed to drag McCoy out of Happy Henke's laboratory and into the hallway, Rutherford prancing along nervously behind them.

"Uh," McCoy moaned. "Wuh-wuh-wuh."

"Get up, Dean!" Marie said. "I'm warning you. Get up or else."

McCoy groaned again and lurched to one knee. "Wuh's going on, Zally? I miss all the fun?" he mumbled.

"Damn right you did," Zalman said. "You're just in time for the part where we get blown to bits and die in horrible agony if we don't get out of here in the next fifteen seconds! The building's gonna explode."

"What?" McCoy said increduously.

"Yeah, Failin' Phalen wired the joint and it's gonna go boomski, Dean. Get up, dammit!"

"Can you make it, Dean?" Marie said desperately, as she checked out McCoy's pathetic form.

McCoy nodded his big head and groaned. "You

bet. I been hit by tougher guys than him," he said, staggering to his feet.

"Follow me," Marie called as she started to run.

"Right behind you, doll," Zalman said.

With Marie in the lead, all four of them ran back down the hall, through the artist's studio, and past the dummy barbecue, then downstairs and through the first floor sweatshop. Rutherford brought up the rear, yipping and yapping at their heels.

"Where are you going?" Zalman called.

"Just follow! I know what I'm doing!" Marie shouted impatiently as she pointed toward a slice of light coming from an open door at the far end of the warehouse. Above them, the sharp crack of exploding glass cut through the building. "There! Go, go, go!"

Marie broke through the gloom of the warehouse, and Zalman saw her silhouetted in the slice of light. McCoy, with his long legs, was right behind her. Suddenly there was a tremendous boom and a terrible groan as the entire building trembled on its foundation, quivering and shaking like a fat stripper doing the shimmy. The walls around them began to collapse.

"The lab's going up!" Zalman shouted as he ran for the light.

Brenda was by Zalman's side, but suddenly a partition fell right in front of her and she screamed wildly, a thin, childish shriek of terror. Zalman saw her stumble and hit the floor as a glittering stream of jewelry spilled from her pockets.

They collided and Zalman instinctively grabbed for the kid as another huge explosion rocked the warehouse with the force of a bomb.

Zalman felt the building shake as the walls buckled and imploded. Plaster, concrete, and timbers fell all around him as the chemicals in the lab erupted. He tried to grab Brenda, but he couldn't find her in the debris. Then he felt her shoulder and thought he had her, but as he tried to pull her out of the wreckage a hunk of collapsing wall hit him on the head. Her face went fuzzy on him, and he couldn't make contact.

Another explosion rocked the building, and as he shook his head free of the litter Zalman saw Brenda lying in front of him, her whole body covered with dust and grit from the collapsed walls. The Picasso medallion was lying on the floor next to her outstretched hand.

He reached out, grabbing for a handhold on Brenda's Camp Beverly Hills sweat shirt. He lost his hold, but kept trying. Time stopped as he reached forward again in languorous slow motion. He finally connected with Brenda, and as he hoisted her over his shoulder, Zalman scooped up the Picasso medallion and stuffed it in his pocket.

He got a good grip on Brenda, and as he ran toward the open door he saw Marie in front of him and heard her urging him on.

"Jerry, this way," she called.

Brenda was very heavy, but Zalman didn't care. He kept hearing a voice in his head saying "Here is the church and here is the steeple" as he staggered through the debris toward Marie, who was outlined against the shining open door.

Just as the warehouse blew up behind him and the night sky of downtown Los Angeles erupted into a brilliant fountain of cascading color, just as hundreds of tons of concrete, steel, and timbers collapsed with a terrible roar, Jerry Zalman and Brenda Henke broke out of the warehouse and onto the dark street.

"Close the doors and squash all the people," Zalman croaked as McCoy grabbed Brenda out of his arms.

"Keep running," Marie yelled. "Don't stop or we'll get hit by—" A hunk of concrete sailed past her and landed in the middle of a dilapidated Ford Fairlane across the street. "Dean," Marie said as she flipped her car keys through the air at McCoy, "get Brenda out of here as fast as you can. I'm taking Jerry home before the cops show up."

"Gotcha," McCoy rumbled as he sprinted toward Marie's little red Thunderbird. "Later, 'gator."

Zalman and Marie ran for the Mercedes and jumped inside. Happily, Zalman inhaled the safe, comforting aroma of expensive leather upholstery and the delightful odor of a good cigar. My world, he thought. I love my world. Suddenly he started to laugh.

"What's so funny?" Marie said as she gunned the engine and expertly swerved around a pile of rubble from the exploding building.

Zalman grinned as he stared out the window at the ruined warehouse and rubbed the painful bruise on his head. "I just realized that Failin' Phalen finally did something right," Zalman said. "But the poor schmuck had to die to do it."

"TELL ME SOMETHING," ZALMAN ASKED AS MARIE unlocked his front door and helped him into the house. "How did you get into the warehouse? I had to pay Pokey Snails a fortune and climb up on a filthy Dumpster. . . ."

Marie looked at him in amazement. "I shot the damn lock off, how do you think?"

Zalman groaned. "Why didn't Dean think of that? What the hell do I pay him for?"

"Beats me." Marie laughed as she let Rutherford out into the backyard through the sliding doors.

"That's another thing," Zalman said as he settled down on the couch. "When'd you learn to shoot? Last I remember, you didn't know which end the bullets went in."

"Daddy took me out to the range and taught me," Marie said uncomfortably. "He said if I was going to hang around with you, I'd better learn to defend myself. I can pop those paper FBI targets right in the sneezer! Target shooting's a lot of fun."

"Isn't it," a woman said flatly.

Annabelle Forrester was leaning casually against the hall door, a pearl-handled Browning semiautomatic .25 in her hand.

Zalman sighed. "I thought I'd be seeing you sooner or later, Annabelle. I just didn't think it would be tonight."

"You're finally calling me Annabelle," she cooed. "But it's a little too late. Where's the medallion, Jerry?"

"In my pocket," Zalman said quietly. "Why?"

"It is?" Marie asked. "When did you—"

"Hand it over," Annabelle said shortly.

"Do you have the medallion?" Marie demanded.

"Yup. Brenda dropped it in the warehouse, and I picked it up. What's it to you, sugar?" he asked Annabelle.

Annabelle looked at him in astonishment. "You don't know," she said, her voice as smooth and flat as a river rock. "You don't know."

"Know what?" Marie asked.

Annabelle smiled. "Take a look at it, Jerry."

"Okay, I'll bite," Zalman said as he pulled the

medallion out of his jacket pocket. "One Picasso medallion, coming up."

"Wrong," Annabelle said, tossing her blond hair like a racehorse flicking flies. "One copy of a Picasso medallion, coming up. Happy made it himself, and it's absolutely perfect, with one important variation. He engraved the formula for the Rubyola on it. The original's in his safe, where it's always been. But he gave the copy to Mary Rose for safekeeping."

"But he didn't tell Mary Rose that he'd engraved the formula on it, right?" Zalman asked.

"Her? That dope? Of course not," Annabelle said, her voice sharp with scorn. "She thought it was a touching little memento. Happy thought he'd try the Edgar Allan Poe trick and hide the formula in plain sight. You see, Mother knew the combination to Happy's safe, and he just didn't trust her anymore," Annabelle said sadly. "I don't know why. She was a wonderful woman."

Zalman sighed. "And after it was stolen from Mary Rose, Happy must have told Doris that it was a copy and the formula was engraved on it, right? So she killed him and stole the medallion." Zalman rubbed his burned arm, watching Annabelle closely.

"Right again," she smiled. "Mother was tired of Happy and tired of playing second fiddle to Mary Rose and tired of that idiot Phalen," Annabelle said. "Mother and I thought that with Happy out of the way we'd be able to start a new life."

"Phalen had the same thought," Zalman said.

"That double-crossing bastard! After the robbery, he wouldn't give Mother any of the jewelry. She couldn't get the medallion back, so she was going to kill him. But he got her first. Then, after he killed Mother he had the medallion with the formula on it all the time; he just didn't know it. I told Bertie I thought you had it, to distract him, and then he tried that fake kidnapping stunt." Annabelle shook her head. "He thought I'd be impressed. Bertie's a fool, but he loves me. So you see, Jerry, I knew where the medallion was all along. I just couldn't get *to* it. Mother and I shared everything," Annabelle sighed wistfully. "Now that she's gone, I wonder if I can ever be close to anyone again."

Zalman shivered. "How did you know I had the medallion?" he asked curiously.

"You mean after that mess downtown?" Annabelle asked. "I played the odds." She shrugged, and her blond hair cascaded over her shoulders. "I've been following you, Jerry . . ."

"Gee, you look swell in a trench coat."

". . . and the way I saw it, there were only three choices. You had it, Brenda had it, or it was lost in the explosion. I decided to try you first."

"Lucky me," Zalman said shortly.

Annabelle's face tightened, and a cold smile flickered over her lips. "Hand over the medallion, Jerry. I don't have time to screw around." She raised the gun, her pretty red mouth twisted into an ugly slash.

"Some fake," he said appraisingly, hefting the gold medallion in his hand.

Annabelle laughed, a cold, slivery trickle. "Say 'faux,' Jerry. Never say 'fake.' Happy was a genius in his own line."

"Fooled me. So much for my ability as an art critic," Zalman mumbled as he turned the medallion over. It shone peacefully in his palm; the woman's three-eyed profile smiled like a hungry Mona Lisa. It was a beautiful trinket, he thought, another in an unending list of trophies splashed with the blood of greedy people.

But Happy Henke's hand had been sure, and his skill as an engraver had been perfection. Zalman knew if he looked through a magnifying glass at the tracery of minuscule engraving, he'd see the formula for the Rubyola written on the wings, concealed in the hieroglyphic pattern.

"Annabelle, don't you want to think about this?" Zalman asked, playing with the medallion.

Quickly Annabelle stepped forward and grabbed Marie's hair, twisting it painfully in her hand. "Don't underestimate me, Jerry," she said, her voice hoarse with anger as she dug the little Browning into Marie's neck. "Mother never hesitated, and neither do I. But Mother's dead and without her, I'm out in the cold. Brenda's going to inherit Happy's estate, Henke's Hideaway, everything. The Rubyola's the only thing standing between me and a swell life as a K-Mart checker. So don't underestimate me."

"I don't think I'd ever underestimate you," Zalman said slowly, holding out the medallion. "Here. This is what you want. Let Marie go."

Slowly Annabelle released Marie's hair. "No tricks," she warned, swiveling the gun in Zalman's direction. "I'll kill you."

Zalman smiled harmlessly and quickly flipped the medallion through the air toward Annabelle Forrester. The blonde's sapphire eyes caught blue fire as the medallion turned end over end in the air and her red-nailed hand reached out for it.

In her brief flash of distraction, Zalman jumped over the low coffee table at Annabelle, shoving Marie to the floor at the same time.

As he grabbed Annabelle's gun arm, she pulled the trigger reflexively, but the shot went wild, thudding into the wall behind the couch like a ripe cantaloupe hitting the ground.

Zalman struggled with Annabelle and clamped his hand around her wrist, but she jerked the gun forward and fired again. The blast caught him in the shoulder.

BLOODY MARY

The sound was incredibly loud, and the pain was incredibly real.

Zalman had never been shot before, and he was amazed that it hurt so much. It felt as if someone was holding a blowtorch on him or hacking a ragged hole in his burning flesh with a dull steak knife. His shoulder was hot and wet, and he heard Marie screaming in the background. But despite the quick wash of nausea pushing through his gut, he continued to struggle with Annabelle, trying to force the little gun from her hand.

Marie screamed again, and there was a terrible pounding in Zalman's head. Except the pounding wasn't in his head, Zalman realized thickly as he tried to shove Annabelle's gun hand away from him with his good arm, it was at his front door.

Annabelle screamed and spat, and there was a shriek of splitting, splintering wood as the front door came crashing down. Captain Arnold Thrasher and Lieutenant Howard Yarrow stood in the busted doorway, snorting like a pair of angry pit bulls.

"Baby!" Thrasher boomed. "Daddy's here!" He ran over to Marie and helped her up off the floor, ignoring Zalman.

"Hold it right there," Yarrow chimed in as he leveled his big Ruger .357 at Annabelle.

Annabelle shrieked in fury when she saw the two cops, but she still wouldn't give up. Her hands fought for control of the gun, and her sharp nails clawed wildly at Zalman's face. He ducked back as she lashed out with a vicious knee, and her white teeth shone as she tried to bite his hand.

"That's it for you, lady," Zalman said as he managed to draw back his fist and clip her full on the chin. "No more Mr. Nice Guy."

"Good one, Jerry!" Yarrow said with professional admiration.

Annabelle's eyes rolled back in her head like the lights on a dizzy slot machine as her knees buckled and she slumped forward, unconscious, into Zalman's arms.

"Darling, you've been shot!" Marie gasped anxiously as she ran over to Zalman and took him in her arms. "Oh, Jerry, I wanted to punch her lights out but you were doing a great job and I was afraid I'd get in your way."

Yarrow came trotting over and peered at Zalman's shoulder. "Boy, that looks ugly," he said critically. "Hurt much?"

"Damn right it hurts. She shot me!" Zalman groaned as he stared down at his bleeding shoulder. "How did this happen to me? Lawyers don't get shot!" His knees were rubbery, and he felt as if he was sweating wax as Marie and Yarrow helped him onto the couch.

"Give her to me," Thrasher said as he took the unconscious Annabelle and propped her up in a chair.

Quickly, Yarrow went to the phone, and Zalman heard him calling the paramedics as he gently eased off his jacket. His shoulder looked like a pound of ground chuck. "She actually tried to kill me," he groaned.

"Too bad she missed," Thrasher said shortly. "Put the cuffs on her, Howard."

"The hell with the cuffs. Drive a stake through her heart!" Zalman snapped as the wail of an ambulance cut through the peaceful L.A. night outside his house. "And don't forget to burn her grave!"

Marie pressed a towel to Zalman's bleeding shoulder. "Thank heavens you showed up, Daddy," she said, cradling Zalman's head in her arms. "How did you know Annabelle was here?"

"I didn't," Thrasher said shortly. "I came to arrest him," he said, staring at Zalman. "We only busted in when we heard the shooting. We got an all-points out on you, Zalman, for that explosion downtown. Some old lady whining about slaughtered snails phoned in your license plate number."

"Pokey, that traitor," Zalman mumbled as two paramedics rushed into the room.

Thrasher piped up again. "Marie honey," the big cop said to his daughter, "this is no place for you. Howard, why don't you—"

"Not a chance, Daddy," Marie snapped. "I'm going to the hospital with Jerry. Don't be a big bully!"

"Besides, Arnie, I want you to be the first to congratulate us. We're engaged," Zalman croaked.

"*What!*" Thrasher yelled in horror as the paramedics loaded Zalman onto a stretcher. "No! Honey, you can't do it! You'll regret it for the rest of your life! It's a terrible mistake. Marie honey, I'm begging you—"

"Daddy . . ." Marie growled ominously, and to Zalman's astonishment, Thrasher didn't say another word.

As he was wheeled out of the house, Jerry Zalman smiled happily to himself as he saw Arnie Thrasher's agonized face in front of him. Then he passed out.

"I've never seen so many flowers!" Marie said as she came into Zalman's room at Cedars Sinai and kissed him on the forehead. "Your room is almost full."

Zalman looked up from his hospital bed and smiled. "I gave half of 'em to the less fortunate," he said. "And all that chocolate made a big hit with the nurses."

"Daddy says Annabelle's down for attempted murder and some other piddly stuff."

"Your dad doesn't say piddly." Zalman laughed as the door opened. "Has he forgiven us for being engaged?"

"Don't think I'm going to marry you just because

you got shot, Jerry Zalman," Marie said. "I'm not that easy. Now, if you get yourself killed, I'll consider it."

"Breach of promise," Zalman said firmly. "I'll sue."

"Hello, Mr. Zalman." It was Mary Rose Peek with McCoy right behind her. "Ah'm so sorry you got shot, Mr. Zalman," she said breathlessly. "Ah think it's just awful!"

"Me too, dear," Zalman said. "But I'm going to be fine in a few weeks."

"Ah can't wait for you to be back in the office so you can set up my TV deal at Paramount. That nice young man who works for you—Albert, ah think his name is—wants me to sign with him, but ah told him ah wouldn't make a move until you were there to help me," she said firmly.

"Albert!" Zalman said incredulously. "You mean that little wuss is trying to scuttle my deal?"

"Kid learns fast, Jer, you gotta give him that," McCoy said.

"He'll go far in this town," Zalman said ruefully.

"I won't sign a thang without you," Mary Rose promised, stubbing her toe on a large plant in the corner. "Ow, darn it."

"Very ethical of you, Mary Rose. I appreciate it."

"Uncle Jerry." Jason Hanning and Brenda Henke were standing in the doorway, laden with flowers. Jason was wearing a pink silk sport shirt and black slacks with pointy-toed black boots. Brenda was chic in beige.

"How can I ever thank you?" Brenda gushed as she came over to Zalman's bedside and looked at him adoringly. "You saved my life!"

"Marie saved your life. She's the one you should thank," Zalman said modestly.

"I know she did," Brenda said. "I thought you were wonderful with the gun, Marie, and I hope you'l give me shooting lessons. I'm the richest little girl in Beverly Hills, and I'll need to know how to protect myself. But when I fell down last night in the warehouse, you picked me up. You saved my life, Mr. Zalman, not to mention getting shot by stinky Annabelle." Brenda sighed. "And you saved the medallion. You were wonderful."

"Thanks, Brenda."

"Now that I'm going to be so rich, I'll have lots of legal business and I'll need your help. I want you to take care of everything for me. I know I'm going to have trouble with Annabelle."

"She won't bother you for a while. She's in jail on an attempted murder charge," Marie said.

"But she didn't kill you, did she?" Brenda said wisely. "And Tehachapi is so overcrowded these days, more's the pity. I doubt they have room for attempted murderesses. I wouldn't be surprised if she's out on probation in six months and she'll be back with her claws out. She's going to sue me, I just know it," Brenda said angrily. "Stinky Annabelle, what nerve!"

"I'm afraid you're right, Brenda. I doubt we've seen the last of Miss Annabelle Forrester," Zalman agreed.

Brenda smiled happily and tugged at her pearls. "But here's the good news," she said. "I want you to be my guardian. I'm going to be the richest little girl in Beverly Hills, and if you're my official guardian, you can be my new daddy and live with me. Won't that be super? Uncle Daddy, I'll call you Uncle Daddy. We can all go to Disneyland together."

McCoy smothered a laugh. "Uncle Daddy?" he asked.

"Disneyland, huh?" Zalman grimaced in pain and shifted uncomfortably in his bed. Somehow the vision of playing Daddy Bigbucks to Brenda Henke, the richest little girl in the Fantasyland of Beverly Hills, didn't fit in with Jerry Zalman's plans for the rest of his life. "I don't know," he stalled. "I'm very busy right now, and I've promised to take Marie on a world cruise as soon as I'm out of the hospital. Hong Kong, Singapore . . ."

Jason leaned forward and frowned thoughtfully at his uncle. "You can go on a vacation anytime, Uncle Jerry. This is a great opportunity," he said. "Once Brenda and I get the jewelry stores back on their feet, we'll all be set for life. See, here's the deal," Jason said seriously. "We want you to come in with us on Henke's Hideaway. Failin' Phalen ran 'em into the ground, but Brenda and I are gonna rebuild the Henke empire. Now that we've got the formula for the Rubyola, it'll be a snap! You'd get a big piece of the action. Isn't that a great offer? We were thinking you could do the legal work in exchange for your cut. That's in addition to being Brenda's guardian, of course. How does that sound? Pretty good deal, huh? We'll all be rich."

"But not as rich as me. I'll be the richest little girl in Beverly Hills," Brenda singsonged.

"I'll think it over." Zalman backpedaled as visions of mountains of unpaid legal work caromed through his head. "After my vacation."

"We'll have plenty of time to talk about business when you're all better, Mr. Zalman. Oh, but there's one more thing. I want you to have this." Brenda reached into her purse, pulled out a little box, and handed it to Zalman. "It's the Picasso medallion. The real one, not the copy Daddy made. I want you to have it."

Zalman opened the box, dumbfounded. The Picasso medallion gleamed in his hand like a dream in the night. "Brenda, I can't take this; it's worth a fortune!"

"Mr. Zalman, I know exactly how much it's worth, and I want you to have it," Brenda said seriously.

"After all, you saved my life, and without you, I wouldn't be the richest little girl in Beverly Hills."

Zalman looked at the medallion, the real medallion, a Picasso original right there in his hand. It was gorgeous. It was the most beautiful . . . "But, Brenda," he said, pretending he couldn't take it, "I can't . . ."

"Sure you can, Mr. Zalman," Brenda said with a knowing smile. "Why not? You deserve it."

Zalman grinned. Suddenly his burned arm, mashed head, and shot shoulder felt a lot better. "You're right, Brenda, I do deserve it. After all, I've been stunned, I've been scorched, and I've been shot. It's about goddamn time I won a round."

Marie leaned over, took the Picasso medallion from Zalman, and held it up in the air admiringly. "It's beautiful," she said softly.

Zalman laughed. "That's right, doll. It's the stuff that schemes are made of. . . ."

ANTHONY AWARD–WINNING AUTHOR OF *NO BODY*

NANCY PICKARD

Join award-winning author Nancy Pickard as she brings an exciting mix of romance, wit, violence and sleuthing to the Jenny Cain Mysteries.

GENEROUS DEATH	70268/$3.95
NO BODY	69179/$3.95
SAY NO TO MURDER	70269/$3.95
MARRIAGE IS MURDER	70168/$3.95
DEAD CRAZY	70267/$3.95

Also Available in Hardcover
BUM STEER

POCKET BOOKS

Simon & Schuster Mail Order Dept. NPA
200 Old Tappan Rd., Old Tappan, N.J. 07675

Please send me the books I have checked above. I am enclosing $_____ (please add 75¢ to cover postage and handling for each order. N.Y.S. and N.Y.C. residents please add appropriate sales tax). Send check or money order—no cash or C.O.D.'s please. Allow up to six weeks for delivery. For purchases over $10.00 you may use VISA: card number, expiration date and customer signature must be included.

Name_____

Address_____

City_____ State/Zip_____

VISA Card No._____ Exp. Date_____

Signature_____ 301-05